'*The Beautiful Ones* capture through the overpopulation le Faure weaves the interconnec the wealthy, environmental poverty, into a thriller that moves from today to 2081 and lays clearly at the readers' feet a challenge for all of us to change current behaviors *now*.'

Paul Ehrlich, author of the *Population Bomb* and Bing Professor of Population Studies at Stanford University

'A tremendously ambitious, thought-provoking and worthwhile project. O. M. Faure has conjured up a colourful cast of characters caught up in an entertaining story in which action is informed by important ideas about our global past, present and future. An impressive achievement!'

Sue Belfrage, author of *Down to the River and Up to the Trees*

'*The Beautiful Ones* is a story that people need to read and a discussion that needs to happen in society. The characters feel like they're alive. The book made me laugh out loud a lot... and it also made me tear up. I would keep the clapping going for a great story with a compelling idea and a gripping narrative.'

Tony King, author of *Fishing for Music* and Australian Songwriter of the Year 2009

'Captivating, unsettling, bold. O. M. Faure's *The Beautiful Ones* isn't afraid to hit you hard with the "first they came for them and now they're coming for you". With such authenticity and heart, this trilogy will touch your life and spark many conversations.'

Isabelle Felix, author of *Deafinitely*

'In *The Beautiful Ones*, O.M. Faure offers us a chilling glance into a world not so very far from our own, and paints a compelling picture of a dystopian future that may be closer than we think.'

Clare Kane, author of *Dragons in Shallow Waters*.

ALSO BY O. M. FAURE

TORN

BOOK 2 OF THE BEAUTIFUL ONES TRILOGY

O.M. FAURE

FORWARD MOTION PUBLISHING, LTD.

ISBN:978-1-9164370-2-9

Published by Forward Motion Publishing, Ltd.

Cover design by Stuart Bache of Books Covered | Cover images ©
Shutterstock

The events in this book are an extrapolation of what the future could be, based on real scientific data, UN forecasts and current studies.

However, this is a work of fiction. Names, characters, places and incidents are either the product of the author's imagination or are used fictitiously, and any resemblance to actual persons, living or dead, or to actual events or locales is entirely coincidental.

If you would like to know more about the sources and data, please consult the bibliography at the end of this book. A list of book club topics will also be provided to readers who subscribe to the newsletter.

Visit www.omfaure.com to join the conversation today.

For my godmother Hélène Quin, who taught me that elegance and femininity should be woven through with strength.

'Unlike plagues of the dark ages or contemporary diseases we do not yet understand, the modern plague of overpopulation is soluble by means we have discovered and with resources we possess. What is lacking is not sufficient knowledge of the solution but universal consciousness of the gravity of the problem and education of the billions who are its victims.'

— Reverend Martin Luther King Jr. (1929–1968)

TORN

1

DEANN

K ampala, Uganda, November 2081

AFRICA.

A half-dozen motorcycles zoom past me with loud blares, racing each other through the traffic, as I look around, bewildered, reeling from the overnight change in scenery. Honking cars inch their way forward in the haze of the morning heat as billows of dust and exhaust fumes whirl their way up toward the sky. The din is deafening. On the congested sidewalk, throngs of people weave their way past or bump into me, completely ignoring me.

The cars are close enough to touch. I try to keep to the sidewalk but after a few feet I have to face the fact that there is no sidewalk anymore, just a strip of red mud next to the busy potholed road. I'm trying to sidestep a mound of garbage without getting run over, when a pair of enormous birds, at least four feet high, emerge from behind it. The intensity of their stare is jarring, their eyes like gouges on their diseased-looking skin, red mottled with black. Their beaks are as long as my forearm and sharp as machetes. As I carefully back away, one of them rushes toward me flapping its enormous wings, looking like Death itself is coming for me. I scream, barely escaping its beak, and find myself on the road. A matatu narrowly avoids me and honks a long protest as it whooshes away, its bumper proclaiming 'God Saves' in a cheerful glittering font.

There are people everywhere, sitting on the floor in front of their shops, arguing, touting their wares, haggling. Hundreds of bodies walk chaotically all around me, with no direction or boundary, no discernable organization. I stop to get my bearings, next to a street vendor who is cooking something on a charcoal-filled oil barrel. The makeshift barbecue emits pungent heat as the woman flattens balls of dough on the round lid. She cooks an omelet and, picking it off with grimy fingers, rolls it in the flattened pancake.

'Rolex?' she asks, wrapping one in paper and holding it out for me with a smile.

'You'd have to pay me to eat one of these.'

Her face falls. Suppressing a twinge, I absorb myself in the map on my wrist. It's just a crowded street. I make an effort to breathe deeply, ignoring the smell of the breakfast omelets and the woman's curious glances.

Glancing at the street, I try to get my bearings. The surrounding buildings are about three or four stories high, painted in beige colors. Most are crumbling. Small balconies are commandeered by bulky AC units and electric cables sag between buildings like lianas. It's early morning but it's already hot, the smog choking me as it hangs like a jaundiced omen above the city. Dust envelops the crowd, coating everyone in a fine layer of red. I purchase a sealed plastic bottle from the woman and sip the tepid water to buy myself a few more minutes before diving into the throng again.

I always thought that when I finally traveled to Africa, I would be coming home, to the motherland. That I would, at last, be the right color. That I would belong. That I would no longer feel like the token black person in an all-white cast. But instead I'm a foreigner in this busy street. Everyone around me is the exact same shade of dark brown; there are no gradations. I feel so pale. People stare at me openly, stopping to gape and point when I pass by. I guess they don't get that many foreigners.

The synthetic fabric of my Programme outfit clings to me in the suffocating heat and I'd give anything to wear linen or light cotton instead. The scents are strange and overpowering. Everywhere I go, it smells of smoke, burnt wood, sweat and shit and in the unbearable heat, discarded food releases the sweet and acrid smell of decay.

All around there are loud conversations, the tone, cadence and volume all sounding strange; they cut the sentences in weird places, emphasize the wrong syllables. Their hair is strange, most people wear it shaved but a few women wear very elaborate buns with braids of vivid green or pink woven through.

A group of women balancing large trays on their heads, laden with bananas, surrounds me and I wave them away. An old man sits despondently in front of a mountain of second-hand shoes, while a block away, a group of young men sits idly by, AK-47s slung on their backs, ogling me. People wear a mishmash of clothes: free promotional t-shirts with preposterous slogans, traditional dresses with strange pointy shoulder pads and elaborate obi belts. By contrast, with my perfectly straightened, natural locks, my body tightly encased in the strict Programme uniform, I feel like a New York news anchor, not a hair out of place and intensely fake.

It turns out I'm only a couple of streets away from my destination, so I summon my courage and plunge back into the mass, pushing with my elbows to earn my space in the flow. Someone grabs my buttocks in the crowd and I turn to slap him but he's already gone. In my second of inattention, I stopped and strangers bump into me and vent their frustration with loud protests and toe crushing. A gaggle of school kids about seven years old or so trot ahead of me, their pristine bright orange school uniforms contrasting with their dusty bare feet.

Finally, I reach the address I'm looking for and ring the doorbell. The rusty blue garage gates screech open and a diminutive white woman with gray dreadlocks and a nose ring comes into view. She's standing in the middle of the red clay courtyard, wearing green hospital scrubs with a stethoscope around her neck. She gives me a once over and frowns.

'You're late.' she says in a thick French accent.

'There was traffic,' I answer sarcastically.

She raises one eyebrow and turns on her heel, gesturing with her raised hand for me to follow, introducing herself as she marches down the medical facility's corridors.

I'm to be stationed here for six months. Then, the plan is to send me to a pharmaceutical plant in Bangalore for the remaining six months. I hate the plan. I protested strenuously when Burke told us. How on earth will I learn about cutting-edge genetics and make it big when I come back if I'm assigned to a French Doctors' outpost in the sticks.

The old doctor gives me the tour and a rundown of the situation as she speeds from building to building, introducing me to the staff as she goes. The hospital is spread over a small hill, where six or seven buildings are connected by covered walkways. Sitting on the ground with vacant expressions, people stare at us listlessly as we pass by, patients I suppose, or maybe their loved ones. They seem to be here for the long run. Here, two women wash their clothes in plastic basins and dry them on the yellow grass; there, another lathers her toddler with soap, his small feet dunked in a bright blue plastic basin.

As we pass by, a breastfeeding woman holds out her cupped hand, begging, but the French doctor doesn't slow down. A little further, an old man with grimy-looking bandages on his feet lies on the ground. I feel the urge to stop and take his pulse to figure out if he's dead, but Dr. Herault is too far ahead already. A group of children playing hopscotch scatters like frightened birds as she marches into the main building, and I hurry in after her.

Inside, it's mayhem, every room is overflowing with patients, spilling into the corridors, sitting on the floor, in various states of suffering, undress and despair. I wonder what's wrong with them. Maybe malaria? The rainy season must have just ended, although the grass outside was looking very yellow. Maybe I made a mistake about the season? I'll have to check later.

I'm not accustomed to all this human misery, shielded as I usually am in my pristine lab. Come to think of it, it's strange that modern medicine has not yet caught up here, sixty-five years on. Didn't Madison say that communicable diseases were now all eradicated?

The other doctors are busy treating patients so they give me distracted waves as I walk past with the brisk French woman. We continue like this through the consultation areas and operating theaters around the building, and she finishes up in the changing room. Here, the old woman rummages in a wooden locker and extracts second-hand green scrubs like hers. They're clean and pressed and she thrusts the folded bundle in my hands without a word, her meaning clear: get changed.

I haven't worn hospital scrubs since my first few years of med school and it feels strangely familiar but also wrong, I thought I'd have outgrown this part of my career by now. What the hell am I doing here? I should be in Baltimore ordering my staff around. Not here, wearing an old woman's hand-me-down scrubs in buttfuck nowhere. What on earth came over me and how am I going to get out of this mess?

I redo my ponytail, then join Dr. Herault, who takes me to a small examination room, where she pats a chair, waits for me to sit on it and then perches on a wheeled stool. When her fingers close around my cheeks, I flinch, surprised at her sudden proximity. I really dislike it when people invade my personal space.

'Calm down, I'm not going to bite you. What's your name again?' Her thick French accent is fucking irritating.

'DeAnn. DeAnn Carpenter. What are you doing?'

By way of an answer, she yanks the Band-Aid off my forehead and I let out an involuntary yelp. Binning the soiled bandage, she moves my face from left to right. 'Open wounds get infected here,' she says, assessing me. 'Did you get hurt in Kampala?'

'No, in London.'

'What happened?' she asks, her eyes fixed on my forehead, as she disinfects the wound.

'People in England don't seem to like blacks much.'

She chuckles.

On second thought, I should get along with her just fine.

She ends up having to stitch my wound the old-fashioned way, as the chemical glue and dainty wound closure strips have both come undone in the heat. Once she's finished, she sticks an enormous white dressing on my forehead. I look ridiculous but so be it.

The day passes quickly and slowly at the same time. I get to know my colleagues over a quick sandwich in the break room. Burke made me memorize the details of my cover by heart, so I hope I sound convincing as I pretend to be a lot younger and not a genetics specialist at all. I tell them that I wanted to find more meaning than just working in a doctor's private practice in Baltimore. A lot of them nod in agreement, like they've had similar epiphanies.

My supposedly mediocre medical career should explain why I don't know much about 2081 operating techniques. That's, in part, why the Programme chose to send me to a field hospital, as my lack of current medical knowledge will be less easily detected here. So in other words I'll barely learn anything new. I ask about the standard of care here and they tell me they make do with the material and equipment available. No kidding.

I spend the rest of the afternoon in the women's wing. Tending infected female excisions, taking rape kits and analyzing the X-rays of battered women's broken limbs. Can't these women learn self-defense and use their kitchen knives, for God's sake? Maybe cut off their husband's dicks and solve two problems in one, I think darkly.

The other doctor, Rosebell, is a local and much more touchy feely than me. A large matronly woman, she converses with the sobbing patients in a low voice, patting their hands, providing comfort and advice. But with me, she's loud and authoritative. Well, she tries to be, but soon realizes that she won't be able to boss me around, so she ignores me instead.

I'm not sure why Dr. Herault placed me here for my first day at the clinic. Maybe it's hazing. I sure hope I won't spend the whole six months in the goddam women's wing.

At the end of my first day, I go back to the locker room to change, already fed up with the hospital, the country and this whole absurd situation. The hospital's supplies are risible. The facilities are worse than 2016 Baltimore and we are in 2081. Apparently Uganda didn't get the memo. We're still operating with X-rays, basic instruments and barely any drugs. If I was hoping to learn any new techniques, this isn't the place to do it.

I'm removing my bloody scrubs and changing back into the stale London outfit when Rosebell comes over, leans against my locker and looks me up and down.

'What?' I say, annoyed.

'You're tough. You'll do.'

I snort, 'Yeah, whatever.'

'Most white doctors come here, dreaming of doing a good deed, helping the poor savages and so on. But you're different, aren't you?'

'Well, yeah obviously. I'm black.'

She bursts out laughing, a cackling, booming cascade of hilarity. Her head thrown back, she's slapping her thigh, wiping tears and I smile despite myself. Finally she calms down enough to slap me on the back. I take an involuntary step forward and catch myself.

'You're funny.' She rubs her hand over her shaved fuzz. The haircut makes her head look too small for her large frame. 'You're as white as they come, *muzungu*.' She yanks my forearm and presses it against hers. The difference is striking; I'm light beige whereas she's the same dark mahogany shade as everyone else in Uganda. I yank my arm back, covering the pink microchip scar with my hand, feeling exposed.

'I'm not white,' I exclaim, outraged. 'People always assume I'm mixed race because of my skin color.'

She smiles at me, mollified, and says more kindly, 'Of course you're white. You're white inside.' She taps two fingers between my breasts. 'And it's starting to leak out on the outside. But I like you, *muzungu*, you're feisty.'

Our first expedition together is to go get me new clothes in town. With her by my side, the crowds that seemed so overwhelming this morning part of their own accord. She weaves her way through the throngs to a modern neighborhood. Here the streets are paved, there are sidewalks and fewer peddlers and food carts.

We undergo airport-level security to get into a large commercial center guarded by uniformed men with modern-looking rifles. I try not to stare and follow Rosebell into the mall; it has seen better days but at least there are normal shops here with fitting cabins and racks of clothes.

We spend the next few hours shopping. The crowd here is noisy but seems more manageable than outside. Rosebell chats with the storeowners while I try on clothes. Then, laden with our purchases, we hail two boda bodas. We zigzag through the traffic, leaving clouds of dust billowing in our wakes, as I cling on for dear life, feeling the paper bags flapping against my back and something like delight fizzing inside my chest.

When the motorcycles finally skid to a halt, I get off with relief and dust myself off as Rosebell negotiates the fees and pays. We've arrived at a brand new French restaurant that's just opened. We walk through the open-sky dining area where uniformed waiters practice their well-rehearsed ballet around tables and cozy sofa areas. The place is full of foreigners having muted conversations in the dimming twilight.

'Hey, there you are!' a blonde exclaims, spotting us. She's wearing a remarkably short dress, given her chubbiness. I sit next to an NGO-girl, who's got multiple piercings. As she raises her hand to rub her shorn hair, I catch a whiff of sweat and notice the hint of underarm hair.

'About time, where were you?' says a slender, dark-brown woman. She's wearing a well-cut black dress and looks like she's just come from a corporate office.

'Hey, Akello. Move over,' Rosebell says, pushing the Ugandan woman and settling her large behind on the sofa. 'This is DeAnn, she just arrived yesterday; she needs friends.'

The elegant woman pretends to protest as she slides along the sofa and winks at me with a beaming smile. 'So where are you from, DeAnn? You don't look like a *muzungu*.'

I turn to Rosebell, 'See?' and then I smile at Akello, 'Thank you. I'm African American.'

'Ha. So you're one of us, then. I like you already,' the NGO girl declares and turning to the waiter, she orders me a drink.

The gap between this environment and the hospital is so complete that I have a moment of dislocation as I gaze around, unsure how to feel about this place. It's obviously a good restaurant and an interesting group of people. How can this coexist with the squalor and the poverty that I just witnessed a few hours ago? I shake my head and take a sip of my drink.

We all order food and while we wait, Rosebell regales us with over-the-top stories about our colleagues and the most outrageous patient stories she can recall.

Most people are usually intimidated by me and I'm not

sure how to deal with someone who treats me as if I were cute. I catch myself smiling at her infectious laughter.

We're well into our third cocktails and are nibbling on our starters when an older Ugandan man strides into the restaurant, a young woman on his arm. Amy, the blonde American, falls silent mid-sentence and her smile falters, as the waiters hurriedly show the couple to a table in the restaurant's far corner.

'Who's he?' I ask.

'A man who gives us all a bad name.' Rosebell watches their progress across the room.

'Why? What did he do?'

'So far? He's fathered about a hundred children.' Amy gives the man a hard, disapproving look.

I whistle. 'How's that even possible?'

'A child with each different student. He runs a girls' school on the outskirts of Kampala. Curse him,' Rosebell says, tsking. 'You should write about him, Akello.'

Everyone in the restaurant is studiously avoiding looking at the couple.

'Are you a journalist?' I ask Akello.

'Nah, I'm the editor at *New Horizon*, one of the national newspapers.' Akello turns to Rosebell. 'You know we couldn't write about it, and even if we did, people would probably cheer him on.'

'Why the fuck would they do that? He's repugnant,' I say.

'Half the people in the capital envy him. Unlimited access to virgins. So many offspring.' Amy shrugs. 'He's the epitome of manliness and success.'

'Aren't there laws against what he's doing? They're minors under his care.'

'Laws?' Cristina, the NGO worker, snorts. 'As if. Take polygamy: technically, it's illegal in this country. But in reality... let's just say that it's a very enjoyable way for men to father as many children as they can.'

A flash of anger flares up as I glance at the pedophile.

'My parents had nine daughters and one son,' Akello says, shrugging.

'I don't get it. I thought the demographic transition would have...'

Cristina bats the thought away. 'You mean that as soon as a country becomes developed, fertility decreases to 1.8 child per woman, of its own accord? Nah, hasn't kicked in yet, their economy hasn't developed enough.'

'I don't get it, we're in a city, shouldn't urbanization have a positive impact on reducing fertility?' I gesture around the restaurant. 'I mean, look around, we could be in New York.'

'It's not so simple. Uganda's population had multiplied by five over the last fifty years and Kampala's grown so fast that they haven't had time to build sanitation, infrastructure and the schools to match the population's needs,' Amy says, adjusting her too-tight dress.

'So basically, people come to the capital but they don't get access to developed world conditions?' I ask, thinking of the women's wing, just a few miles away from this opulence.

'Pretty much. Urbanization and development can only have a positive impact on demography if they're paired with education and empowerment for women.' Amy finishes her drink. 'And guess what?'

'None of these have happened...'

'Exactly.'

Rosebell chimes in, 'There's actually more inequality here than in rural areas, so urbanization doesn't have the expected effect of reducing poverty. By and large, people continue to live according to traditional family structures, even in the cities. So poor couples are still having a large number of children to counteract child mortality and provide a safety net for their old age.'

'But isn't child mortality decreasing by now?' I ask, puzzled, remembering what Madison told me in London.

'Yes, of course, on average, but in the slums and shanty-towns, not fast enough. So overall, fertility continues to be much too high,' Rosebell says.

'Ha, slums, that's a good one,' Cristina says. 'Kampala is pretty much one giant slum these days. We've absorbed Entebbe and grown all the way to Kome Island. It's only a matter of time before the city grows like goddam fungus over the rest of the muddy swamp that used to be Lake Victoria.'

'Come on, that's enough doom and gloom, ladies,' Akello says. 'I don't care if you *muzungus* all think my home-town's a slum. Very rude of you, by the way. *I* say Kampala's the party capital of Africa and it's high time we enjoyed it.' The slender Ugandan woman laughs and calls the waiter. 'Another round of shots.'

Sometime later, disinhibited and happier, we all pile into a cab and they drop me off at the compound.

I stumble into the kitchen to search for a bottle of water and instead find Olivia and Burke flirting on the balcony. His feet are propped on the balustrade overlooking the garden and she's laughing at something he said while nursing an empty bottle of beer. They look up when I come in. I'm clearly intruding. What's going on between these two? Can Snow White really be that desperate to get a man between her legs? Seriously, the Nazi soldier boy – that's who she's going for?

I don't know what to make of her. Maybe she really is as sweet as she appears. Although in my experience, people who are always chirpy and bright are just phony.

I learned from the soldiers we bunk with, that Anthony's specialty in the military was to infiltrate and to find things out, like the Gestapo. He's an expert investigator. Snow White's probably an open book to him, and we've got much to hide. She's playing with fire.

Olivia and I haven't had a moment alone yet. I need to find a way to talk to her. Maybe tonight, I'll sneak into her room and we can have an honest chat. I need to know if I can count on her if push comes to shove.

2

OLIVIA

Kampala, Uganda, November 2081

'YOU OK? It's a lot to process.'

I'm sitting on the balcony, looking out at the garden without seeing it. The city sparkles with a thousand lights against the vast darkness, the night simultaneously warm, terrifying and electrifying.

'I'm sorry? What's a lot to process?'

Anthony must have come out quietly because I didn't hear him. He's standing very close, his muscular frame towering over me, holding two beers.

'Africa, you know: the heat, the noise, the poverty, the smells...' He smiles and sits down on the wicker armchair next to mine, handing me a bottle. I hate beer but I accept his offering, curious to see what he wants.

'Oh no, I'm fine.' I take a sip and grimace; he laughs.

He looks as if he's trying to guess my thoughts; I squirm

in my seat hoping he can't really read minds because I was debating what to do about the Cassandra Resistance. They just sent me their first instructions. I'm supposed to gather the names and ranks of all the soldiers I'll be living with over the next six months.

My new 'home' is surrounded by concrete walls, topped with rolls of barbed wire. Several buildings are enclosed within the perimeter and the one we're in is the largest, five storeys high, with dormitories, communal bathrooms and an entertainment room at the top.

Given the comings and goings, I think there's a weapons room and a gym in the basement floors. There's probably more but I'm not allowed below ground. My pass doesn't work on that door and even if I snuck in, I couldn't justify my presence there.

Security cameras are everywhere, monitoring inside and outside the walls of the compound. At the corners of the compound, sentry boxes are manned by soldiers who take shifts, armed with heavy duty machineguns, the kind with legs. I guess I should feel safe, surrounded by so much fire-power. But I've never felt less safe in my life.

Pushing down my anxiety, I consider Anthony's profile and wonder what his intentions are. He's in his forties and his pale grey eyes are striking against his tanned skin. He looks like he's spent a lot of time in places just like this one. Stubble is growing on his jaw now and he seems more at ease in army fatigues. I'm guessing he must relish being back after his short stint at the London headquarters. There's an air of no-nonsense competence about him. An ease that's both attractive and intimidating.

For some reason he seems to like me and treats me with kindness, but coiled inside him, I sense something like power or maybe anger. I dismiss the thought, admonishing myself. With the kind of world he lives in, it's a wonder he came out so nice. I noticed how factual he's stayed during the political debates DeAnn insists on starting. He's not as bad as Groebler or Darren. I see good in him.

At any rate, Anthony seems to be in charge here. The Colonel left us as soon as we landed to go to a military base somewhere in the countryside. Even though Anthony is the commanding officer in Kampala, I'm not sure where the men's loyalties lie, with him or the Colonel. Probably with Groebler.

Anthony gets up to fetch two more beers. When he returns, he sits in his armchair and drains half of his bottle with relish. I'm still working on the first; it's disgustingly bitter.

'Here.' He holds out the second one to me.

I smile. 'You go ahead and drink it. I hereby donate all my beer rations to you.' Both our iModes flash blue, startling me.

Looking surprised and touched, Anthony clinks his cold bottle against mine with a smile. 'To Kampala, then.' There's a slightly coarser accent detectable under his voice's veneer and a roughness around his edges.

I think I might have unintentionally just made a more significant gift than I realised. Food matters here.

'So, Olivia Sagewright, daughter of the famous Alastair Sagewright, what brings you to this part of the world?'

I burst out laughing. The last few days' accumulated tension is getting to me and beer on an empty stomach isn't helping me keep my act together. 'Mmmh. Oh, I don't know, Anthony, I got tired of my job as a lawyer in a boring London law firm, so I thought it'd be a great idea, you know...' I carry on laughing in fits between words, as the ridiculousness of the situation dawns on me. 'I thought I'd become a bloody field agent,' I chuckle, 'in a secret organisation' – giggles – 'so they could make me *time travel*,' I struggle for breath, 'to bloody Africa.'

My words stumble and I laugh until my belly hurts and tears start streaming. Then I catch my breath in long comical gasps and finish, 'Let me just put it this way, I certainly didn't think I'd ever end up doing this with my life, that's for sure.'

'Well, it's not over yet, is it?' His smile stretches into an amused glance. I catch the double entendre. He thinks I don't know about the Programme's plan to kill us and now he's joking about it to my face. That's a sobering thought but I can't decide what he means. Could he be with the Resistance?

'You're so bloody cute, Olivia.'

'Why, thank you, Captain Burke, that's just what every trained Programme agent always dreams of hearing.'

He laughs and leans back in his chair, balancing his feet on the balustrade, crossing them casually at the ankles. The beer tastes bitter on the back of my tongue. I sigh and sit back as well, looking at the stars. The sky is full of little twinkling lights that shine intermittently against the black velvet night. The air smells vaguely of wood smoke and dried straw.

'So what are you doing here, Anthony? Come to keep an eye on us, have you?'

He looks taken aback, but when he sees my smile, he relaxes. 'Well, you *are* an unknown quantity...' His eyes linger on my face, trying to read me.

We're dancing around each other carefully. So I help him along by playing up my silliness. I fake outrage, my lips part and I raise a hand to my heart. 'Unknown quantity? I thought you'd welcomed us into the fold.'

A shadow passes over his face and I know what he's thinking. To him, we're just walking, talking chip-casings, aren't we? Disposable.

'I'm overseeing a project here and it was just practical to send you girls here too, so I could support you wherever possible, as I was stationed here anyway.'

'Oh, what's the project about?'

'Sorry, I could tell you, but then I'd have to kill you.' He wriggles his eyebrows. 'Maybe I'll show you one day, but you probably have enough on your plate at the moment.'

I need to get to the point where he trusts me enough to show me what his team is working on.

'So how was your first day at work?' he asks.

As I'm a lawyer, I've been placed at the KEW High Commission in Kampala, where I work in the department of international trade. I spent the day getting acquainted with my new colleagues, a bunch of pasty dad-bod expats with a dubious sense of humour.

I sigh dramatically. 'It was *fabulous*, Anthony, just what I always dreamed of. Working in a stuffy office that smells faintly of mothballs, with people whose objective in life is to get to five p.m. having accomplished as little as possible. We all had lunch at our computers and later I had coffee with a guy who stared at my breasts while he spoke to me about taxes. Living the dream, my friend, living the dream.'

He chuckles and looks at me, clearly reappraising me. 'You're funny,' he says, talking more to himself than to me, really. His eyes linger on my lips.

'You sound surprised. I fooled you with my *femme fatale* looks, didn't I?'

He laughs, throwing his head back.

'Well, there's really no need to enjoy the joke quite that much, thank you.' But I smile despite myself; I'm wearing loose pink pyjamas bottoms and a fluffy hoodie with pompoms.

After a while, his laughter dies down and we just sit in silence, catching our breath, watching the city's lights in the distance.

He tells me a few stories about his Forward missions. I ask him what the future looks like and he tells me. I wish I hadn't asked but it's too late: now the catastrophic outcomes that await us are seared in my brain. The night is warm and calm, enveloping us in the sense that we're alone in the world. It's completely dark on the balcony but our eyes have adjusted to the night. The city's sounds are muffled and all is quiet. He stays silent for a long time, his face thoughtful. Then he turns to me and says quietly, 'Olivia, there is something I should tell you...'

And that's when DeAnn slams open the balcony door, spilling the kitchen's light all over us, making us blink in the sudden glare.

'Ah. There you are.'

The volume of her voice is normal but it sounds extraordinarily intrusive and loud after our whispered conversation. Startled, we both jump back and under the stark light of DeAnn's glare, I feel foolish.

I excuse myself and go to bed. I try to brush my teeth but no water comes out of the tap. There's a sign taped to the bathroom door, which says that water is cut every day from 8 p.m. until 6 a.m. Mmmh. Water shortage? Weird. I brush my teeth and wash my face anyway with some bottled water.

In the dark, I lie wide awake, staring at the ceiling as I play back the conversation. What did he want to tell me?

I'm mulling it over, feeling exhausted and out of my depth when the handle of my door wiggles. Oh my God. Is it him? I sit up, my heart beating a panicked little jig in my chest. A figure enters and closes the door. But it's only DeAnn. I sigh with relief. Not sure what I'd have done if it had been him.

'How was your first day?' I ask her. I think she's had a few drinks.

'Not too bad.'

She doesn't ask about mine.

'Our assignments are a fucking joke,' she says.

'Do you think it's safe to talk here?' I ask, trying to hint that we shouldn't.

But I guess my English subtlety flies right over her American head because she shrugs and plops herself down at the foot of my bed. Soft moonlight pours in through the window and I can't make out her features very well through my mosquito net. Her whisper is really low, yet seems loud in the compound's silence.

'I'm not going to learn anything at the clinic where they've parked me, that's for sure.' She slurs her words a bit.

'At least you're doing some good. I'm stuck at the consular department that helps English companies do business here.' I hug my knees, worried about what she might say and who might be listening.

She thinks about it for a while. 'Clearly they're keeping us in the dark on purpose. I'm sure of it.'

'Yes, that crossed my mind as well.'

I open my mouth to tell her that we need to make them think we're innocuous, that we have to be careful or they'll kill us. But I'd have to tell her about my night-time excursion to the London headquarters' top floor. I'd have to explain about Madison and A., the mystery woman, and they specifically instructed me to withhold it from DeAnn. I close my mouth and think about how I could warn her without revealing anything crucial.

She looks at me curiously and as I don't add anything, she frowns. I try to think fast but this is out of my league. My days are usually spent drinking tea and preparing legal opinions.

'We need to be careful,' I add unhelpfully.

'Yes, Burke... he's dangerous. He wouldn't mind if I disappeared from the picture altogether.' She looks at me with furrowed brows 'Why are you fraternising with him? Doesn't it bother you that they're all racists?'

'Yes, of course it bothers me. Who do you think I am?' I whisper. Then add louder, for any potential eavesdroppers, 'Anthony said that he has a project going on in Uganda and that's why they sent us here with him, so he could help us. I suppose it's better than sending us somewhere random to fend off for ourselves on our own. Anyway, Anthony's not like the others.'

'Not like the others?' she sneers. 'Wake up, Snow White, you're flirting with a Nazi Programme agent.'

I want to explain to her that I need to get close to him so that I can find out what's going on in this future and save both our lives but I can't. Not here, Not now. I have to get Anthony to trust me but I won't achieve that if he hears me whispering to DeAnn every night about how wrong his ideas are. Plus, I hope I can change his mind. We need allies.

I remember how DeAnn betrayed me to Critchlow at the first opportunity. So I decide to follow Karen and the mystery woman's advice. I can't loop her in.

'Maybe Anthony is just the product of his era. His ideas match his cultural context. I can't fault him for them. I'm sure he's a good person underneath it all.'

She visibly recoils from me at that point, a hurt look on her face. 'Wow, you're just like the rest of them, aren't you?' She gets up, her lips pressed together and walks out.

Darkness envelops me once again and I lie back down, staring at the ceiling. I'm really alone now. I didn't realise how much I'd been counting on her until now, tenuous as our bond was, it was the only certain thing I could rely on in this world. Now I'm completely and utterly on my own in 2081. What have I done?

3

DEANN

ampala, Uganda, November 2081

'HOW CAN THIS BE? Yet another cancer.' Rosebell's voice reaches me through the ear bud, startlingly close.

'Squamous cell carcinoma?'

'No, epithelial again.' I see her frown through our iBubbles. 'I'm telling you, such a high incidence isn't normal, I'm sure of it. My research says there's at least double the number of cases here, compared to the national average.'

'Maybe it's just that the data is unreliable. I mean, how do they gather the figures?' I raise my hand to touch my forehead but it hits the glass instead. Cursing under my breath, I retract the damn fishbowl and the scan disappears with it, leaving only the patient's abdomen, her brown flesh taut against the protruding ribs.

'Still, something isn't right.' Rosebell gives me a look and then retracts her iBubble as well.

'Could this be related to the slum environment? They all seem to come from Bwaise.' The woman we're treating tilts her head, I don't think she understands what we're saying. She's so young. They're all so young here. The vast majority of the population are little more than teenagers. Sighing, I pat her shoulder and gesture for her to get dressed.

Rosebell breaks the news to her but the young woman doesn't seem to understand what it means. She only has weeks to live and she doesn't know it. Feeling a surge of guilt, I start to leave the dingy consultation room, when a nurse barges in.

'Come quick, we need an available doctor. You've got basic ER skills, right?'

'Rusty but yes.'

I look at Rosebell, who nods. 'Go, go, I'll finish here.'

The nurse and I run to another building. The metallic smell of blood punches me in the nose as soon as we pass the threshold. Screams bounce off the walls of the small room, deafeningly loud. Trying to ignore the chaos, I look for somewhere to wash up but there is no operating room, no sink, no process, just the piercing sound of pain.

A group has just been brought in; ambulance drivers are carrying the wounded from the back of a jeep, dumping them unceremoniously on the ground and running out to get more.

The doctors crouch near the squirming bodies, trying to triage this blood-spattered mess into a semblance of order. A nurse slips on the blood-slick tiles; wincing, she gets back up and continues running, a red stain now smeared along the side of her scrubs. A baby is crying somewhere and a woman howls with pain or sadness, it's hard to tell, rocking back and forth as she holds a child on her lap. An elderly man lies unconscious or dead on the floor but EMTs just step over him as they bring in more mangled bodies. Desperate people try to catch the leg of my pants as I pass by, feeble attempts to get my attention. Fishing rubber gloves from my pocket, I bend to examine one of them, but someone calls me.

'You, over here! The doctor sounds German. I hurry over to him. 'Take care of these two.' He points to a woman in her thirties and a young girl of twelve or so, and dashes to triage another group, while the nurse stays with me.

We flop the mother onto her back and lift her shirt. The bullets ripped through her abdomen, shredding fist-sized holes through her skin and muscle tissue.

'Not worth the effort,' the nurse mutters.

The woman just won't stay still. She's trying to grab something that's just beyond her grasp. She clutches my wrist and stares at me, speaking in a dialect I can't understand, her eyes wild, white showing around her irises. Then she starts twisting again madly, reaching a few feet away from her head. The nurse roughly holds her down but I can see it's no good.

What does she want? Her bag? I reach for it so she'll stop fidgeting and as I pull the bundle of rags toward us, I realize it's an infant. The child's jaw has been ripped out by a bullet and half his face is missing. Suppressing a heave, I cover his head. But it's too late – the mother has seen it.

A shriek explodes out of her, a strident sound that doesn't seem to end. The sharp siren of her scream pierces through the fog of adrenaline and then I see her. I really see this woman. Not her wound, which I'm pressing down on, trying to stem the flow. Not her poverty or the dirt of the road on her feet. I *see* her. She could be my sister, my friend, my neighbor. She's just a few years younger than me. Her eyes roll back and she starts to convulse.

'Nurse!' I yell as the nurse starts to leave, shaking her head. She stops and glares at me.

'What?'

'Bring me anti-seizure medication.'

She snorts, 'We don't have any here.'

A few feet away, a doctor pours a yellow powder into a man's gaping wound. The yellow powder foams in the exit wound as it hardens. The doctor holds the ragged lips of flesh together, holding the man down and counting under his breath. A sharp chemical smell wafts over, nearly over-powering the smell of sweat, shit and blood.

'How about that?' I point with my chin, holding my sleeve to my nose. 'Can you bring me that? What is it? A coagulant?'

'Too late for this one. No point in wasting it.' With a shrug, she walks away.

Anger's rising in my nose, hot as mustard, I scan the room. Complete and utter chaos. I'd lose too much time going to look for either of those medications, I don't even know where they store it. Making my decision, I wrestle the patient, pin her closest arm down with my knee and, taking a deep breath, plunge my hand in the gaping wound. Or more accurately, in the bubbling pool of blood. As I grope blindly, the red liquid rises, lapping warmly against my fingers, then my palm. Now it's nearly at my wrist.

There.

My thumb and forefinger close around the slippery tube of the ruptured vessel. But it's too late. She goes limp and her head lolls back. Unable to let go, my fingers stay clamped inside her, as I take her pulse with my free hand. She's gone. I stare at her empty shell, wondering whether she's better off. The infant's cadaver has come uncovered, so

I remove him carefully, my hands dripping with red, and place him at her side.

Breathing shakily, I get up yanking my gloves off. More patients come in, wailing for help. Someone pushes me and I stumble.

Wait, the surgeon said there were two patients. Wiping my hands on my trousers, I hurry over to the girl. Her small body is completely unresponsive. She looks dead.

Hands slippery with blood, I take her pulse; it's weak but definitely there. The girl's alive, she's just fainted. Relief washes over me; I can at least save one of this woman's children.

Probing anxiously for wounds, I uncover a bleeding hole in her upper arm, the size of a quarter. I carry the girl over to a gurney and disinfect the injury as best I can, then rush her over to the X-ray machine to check her bone; shattered. And there are bullet fragments. But she got lucky, it could have been of a bigger caliber and given the size of her arm, it would have been shredded to a pulp.

Her t-shirt is torn and stained with gore, so I cut it off to clean her torso and neck. I administer an anesthetic, disinfect and cut open the wound, then tug on the bullet fragments, periodically consulting the live fluoroscopy view through my iBubble, to make sure none of the fragments is pressing against vessels or tearing up muscle and nerves.

Her skin seems to surrender the fragments reluctantly, clinging to the dull, jagged pieces until finally I locate and wrestle them all out. Broken bone surgery is above my skill level, so I abandon the girl on the table and sprint back to the ER.

The German surgeon is sitting on one of the waiting-room chairs with his face in his hands.

I rush to his side and snap him out of it. 'What happened?'

He blinks at me. 'See for yourself.'

Now that my one-track focus lifts, I realize he's right; the noise has receded. The hospital staff are removing the bodies and a janitor has already started mopping up the blood. Soon the tiles will be white again, while they wait for their next red offering.

'They're not all dead,' I say.

He looks up with something like hope wavering on his face. 'Really?'

We rush back to the girl's side and, as I show him the X-Rays, a tired smile breaks on his face. He claps me on the back and says, 'I can fix this.'

A breath shudders out of me that I didn't even realize I was holding. Smiling like loons, we help each other into gowns and wash our hands, then work on the frail girl's arm in focused silence. Finally, after a long, fiddly procedure, he loops thread in a surgical needle and holds it out to me. I distinguish a smile behind his blue paper mask.

'You can finish here?' he asks.

I nod. 'Thank you, Doctor.'

'No, thank you. I needed this today. Sometimes...' He removes his gloves and rubs his wrinkled forehead. 'Sometimes it's too much.' Then he pulls his mask off and a nascent smile is definitely there. 'Welcome to Kampala, Doctor Carpenter.'

I chuckle as he exits the room. I haven't done any sutures since my residency, but I manage. It's not pretty or perfect but it will do.

After much fiddling, the 3-D printer agrees to construct a pink, webby device similar to the one which I saw Rose-bell place on a patient earlier, so I figure out how to carefully slide the synthetic brace on the girl's skinny arm. Despite the bandages and the strange material, her limb is completely immobilized and better yet, the cast is customized to her measurements.

She's stirring, so I wrap her in a too-big paper gown, then carry her out to the women's wing to make sure Rosebell or I can keep an eye on her. She weighs nearly nothing.

When the girl blinks slowly awake, Rosebell speaks with her in soothing tones and translates for me: the kid's family was displaced by the famine and lack of water. The entire family was just walking along the road, trying to get to Kampala, when roamers attacked them and shot everyone. Her name is Kitsa.

I try to avert my eyes but it's there, on her face, the moment she realizes that she's the massacre's only survivor. Her pain morphs into sorrow as Rosebell does her best to comfort her. She'll pull through. She'll live. She'll be OK. But the young girl can't hear it. She's drowning in despair and terror. What will a twelve-year-old do, all alone in this fucking horrible country? She'll probably get raped and killed before the year is out. And she knows it.

What would I do if I were her? Deprived of all the opportunities that I was afforded at her age? No home, no family, no education, no infrastructure, no police, let alone food, water. She has nothing left.

When the evening comes, we have to leave her lying on the hospital bed like a broken doll. Her slight body drowning in the large hospital gown, she stares at the ceiling, as tears roll, unchecked, on either side of her face. Yet she doesn't make a sound.

4

OLIVIA

 ampala, Uganda, December 2081

COMPARED with the frantic exit from 2016 and the cloak and dagger of the London headquarters, working at the KEW High Commission is mind-numbingly boring.

Gossip is amplified by the fact that there are less than a hundred of us here. So by now I know about all the extra-marital affairs, the perverts who make their maids vacuum in the buff, the stapler thieves, the swingers and the rations hoarders.

Catfights break out over who ate whose packed lunch. The squabbles are becoming bitter as food scarcity starts to sting. Let's put it this way: in this era it's not the cream of the diplomatic crop who get sent to Africa.

'Congratulations are in order, I'm sure.' Violet's wearing an unflattering smirk on her plain face. I wonder if she's going to try to assert her slight hierarchical authority over me again. She adjusts her tartan headband in the mirror.

I hold my breath, disinfecting my hands with gel as fast as possible. 'I have no idea what you're talking about, Violet.'

The loos have become the seventh ring of hell since there's no longer any water to flush. The night shift do their best to clean up but we're nearing the end of the day. I just couldn't hold it anymore.

'So what did you do to get that promotion to Senior Trade and Investment Officer in under four weeks?' she says with a sneer.

I tighten my lips in the approximation of a smile and escape to the corridor, taking a breath as soon as I'm out. But Violet follows me, wiping her palms on her sturdy thighs, encased in riding breeches.

'Hugh hasn't told you yet?' she says.

'Violet, I'm really not interested in this supposed promotion... or in Hugh for that matter.'

My colleague Hugh has aristocratic blood and slurs with an Etonian accent, so the girls are quite keen on him.

'Right. I'm sure you aren't,' she says, giving me the once over. 'And you got that promotion based merely on your stellar work. However did we manage before you arrived, I wonder?'

The smile congeals on my face. Through the slats and the steel bars of the barricaded window, I can see a piece of sky, laced with barbed wire.

'I really should start thinking about making a move.'

'Yes, tick tock, tick tock, we're no Spring chickens.'

'No, I meant the shuttle.'

'Oh bless. Of course you did.'

Escaping her clutches, I hurry to the exit just in time to

catch the Embassy shuttle. Panting, I take the last available seat and realise with a wince that Hugh is in the seat next to mine, with his curly thinning blond hair, his chinless profile and ridiculous moustache. He's wearing a knitted tie and a short-sleeved shirt with shorts. His flaccid arms hang at his sides and he's listlessly gasping for breath in the sauna of the crammed van. We pass the security gates and Kampala starts to unfurl outside our dusty windows.

Hugh has a car and a driver, though. He doesn't usually stoop to take the High Commission shuttle. I'm pretty sure he only boarded it today because he knows I'll be trapped in here with him for over an hour. He's probably hoping to get his moist mits on me.

Hugh invites me for a date, as I thought he would, and I accept, as everyone thinks I should. Then he tells me about the promotion. I'll be working every day with him from now on. Oh joy. He's dripping with sweat as he climbs out of the van. He wipes his forehead with a folded handkerchief, his signet ring glinting in the sun. The sweat flattens some of his sparse hair on his shiny bald forehead. Sexy. He struts away, bathed in the glow of victory. Or sweat. Or both. I bet he'll tell everyone that we're having sex. Wanker.

I'm the last stop, as always. I say goodbye to Edmand, the shuttle driver, and he waits until I'm safely inside the perimeter before he leaves. Back at the compound, I start preparing dinner for everyone. I love to make food for my Lost Boys, it makes me feel a bit like Wendy.

Something very odd has happened here. In 2016, in London, I was at best a five. I felt invisible and I couldn't get a second date to save my life. But somehow, in Uganda in 2081, I've become at least an eight. My curves are appealing in a society where famine is rampant and my whiteness is attractive to the bigoted expats and to the

Ugandan men, who see it as rare. My red hair is growing long and people try to touch it on the street. I get catcalled. Me! It's surreal.

Maybe it's the danger that's making everything seem more important, urgent even; that's making me feel somehow more alive.

Sometimes I wonder what's wrong with me. Am I so obsessed with finding love, that I'm interested in little else? I mean, if any situation deserves to retain my utmost attention, surely it should be this life-threatening one? Bloody exploding country all around us?

Meh.

SOMEONE GRABS me by the waist and starts to tickle me. I squeak and try to wriggle out of the embrace but I only succeed in giggling and panting until my sides hurt. Finally, Tom lets me go when I start hitting him with my wooden spoon.

'Hey, Red. What's for dinner?' Jarrod sits on the kitchen counter and nicks some bread while Tom tousles my hair and makes a show of nursing imaginary bruises.

'Ow, Granny, you hurt me!'

'Oh, shut up, Tom,' I laugh, tidying my hair back into place. 'Show some respect for your elders.'

We're all part of the Programme and they've sort of adopted me as a mascot by now.

'Also you stink,' I add, wrinkling my nose.

Tom smells his armpits. He's quite big, his steroid-enhanced biceps bulge out of his uniform and he could probably break me in two. But he has a soft spot for me and his cheeks are still dotted with acne.

Jarrod, humming a Christmas carol that's been stuck in

my head all day, gets two beers out of the fridge and hands one to Tom. I wonder where he's heard it.

'Fuck me, Bwaise was gross today,' says Tom, opening his beer. 'I can't wait to go home. We've already been working on this goddam project for six months. I. Am. Done.'

'I'll see your six months and raise you a third rotation in this shithole,' Jarrod replies, rolling the bottle against his neck, eyes closed. 'But at least we're nearly about to start testing.'

Interesting, I didn't know where they were conducting the tests, but it sounds like it must be Bwaise.

'About fucking time. If there's no snafu, we should be out by March,' Tom says.

Humming the Christmas carol to myself, I wonder for the hundredth time what their project is and why they need to test it here. I tap on with my iMode bracelet and send the location of the tests to A. and let her know that they're imminent.

The spaghetti fans out in the boiling water. 'Why don't you boys make yourselves useful and get some bowls out? We're eating in the cinema room tonight.'

Tom hops to it with a grin, but Jarrod leans back against the wall, feet dangling off the counter and drinks from his beer bottle. His narrow lips make a smacking sound as he observes me. I hope he didn't see me text.

I get the sense that they're testing a technology that they got back from one of the future missions. Apparently, the Helenus only sends soldiers on mission now. You only get to travel forward when you reach a certain military rank. The main objective of this new breed of field agents seems to be to bring back military technology, schematics for weapons and any civilian advance that can be used to kill and maim.

I'm really concerned. Could Burke's mystery project

involve building a weapon based on military technologies brought back from the twenty-second century? That would explain everything I'm witnessing. It explains why all the boys are Programme operatives instead of just run-of-the-mill soldiers. It also explains why Anthony, a senior Programme agent, is supervising part of it. They probably all need clearance to know about time travel and the future technology that has been brought back.

It just doesn't seem to make any sense why they'd build it here though, in a country on the verge of collapse. I've been trying to figure out that part for the last week or so. What on earth does the Programme want to test here that can't be tested anywhere else?

'Jarrod, could you please? It's too heavy for me. Oh, thank you, you're my saviour.' He lifts the large boiling pot, his thick eyebrows furrowed with concentration. 'Wait, save the water.' I slide another pot under the colander. 'I'll water the herbs with it later.'

I often think of Professor McArthur and the rest of the 2016 Programme. I hope they survived the attack. I wish we'd had more time to get trained; heck, I wish I were a real agent and not desperately in over my head. I hope I'm gathering the right sort of information.

'What's cooking?' Anthony strides in looking less intense than usual.

'Hi there, boss,' I say distractedly.

He steals my wooden spoon and tastes the sauce, an appreciative look on his face. 'Spag Bol? Where on earth did you find tomatoes?'

I try to be as friendly as I can. Hopefully I can drag this out a little longer because I don't have a plan yet for when our time is up and he kills me.

'Hey. Chef's secret. Hands off.' I steal the spoon back, taste it myself and decide to add some salt.

The boys skulk out of the kitchen. I've noticed it before; they aren't the same around Anthony. In London, I was usually surrounded by women, at church and at the IVF clinic. I've never lived in all-male environment before and I'm learning the rules. It feels like Anthony has marked me; I'm his territory and the others stay away. So what am I? Prey? Enemy? Pig for slaughter? I'm not sure.

My iMode pings, I glance at my bracelet and feel the blood drain from my face. Shit, a message from the Resistance.

'Very important. Find out what they're doing in Bwaise.'

Since our arrival, I've been reporting on what's happening here and the old woman, A., gives me instructions on what to look for. Find this file, learn more about this company, beware of this person. It's dangerous but I don't have much choice, do I? She's my best chance of getting out of here alive and if I don't give her what she asks for, she'll probably abandon me and steal the chip later. Once it's been... extracted.

Shit, shit, shit, how am I supposed to find out what they're doing in Bwaise?

'Drinks later?'

'Mmmh?' I pour the sauce over the large pot of pasta. I don't even know where that slum is. I need to look at a map.

'Beer?'

'Oh yes, in the fridge,' I say, distracted as I try not to burn myself.

'Thanks.' He takes a bottle and, frowning, leaves the kitchen.

Maybe I should tell DeAnn about what I'm discovering. On the few evenings when she's home, she ignores all the soldiers, has dinner on her own and locks herself in her room. I asked her what she was doing and she said she was catching up on medical advances over the past sixty-five years. That's really sensible. But sometimes I wonder if we're meant to learn about other areas as well, like the way people think, the political developments, the human aspects. DeAnn sure doesn't look impressed with my methods.

I plug into the iMode group and yell, 'Dinner's ready!' in everybody's earbuds.

A few minutes later, my Lost Boys rush in, loud and cheerful, jostling each other, loading up on garlic bread and trying to figure out which bowl is fuller. I've set one aside for DeAnn. Maybe she'll come back tonight.

Then we climb to the top floor of the compound and watch idiotic movies about fast cars, exploding stuff and virile men saving well-endowed girls. I really enjoy being part of this easy camaraderie.

Anthony's nowhere to be seen, working in the basement again. I should find a way to explore the basement at some point. I bet I'd find explanations there and maybe even a prototype of the armament they're about to test. I glance at the moon through the skylight. Something is nagging at the back of my mind. Something Burke said earlier? Probably just nerves.

5

DEANN

K *ampala, Uganda, December 2081*

THE VEIN IS ELUDING ME. Or maybe there's sweat in my eyes and I can't see very well. Cursing under my breath, I finally manage to plunge the IV drip in the crook of my patient's elbow and feel the room spin when I lift my head up.

Just then, Kitsa's small brown hand appears under my nose, holding a couple of triangular sandwiches. 'Look, Doctor DeAnn, lunch.' The white corners smushed by the saran wrap have melted into an indistinct ball.

She stuck around while her arm was healing and no one had the heart to tell her to scoot. Admittedly, she's barely twelve years old and has nowhere to go, but the medical clinic isn't an appropriate place for a child. She's taken a shine to me, for some reason, and follows me around everywhere. I shoo her away every time she gets too close, so most days she just hovers around the edges, looking sad.

'Get that away from here, the place is disgusting. I'll come to the cafeteria when I'm ready.'

'But Doctor DeAnn, it's three o'clock and all the sandwiches are gone. I kept this for you preciously.'

There's hope and something else in her eyes.

'I didn't ask you for anything.'

She looks as hurt as if I'd kicked her. Kids are so fucking annoying. And fragile. They haven't had the time to build a hard shell around their hearts like adults. I don't have time to deal with this.

'OK, give it to me.'

She perks up and a tentative smile blossoms on her face. I try to ignore it as I wash my hands with alcohol and then, emerging outside the building for the first time in hours, I sit next to her on a bench, dazzled by the sun. Endless crowds of people stream into the hospital's courtyard; some sit on the dry, yellow grass, others line up in silence, despondently waiting for life to finish beating them into submission.

People come to the hospital and tell us they haven't consulted a doctor for twenty-seven years. They arrive from miles around. They wait until their conditions are so severe that they're half-dead from things that should have been treated five, ten years ago – and we see them when it's nearly too late for us to do anything about it. People don't trust modern medicine and, frankly, who can blame them? Africa has a long history of being used by the West as a testing ground for experimental treatments. So they stay away from us, convinced that the vaccines contain diseases, that our doctors are not as good as their sorcerers, that we're a last resort. Anything is better than admitting defeat and coming to the French Doctors for help.

It fucks you up a little. Maybe a lot. Knowing that you

could have saved them if these had been normal circumstances. But nothing about this is normal.

At first, I was so frustrated about this; the missed opportunity, the absence of medical progress here. But now I just don't have time to think about it. We start the day at 6 a.m. and barely take any breaks, working through to 8 p.m. There are so few of us that the longer you take for yourself the more people die. I stopped for fifteen minutes the other day, to have lunch, and my patient crashed because of it. There's just no one else to take care of anything, to take responsibility for it. It's gut-wrenching. Then you get used to it. So I take shorter lunch breaks, stay until I have reached past my exhaustion point, forego weekends.

When I worked at the IGM, we used to share the responsibility of the diagnosis with six or seven other colleagues. The hospital provided committees, insurance, back-up. Here, when I first arrived I soon realized that I was the only person in charge of thirty or forty patients and their lives were in my hands. The weight of responsibility was chilling.

In Baltimore, I was far removed from real medicine but I didn't know it, working as I was, in my ivory tower, surrounded by glass beakers and mass spectrometers. But now, I'm elbows-deep inside my patients' guts and gore, learning about their lives, experiencing their dramas and it's fucking awful, yet I have never felt more alive.

I can't believe I balked at the thought of walking on the street to get to work on my first day. What a joke. How far I've come since.

When I started out in the women's clinic, I found the experience distasteful but relatively calm. Then water got scarce, people started drinking what they could find and soon we had an outbreak on our hands. Things went sideways, fast. I'm in the main hospital now, doing the best I can,

like all my colleagues. Triaging, treating, arguing with the
nurses and locals, chasing down a translator, a missing piece
of equipment, a drug that ran out. The logistics and
procurement team does their best but we still run out of
everything. It's not that MSF is too small to cope, it's that the
situation is too overwhelming for any NGO to solve.

Rosebell knew that crowds were hard for me, so she
started coming to pick me up every day in the MSF jeep.
She also got me one of those ridiculous white jackets, the
ones with the big red Doctors Without Borders logo on
them. She knew that I refused to wear them and so she got
one for me on purpose, so I'd have to. Because it was a
present. Idiotic Rosebell. I smile remembering her grin as I
tried on the sleeveless jacket for the first time, feeling faintly
ridiculous. Who would have thought I'd ever wear anything
with a garish logo on it? Why not a hairnet while we're at it?
But the vest is an all-access pass to whatever is worth
having in this country. So now I wear it everywhere I go.
People respect the organization and they help me when I
wear it.

Rosebell manages the department with an iron hand but
she's also the mother we go to when we have an issue. I'd
never admit it to anyone but she gives the best hugs.
Engulfing me in her large arms, the cushion of her large
bosom comforting me when I need it most. I make mock
noises of protest, of course, because I'm me, but she knows
when I need one and she won't let go of me until I feel
better.

Now in hindsight I realize that Kampala was stable
when we first arrived. People went to work, earned money,
spent it in restaurants and shops. OK, admittedly it was so
crowded that I couldn't set foot on the streets without
having panic attacks, but the city was fine, purring away

with the routine of peacetime life. Kampala has descended into chaos now.

I sigh, thinking of this afternoon's workload. The line of patients looks half dead, exhausted from days of walking, thin as rails, sometimes wounded and bleeding.

I start to eat and notice halfway through that Kitsa's staring pretty intently at the moist sandwich, on its way to my mouth.

'Have you eaten today?'

'Yes, Doctor DeAnn.'

'Don't call me that. It's ridiculous. Call me Doctor Carpenter or DeAnn.'

'Yes, I have eaten, Doctor DeAnn,' she says, and I can't help but smile.

'Don't lie to me.'

'I did. A nurse gave me a piece of chapatti for breakfast.'

'Here, have this, I'm done anyway.'

She devours the disgusting sandwich, her huge black eyes for once not trained on me, not following my every move. She's too thin, her torso is floating in a filthy pink t-shirt and her scrawny legs are dangling from the bench, knees swollen and thighs no thicker than my forearm. I try to remember what she looked like when she got here two weeks ago, but I can only visualize her wound and her strength of character as she cried silently looking at the ceiling.

'What have you been living on?'

'I don't understand, Doctor DeAnn.'

'Where do you find food?' I doubt she's been allowed to eat the staff's rations; we need to maintain our strength to face the mounting health crisis here. And none of the patients' families who loiter around the hospital would feed her. She's not one of them either. She's got no one.

'I find enough.' She crams in the remaining mouthful with both hands.

'Why don't you just leave and try your luck elsewhere?'

'I want to be a doctor like you.' Her little chest puffs up proudly.

I laugh and then stop when I see her pained face. 'You're serious.'

'Yes, I want to be like Doctor DeAnn.'

For a moment, all words get stuck in my throat. Nobody's ever said that to me. Pushing down the emotions, I reason that I'm the only expat here who's African American. Maybe for her I embody the unreachable wealth of foreigners, but also through the color of my skin, the familiar and achievable.

Tapping my fingers on the bench, I watch the throngs of people streaming in and think. I could justify her presence here for another two weeks or so, while she wears her cast, but after that, it will be obvious that she's healed and she'll be kicked out. I mull things over for a while as she looks at me hungrily, her huge eyes drinking in everything about me, from my hair to my lips to my clothes. I know because her gaze follows me all the time. Like a heavy burden of expectation. I want to yell, 'I'll never love you, just go away.' But for some reason I don't.

I root around in my vest's pocket and find what I'm looking for: a paper ring with measurements along its rim ranging from green to red. I slip it on her cast-free arm, pulling it until it's reached just below her armpit. She's in the malnutrition range for a kid her age and size. Quite simply she's reached a stage where she could die if we don't keep her. She observes the ring curiously, her eyes full of love and hope.

'OK, here's what we're going to do: you're going to stay

near me and follow what I do, so I can teach you how to become a doctor. Every day, you'll remind me when it's time for lunch. I'll take you to the kitchen myself and we'll make sure you get a meal.'

'Thank you, Doctor DeAnn.' She lunges for a hug but I stop her and instead unclasp the synthetic brace to have a look at her scar. That's healed well at least.

'That's our...' She struggles to find the right word and then just makes two Os with her curved fingers and links them together, so that each circle is within the other, forming a chain, a bond.

'I get scar to remind me every day about you, Doctor DeAnn.'

Her eyes are too shiny and her smile's wavering. For a second, I wish that I knew how to interact with this child. I'll just have to settle for keeping her alive.

'Where do you sleep at night?'

'I have a place.' She's too vague.

'I'll speak to Doctor Herault and find you a corner to stay.' I hold my hand up before she has a chance to thank me again. 'Alright, first lesson: you have to wash your hands before you touch anything.'

We go back inside, I disinfect her hands with alcohol and mine as well, showing her how to rub the liquid in.

The rest of the afternoon passes quickly. I might enjoy seeing her learn but it's hard to tell. She annoys me more than she pleases me. I should buy her some clean clothes tonight, after my shift.

6

OLIVIA

ampala, Uganda, December 2081

I STARTED GOING to Mass every Sunday, when I first arrived in Kampala and it naturally evolved into volunteering, as it usually does. Father Opok, a lovely plump man in his seventies, noticed me and asked if I had time to help. Weekends were long with the soldiers working on their mystery project in town and DeAnn absent or locked in her room, so I agreed to help out at the church.

I knew that I was supposed to be spying and finding intel, being a time-travelling field agent and all. But I was quite out of my depth in that department and surely it didn't harm the mission to help out at the church in my free time?

So, I began helping with the children's liturgy, such a wonderful, joyous affair here. Hundreds of children, crammed in a bare room, sang, jumped, danced and prayed, their bright school uniforms a riot of colour and their voices a harmony of laughter and happiness. They gathered around me crying, '*Muzungu, muzungu!*' touching my hair, my hands, my clothes, trying to comprehend my foreignness.

'*Muzungu* means "wanderer",' a beautiful woman in her early thirties said to me as she shooed the kids away. 'Ugandans didn't travel all that much, so when we saw missionaries come and go, we called all white people *muzungus*: the travellers.'

'Oh, I like it,' I said, thinking, *If only she knew how far I've come.* Wanderer seemed apt.

The woman picked up her two children at the end of service but she didn't come the following week, so I looked after her kids. When I realised that they lived in the slums, I sent the children back home with treats and little gifts. The following week, Edigold waited for me at the end of Mass and we chatted about her children, their singing and their sweet personalities. We went from there and became friends.

'We had to go,' was all she said to me about why she's a refugee.

Other parishioners told me that she was a respected Mukiiga teacher who managed a primary school until an armed group took over Katojo, her village. Nobody knows whether it was the Batooro or the Congolese who killed her husband, set fire to the village, and massacred everyone in sight. Edigold and her two children escaped with only the clothes on their backs. They walked 400 kilometres to reach the relative safety of Kampala.

Kind, upbeat and hopeful, she managed to keep her faith through this ordeal and she even rebuilt a life here, setting up a small school in the slums. I'm in awe of her strength.

'Life has no spare parts,' she said to me the other day. 'You do your best with what you have and take care of the people you love, because you can't replace them.'

Other refugees and displaced families wash up in our parish every day. I try to help by organising collections for them. Then, a few weeks ago, it dawned on me: I could participate in the runs to Bwaise in an inconspicuous way with other parishioners. So over the last few weeks, I've distributed food, clothes and water, all the while keeping an eye out for any suspicious military activities.

In her free time, Edigold goes around Bwaise and tries to help other women, so I tag along when I can to widen my perimeter and gather more gossip. But so far I've heard nothing about white soldiers, what they might be doing here or where their operations might be based in the slum.

That's why I'm here today, sitting on an overturned bucket, watching my friend talk a young mother into accepting a packet of contraceptive pills.

'Come on, Goreth, you told me you don't want any more children. You've had two beautiful girls already. God has smiled on you. Isn't it enough?'

Wide-eyed and inscrutable, the young mother caresses the head of her newborn, who is breastfeeding peacefully.

'I can't, sister. Milton wants a son. He'll be so angry if I take them.' She waves a fly away from the baby's face and shakes her head, refusing the pills gently but firmly.

'But, Goreth, how will you feed the little ones? You know it's not easy these days, aren't you worried about—'

The young mother looks up in alarm, past us. I turn as a lanky man enters the hovel, frowning. Swaying on his feet, he starts to reprimand the young woman in Luganda.

The young woman looking slightly panicked, closes

Edigold's hand around the pills and pushes my friend away. 'You need to go, sister. Please don't come anymore. *Jebaleko*.'

The man turns to me, bending, so his face is very close to mine, anger making his inebriated slur more pronounced. 'Poison. Out! Out!' His tongue has a strange mottled black coating and he's shaking a pipe in my face.

Uneasy, I glance at Edigold, who sighs, touches the young woman's arm and kisses the baby's forehead.

'Come, Olivia, we'll let her rest for now. We'll return next week.'

Completely ignoring the man, my friend stands up and makes her exit, dignified and silent. I hurry after her, relieved that the man didn't do any more than shout. We set off towards Edigold's home.

'You OK?' she asks.

'Yes, I'm fine, don't worry about me. Are you OK? You're acting a bit strange today.'

She smiles fondly at me. For some reason, she always looks surprised when I acknowledge her presence or care for her in any way.

'Yes, yes, I'm fine. Please let it go.' She sticks her hands in her pockets and looks down at her feet.

But she's not fine. Her hair is different today, she normally wears a bright purple wig but today her hair is in a short afro. Her eyes are shiny and she looks like she's having trouble swallowing. She's withdrawn and silent, whereas she's usually so formidable. I throw her a worried glance. 'Did I do something wrong?'

'What? Oh no, of course not. It wasn't you,' she says, as we walk along the slum street.

It's not really a street, more of an open-sky gutter dug in the red ground and full of potholes and stones. A chicken spray-painted blue darts past us and disappears down an alley.

On practically every corner, barefoot children follow us, chanting, '*Muzungu, muzungu!*' as they grin and point. These days, I come prepared, so I stop and give each child a lollipop. Most just run away with their prize, but as we're about to set off, I notice a tiny boy who is trying to eat the lollipop with the wrapper on it, so I fish it out of his mouth, remove the paper and return it. He watches me, astonished, his gorgeous round face illuminated by a smile as soon as I return the sweet.

We start again, walking briskly and I nearly don't hear Edigold when her voice goes quiet, and she says, looking fixedly ahead of her, 'Yesterday evening when I went home, there were two men in my house; they attacked me.'

'What? Are you alright? Did they hurt you?'

'They tried, but I escaped. I'm so angry.' She clenches her jaw and winces, rubbing her hand against her side. I think they did hurt her but she doesn't want me to know. They probably got close enough to rip her hair off and give her bruises.

'Angry?' I say, puzzled. I'd be terrified, crying. But she does look angry. She rubs her face in her hands and shakes her head, groaning with powerless rage.

'The men think that their wives cheat on them if they ask to use condoms. Husbands blame me for offering temptation and sin. I only managed to save a bagful of pills. They took the rest and burnt it.'

'Are the kids OK?'

'Yes, yes, they weren't at home. But I don't know if I can keep doing this...'

I glance at her, marvelling at her strength of character. If someone attacked me physically and threatened my family, would I still stand up for an idea, for a principle?

'We must tell the police or the church...'

'No, absolutely not! No one can know about what I'm doing for the women. I'd lose my job, Olivia, do you understand? Promise me you won't tell anyone.'

I nod and we walk for a while in silence. Finally, I understand what white privilege means. It's a bubble of protection and special treatment that surrounds me everywhere I go, here. Edigold gets attacked in her own home because she's Ugandan, she's poor and she's a woman. I'm a woman too but I'm white and comparatively rich, so I can do and say things that she can't and I'm always relatively safe, even here in Kampala. Protected by everyone as if I were precious, as if I were special. But I don't feel special, I feel ashamed and guilty.

'Edigold?'

'Mmmh?'

'I don't get it. Why don't they take the contraceptives? You're giving it to them for free.'

'The problem's not contraception, it's education. I gave a pack of pills to Prossy the other day,' she says, pointing to one of the huts as we pass by. 'When I came back the next time, I realised she'd taken two tablets and saved the rest for the next month.'

'You can teach them.'

'It's not that simple, it's not just a matter of giving them information. We also have to change the culture. People just *want* children. A lot of them.'

My IVF days seem so far away now, yet my yearning for a child still has its jaws firmly clamped around my gut. 'I understand. Even where I'm from, people think a woman isn't a woman until she's had children.' I square my jaw and blink a couple of times to remove the tears that are welling up without my consent. Surrounded by so much misery, my hands itch to hold a baby in my arms, to feed these children, to hug a toddler and tell her that everything will be alright. But there are too many to help. Overpopulation is killing these kind people little by little. I look at my dusty shoes and swallow, willing the knot in my throat to dissolve. 'Your school and your efforts will help, though. Won't they?'

'I don't know anymore, Olivia. My funding's about to be pulled. The Americans don't want me to offer any type of fertility control except abstinence.' She snorts. 'Stupid, fanatic *muzungus*. Even the school might close now.' She shakes her head and sinks into silence again.

Every week, we stop by an elderly couple begging on the street. The man is a painter who spreads his canvases on the ground, where passers-by trample them. His paintings are incongruously beautiful, naïve depictions of a time gone by, of animals long extinct, dreams of simpler life. Today, he's alone. I greet him and take my time looking at his work, as I know he likes the company. I don't think anyone else really talks to them much.

'Hello, Enok, how are you today? Where is your beautiful wife?'

His mouth works silently but he doesn't say anything. His hair is very short and completely white; his once tall frame is spent. He struggles to get up and I help him to his feet.

'Enok? Are you alright?'

Last time I saw his wife, she had one of those ports for IV drips on the back of her hand. I hadn't asked anything, though; it didn't seem right to pry.

'Itungo is sick. Hospital.'

Edigold speaks with the painter in fast dialect as I

choose a vivid blue river scene with a vibrant jungle at twilight, full of Douanier Rousseau wonder and shiny-eyed creatures.

'Let's go, Olivia.'

I shake his hand with both of mine, and press ten times the usual price into his palm, feeling indecently rich and voyeuristic. As we leave, he hunches over his hand, counting the folded bills. I hope it will make a small difference. Everything seems so futile today.

'Itungo's not the only one who's sick,' Edigold says.

'I can only give to a few people, I don't have enough money...' I say, feeling a surge of guilt.

'No, no. You don't understand. There are so many sick women... they get cancer. I have many friends who died.'

'Enok's wife has cancer?'

She nods, looking straight ahead, her forehead creased.

'What will happen to them?'

'Enok and her didn't have any children. Now they're old and there's no one to take care of them. They'll die.' Edigold shrugs. 'Damned if you do and dammed if you don't.'

'I'm sure what you're doing is making a difference, Edigold. You're just discouraged because of what happened yesterday... I'm sure...'

Her children have spotted us coming down the rubbish-strewn street. 'Olivia! Olivia!'

The kids throw themselves into my arms and I hug them fondly. They dive into the basket of goodies I brought; there's food, clothes and more importantly a football, so the kids run outside to play. I sit with Edigold on the beaten-earth floor of her hut. She rekindles the embers in a small stove and pours water from a plastic yellow jerry can into a pot then she sets it on the stove to boil with a few tea leaves in it.

Burke's soldiers were very clear when I first arrived: under no circumstances should I let my mouth come into contact with water that isn't bottled. Not even boiled, not even to brush my teeth, not even if I spit it out.

Edigold pours the brown steamy liquid in two glasses and hands me one.

'Is it always so hot this time of year?' I ask, fanning myself with a piece of cardboard. 'There hasn't been a drop of rain for months. Do you know when's the rainy season going to start?'

'It's over, it was from September to November.'

'But it didn't rain. Not a drop in the month and a half I've been here.' I frown.

'Mmmh,' she says and then glances at my tea, as I set it down on the floor, having drunk not a single drop of it.

'You know, in Kampala we have a saying, "Water is life... unless you live in Bwaise." That's because floods used to wipe out all of Bwaise every rainy season, drowning hundreds of people in their path. Now it has a different meaning.'

There are things in the water that don't bear thinking about and yet all the children within a three-mile radius fill their jerry cans at the same public fountain. It's muddy and filthy. To avoid getting whatever bacteria and larvae are teeming in in the fountain water, some enterprising kids have punched a hole in the main city pipes. I know that's where Edigold's kids get their water from, but still I'd rather not risk it.

'So if there's no rain, will Kampala have enough water this year?'

She shrugs. 'Only God knows the answer to that question.'

'What about Lake Victoria, can the city use that for drinking water?'

'Most of it's been emptied over the last few decades. Tanzania built a dam on the Kagera River and what little inflow of water was left on our side of the border was drained to supply the capital with running water. What's left of Lake Victoria is mostly a swamp these days.'

'Can't you treat it or boil the water or something?'

'Are you mad? Do you know what's in there?'

'What? Crocodiles?' I chuckle.

'Shit, cholera, dysentery... Heavy metals, chemicals, pesticides. Trust me on this, the water that's left is not drinkable.' She looks at the biscuit in my hand.

I eat just a small bite, leaving the rest for the children. I don't want to deprive her but I don't want to offend her either.

'So, no man yet?' she asks me, teasing.

'Nope.' I smile.

'God knows what he's doing, Olivia – he'll send you a good man when the time is right.'

'Well, he sure is taking his sweet time.' I shrug.

A burst of machine-gun fire interrupts us. We tense up and fall silent, listening to the wind as it plays with the tinkling bead curtain made of folded bottle caps that serves as a door to Edigold's home.

'You can't come here anymore, you know, it's too dangerous now,' she says.

Bwaise is divided into several districts and we're in Bwaise One, the least decrepit. But it's becoming more dangerous every week. If Anthony knew where I am right now, he'd blow a gasket.

I want to protest but think better of it and nod; she's right. She's also too kind to mention that I'm probably putting her family in danger. If her neighbours think I've given her any valuables, they could be killed for them.

'Olivia, before you go – I heard a rumour.' She stops, hesitating.

'I wouldn't have asked if it weren't important,' I reassure her.

She shudders and makes a sign of horns with her fore-finger and little finger to ward off evil. I look at her curiously, wondering if she really believes in sorcery.

'*Muzungu* soldiers. That's what you're looking for, right?'

I nod, holding my breath.

'They've been seen. Near Mazzi.'

'What's there?'

'Not much. It's an industrial zone with hangars by the canal.'

That would fit. If they wanted to test a large weapon or some sort of device, they would need a lot of space. Progress. Finally.

We chat some more but her mood is sombre today and despite my questions, I don't learn anything else.

She walks me back to the main road. Here, the street is paved and there are a few shops with basic necessities. Brightly coloured bowls and t-shirts dangle from awnings, and a woman washes her hair in front of her hut's entrance. A few meters further on, a couple of dogs sleep on blue tarps covered with peanuts that have been left to dry in the sun.

As we chat, I notice a veiled little girl and her mother are following us. The child is running as fast as she can to catch up with me; then she stops and stares at me with a big grin. When we pass by her, she starts running again until she's in front, then she stops and watches me again. Amused, I stop and the mother says, slightly out of breath, 'She just wants to say hello.'

'Yes, of course!'

I stop and crouch. 'Well, hello there.'

The little girl curtsies.

Horrified, I swoop her into my arms and plant a kiss on her cheek. Her eyebrows shoot up with surprise and a delighted smile stretches on her lips as one of her hands goes straight to my red curls while the other touches my cheek.

'Never kneel again, do you hear me, sweetie? Never kneel in front of anyone.' I deposit her carefully on the floor, fish a lollipop out of my pocket and, smiling, give it to her and walk away, embarrassed.

'How could we let the situation get so unequal and unfair that this little girl thinks it's OK to kneel in front of a white person?' I say to Edigold. Tears well up again but I push them down.

'You're funny. You think you can change the world.' Her laugh sounds bitter.

'Don't you want things to change?'

'I just do the best I can with what God sent me.' She shrugs. 'You think too much, Olivia.'

7

DEANN

ibale, *Uganda, December 2081*

THE NURSE IS YELLING at me. I'm used to sarcastic comments and backstabbing. But this full-on-in-my-face-yelling is new. In a way it's refreshing. Apparently, I took the last of the metronidazole and administered it, and now she's blaming me for the lapse in process.

'What the fuck do you want me to do?' I gesture to the crowd in the waiting room. 'Let them die?'

The nurse gets tired of berating me and leaves, but I stopped paying attention to her a few minutes ago anyway. The air doesn't move an inch even though the windows are open. My hands are sweaty inside the rubber gloves and I'm wearing a mask to try to block out the smell of vomit and disease.

I'm on triage shift today, and frankly I'd rather break a limb than stay a minute more in this stifling, stinking chaos.

People are amassed in no discernable pattern, all clamoring for attention and too far gone to help, for the most part.

I undress a bandage and find gangrene. I place a red sticker on the man's forehead and move on. Red for 'not worth the effort anymore', orange for 'treat this mess as a priority', green for 'this can wait'.

The situation is getting unbearable. Lately, the number of patients has become more than we can cope with. It started with water. Pretty crucial to have drinking water when you stop to think about it. But I never even gave that a passing thought before I came here.

It started a few weeks ago with water cuts for several hours a day in Kampala. Soon after that, we reached a point where there was no water at all coming out of faucets and from the public fountains in the slums. The price of bottled water soared. Then the price of food became too expensive for most people. We weren't really affected at the compound or at work, because, as expats, we got our rations flown in and we had enough money to buy bottled water. But the city's population didn't fare so well.

People started to get sick; from drinking dirty water, from not having enough water to drink at all. The first to die were the children and the elderly. Mothers not getting enough food to breastfeed started making bottles using dubious water and their babies died. A whole lot of them.

Everywhere I go now, there are groups of young men riding on the back of pick-up trucks and wielding machetes or machine guns, looking for their next target to loot. We've had to organize ourselves into going home in groups and by car. No one is allowed to go home on foot past 6 p.m. anymore. Some nights we can't go home at all and have to stay at the hospital, barricaded behind our rusty gate, our new armed security personnel taking shifts to protect us through the night.

A woman is pushing through the crowd, elbowing the other patients to get to me; she's carrying an unconscious toddler, dragging three kids in tow and she's pregnant.

'Sick, sick,' she says as she thrusts the child into my arms. The toddler's one and a half years old at the most. He's passed out. I shake my head, making it clear that she has to continue holding him and then I examine him, uncomfortable in the overcrowded room, with people pressing around us on all sides.

His ripped t-shirt is disgusting and he's not wearing anything underneath, no diaper, no trousers, no shoes. His breathing is quick and shallow and there's a spatter of white liquid diarrhea along his leg. Cool, clammy skin. Not good. Cholera. He's already gone into hypovolemic shock and we're out of IV drips and antibiotics. He's going to die within the hour. Nothing I can do. With a twinge, I put a red sticker on the kid's arm and, biting the inside of my cheek, move on to the next patient, the next emergency.

'Wait!'

The woman holds my arm, her grip digging in my flesh. One of the children in tow starts to cry; the noise feels like a cheese grate is being scraped along my nerves. I sigh and turn to her, expecting a litany of woe. Instead she starts to shriek, thrusting her enormous belly forward, her makeup melting in the heat. The smell of shit and vomit is invading every fiber of my being. My shirt is drenched and drops of sweat roll down the side of my ribs.

'You evil *muzungu*! You let my child die!' She shakes the red sticker on the kid's arm in front of my face. 'Where is the drug?'

'I have no drug left. It's gone. No more.'

'You have. Where?' She pushes me backwards. Some people protest as I stumble into them and catch my fall.

'There's nothing I can do.' I'm so fed up with this shit. If I give them drugs, the nurses criticize me for being too lax, and if I don't, the patients assault me. 'It's too late. You should have come earlier.'

'You fat *muzungu*, come here to steal from us, you eat our food and take drugs from my son. Look at her,' she shouts to the crowd. 'She's strong, she's clean, she has enough food.'

A handful of men turn toward us, looking belligerent, and hands start grabbing at me, as the woman wails. Cries of ascent rise up and the crowd surges forward, pinning me against the reception desk.

'You know what? I've had it. You people can just fucking croak, for all I care!'

She stares at me, dumbfounded, but I don't wait to see what they'll do next. I elbow my way through the crowd, stamping on feet as I burst out of the hospital. Then, I run.

Ten minutes into my impromptu excursion, it dawns on me that the street is probably just as dangerous and I decide to walk back to the hospital to get a ride to the compound. I'm turning a corner and starting to head back when I spot a parked water-cistern van distributing drinkable water in yellow plastic jerry cans. Some armed guys are dispensing the water, probably opportunistic assholes making desperate people pay through the nose for clean water.

The amassed crowd is clamoring to get their share, brandishing handfuls of cash and crying for help. The armed thugs keep everyone back, but they're looking increasingly uncomfortable. That's when it happens. The guard nearest the cistern shakes his head and yells something to his colleagues. Out of water. Shit. I try to back-track and return to the street I came from, but more people have arrived and I'm in the middle of the crowd now.

The mob starts baying for blood, the armed men throw down the empty jerry cans and swing their machine guns to the front of their bodies, screaming at people to get back. I've seen these sorts of images on the news and they're eerily familiar, a scene I've witnessed a hundred times before; a desperate crowd pushing forward and cornered men waving battered AK-47s in the air, yelling, their torsos shiny with sweat. But now, it feels like I have stepped through the TV screen into the dusty, sun-beaten square.

The first few shots fired in the air are startlingly loud. Shouts erupt throughout the mob. I freeze, taking in the faces around me, the screams of fear, anger, hate. Unwashed bodies all around, the smell of animal shit and garbage wafting from the open sewers. The unbearable heat. Rubber gloves still on my hands, forgotten till now, my hands slippery with sweat inside them.

Then they lunge, tearing the men from their weapons, and the handful who are still armed try as best they can to defend themselves, firing into the throng. A woman next to me falls, her face a mess of exploded flesh. Her blood splatters my face, its warm slickness trickling down into my eyes, as I scream and turn, pushing against the mass of people, trying to get through and out. But the crowd has become an impassable wall of bodies, pushing in the wrong direction, toward the cistern, the men and their rifles. Someone punches me in the stomach, I double up, my breath cut short, unable to move. Another shove and I lose my balance and fall.

I try to get up and am trampled back down. Somebody kicks my face and a blinding pain bursts in my nose. I'm inhaling clouds of red dust and I'm starting to choke.

Gagging and panicking, the only thing I can do is curl up into a ball and cover my head with my arms, to try to protect it. Behind my back, the woman's lifeless body partly shields me, moving with the ebb and flow of the crowd. It's as if she's drowned and now her body is dancing, caught in the reeds of this strange tide, this river of people.

Finally, the kicking stops. One moment I'm huddled and suffocating, swallowing dust, and the next, I can breathe again. I let go of my head and look up.

The square is empty except for dead bodies.

In front of my face, incongruous among the brass cartridges and the road's packed dirt, a pair of clean leather lace-up shoes shines in the sun. I follow the pressed crease of impeccable black pants to a white linen shirt and an extended hand.

Standing over me is a Ugandan man, his shaved head shining in the sun. His penetrating gaze is focused on me as I heave and spit out the red dust and the blood. How much of it is mine? I ignore the hand and struggle to get up on my own, before my elbows buckle.

Trying to get my bearings as I stand up on wobbly knees, I dust down my white Doctors Without Borders jacket, then use it to wipe my face. He offers me a plastic bottle of water without a word.

I grab it more greedily than I intend to, but my hands are shaking too much to open it. Careful not to touch me, he slowly removes the seal and twists the cap open. I gulp the water down in seconds and then take long breaths to calm down.

The man observes me, still silent. He's clean as a whistle. I can't even remember the last time I saw someone so clean. He stands a respectful distance away, allowing me to regain my composure, as I tie my hair into a quick ponytail and walk around the square looking for vital signs. Everyone is dead. Trampled, shot, beaten to death. Doesn't matter, the result is the same for all these poor bastards.

He leans against a black armored sedan, contemplating me and then gives orders to his chauffeur and bodyguards. They help me as best they can but nothing can be done. Once I'm finished, I come back to stand in front of him and remove my gloves. Somehow, he manages to make me feel like I'm the one who's inappropriate with my disheveled hair, blood-stained clothes and dusty face. I'm struggling with the words of thanks, getting flustered and starting to lose my shit when he grazes my arm.

'If you'll allow me, I'd like to take you somewhere slightly... safer,' he says in an elegant British accent. 'I believe you could also use a shower.'

I let out an involuntary laugh that threatens to turn into a sob. Gunfire bursts in the distance, maybe two streets away, making me flinch. Unsure whether to trust him and feeling like I've stepped into a weird dream, I take his proffered hand against my better judgment and climb in the sedan. As the door closes, its quiet luxury surrounds us, shutting out the world. It feels safe. It feels normal. We ride in silence to his property, which sprawls over a small hilltop in the best neighborhood of Kampala. The gate opens automatically, revealing a vast, manicured garden and several outbuildings gathered around the main house.

As soon as I close the door of the pristine bathroom, I yank all my clothes off as quickly as I can, repulsed by the disgusting mix of blood, garbage and mud. My hands are shaking and my teeth are chattering but I don't stop until I'm standing naked in front of the floor-length mirror. I have a bruise the size of a basketball on the left side of my ribcage and nicks and cuts all over. My nose feels broken and blood has caked into dried brown rivulets around my mouth and jaw. I touch the scar on my forehead gingerly, grateful that it has healed by now or it would surely have split open again in the violence of the stampede.

Nearly two months in Africa have taken a toll; I'm tired, thinner, my hair is dull and my skin too dry. The dead woman's exploded face flashes in front of my eyes, superposing itself on my own reflection. That could have been me, my face could have exploded like a ripe watermelon. I touch my swollen nose and shiver when the jolt of pain electrifies me. I look like shit but at least I'm alive. Time for a clean-up.

The shiny blue enamel scales of a large sculpted fish feel cool under my fingers as I walk down the three tiled steps into the huge shower. My hand trembles as I turn on the water and when blood accidentally makes its way into my mouth, I retch and nearly slip at the bottom of the vast shower, barely catching my fall. I crumple into a small ball, hug my knees and let the water pour in a cascade on my head as I sob.

It feels wrong to waste so much water but I can't get up and I can't stop crying. A long time goes by. When my skin starts to feels warmer and I stop shivering, I clean myself up, then turn off the water and step out carefully.

Feeling better, I wrap myself in a soft white towel and look for my clothes, but someone has already come in to take them away and I didn't even hear them. With a shudder, I wonder if it was him and whether he's seen me weak and naked. But I reason that he's the sort of man who would have a lot of very efficient house staff.

Near the sink, on the mosaic surface, I find a pristine caftan with an embroidered collar and I slip it on. It's too large but it floats pleasantly all around me, only skimming my bruises and cuts.

The bathroom's stocked with all the necessary toiletries so I do my best to look presentable. A while later, I venture barefoot into the corridor, the caftan's soft white fabric caressing my skin as I walk.

Night has fallen and the huge house is plunged in darkness. Kampala's distant hum spills in through the open french windows as the humid night air clings to my body like a hug. I poke my head through a few doorways, taking in one gorgeous room after the other. The house's style is a blend of colonial and classical, with canopy beds in exotic wood, draped with white mosquito nets and crisp white cotton sheets. Beautifully crafted Chesterfield sofas and walnut-burl breakfast tables are matched with animal-hide carpets and ceiling fans. The whole place exudes an air of self-confident wealth and style.

I glimpse a light and walk toward it through a deserted living room, my shadow reflecting in floor-length mirrors as I pass. The scent of rich bouquets mingles with the evening breeze, as it billows through the raw silk curtains. I push open the glass door and there he is, resting in a rattan armchair, contemplating the garden, calm and peaceful like a panther in a tree, swishing its tail lazily after a meal.

I lower myself onto a sofa, wincing at my bruised ribs, and curl my legs under the caftan, feeling vulnerable and jarred. The garden lurks in darkness, the trees and landscaped bushes barely visible as the twilight's symphony builds toward a crescendo. His comfort with silence is like water after a long drought, so I stay silent too, grateful for his respectful restraint.

He isn't exactly handsome but he exudes charisma and intensity. His tall, muscular frame looks less gym-pumped than an American man, yet he also seems stronger, more powerful. My eyes linger on his lips and I imagine running a finger on the sensitive skin as they part under my fingertips and... At last he looks at me.

'Are you feeling better?'

'Yes, thank you for your hospitality and for the clothes.' I gesture to the caftan and he nods without smiling. Assessing me.

A diminutive servant tiptoes in with food, her gestures unobtrusive and darting. Her eyes remain fixed on her task and soon the low table in front of us is piled high with colorful dishes, sweets, a water pitcher and bread; altogether more food than I've seen since leaving 2016. The evening hangs, suspended out of time, the constraints of famine holding no sway over this man. Who the hell is he?

'My name is DeAnn Carpenter. I work at the French Doctors' hospital in Kampala.'

'I know who you are.' His deep voice is warm and chilling at the same time.

'I don't.'

His eyes narrow and for a moment, I feel like a butterfly being pinned to a board. Then he relaxes and I breathe.

'Of course, I should have introduced myself.' He doesn't smile. 'I'm Omony P'Ladwar.'

'Well, thank you for saving my life, Omony P'Ladwar.'

He nods and we start eating in silence.

Inside, the ceiling fan chops the air rhythmically, its whir mixing with the night's warm breath.

'You were lucky to survive today,' he says.

'I knew things had worsened, but I hadn't realized how bad they'd gotten until I was in the midst of it.'

He shrugs. 'There's no more water. The rivers have dried up, Lake Victoria has practically evaporated.'

'What about ground water, that shouldn't be affected by the rising temperatures, should it?'

'Most is unusable for human consumption. Fertilizers and pesticides have seeped through the water table, contaminating it.'

'Here too?' I ask.

'Especially here. Multinational food companies have a free rein in Africa. In Europe or the US, you at least try to impose some limits on the chemicals they use.'

I eye the glass of water I've just drunk from. A bead of moisture slides lazily down toward the wooden table.

'It's well water, clean and filtered.'

For the first time he smiles and I take in his white teeth, the way he looks at me, eyes smoldering, his hand holding his ankle. Relaxed yet ready to spring.

Breaking the uncomfortable eye contact, I tentatively touch the bridge of my nose and wince, holding back a cry. I should be careful; he's much too sure of himself. In fact, come to think of it, I've never met a man who isn't impressed by me and scrambling to please me. I can't remember the last time I haven't been able to read a man like an open book. My American boyfriends were usually little boys posing as men. I vetted them before I even considered granting them a first date. There was no unknown, no danger... and no excitement. This guy is a completely different story. I'm at a loss to know what to do about him, I'm not in control and not sure I like the feeling at all.

He takes a sip as well, as if to reassure me that the water is safe to drink, all while evaluating me. I wonder what it would be like to taste his full lips. I bite my own, putting away the thought.

'What were you doing in that part of town?' I wonder out loud as I touch my rib, soothing the tender bruised area with a tentative rub, suddenly aware that no one knows I'm here.

'I own a company that delivers water by cistern-truck to underprivileged neighborhoods. I was supervising a delivery, gauging the viability of the situation. Our trucks regularly get attacked so we then have to repair the trucks, replace the drivers and increase security staff, with the result that the water often ends up costing more after each riot. But they can't understand that, so they keep rioting.'

The murdered woman's face grimaces in front of my eyes, her caved-in skull swaying violently back and forth as people ran and kicked us.

'Today's mob was out of control,' I say.

'They nearly killed you.'

It sounds more real now that it comes from him. I shudder. He picks up a blanket and wraps it around my shoulders, then sits back down.

'I don't blame them. They're dying.' My mind conjures up the angry crowd and the powerlessness I felt as I was trampled. 'Could you get more water delivered?' I ask, trying to steer the conversation away from my death.

He shakes his head. 'There's barely any left. It's hard to believe there once was enough for all of us. Westerners used to put drinking water in their toilet flushes, in their showers, in their washing machines. Can you imagine? *Drinking water* being flushed down toilets.' Outrage seeps through his words.

'When's the next rainy season?'

He rubs his chin and jaw. 'It's supposed to start in March but even assuming it comes, I don't know if the city will make it that long.'

Our assignment here ends in April, then we go to India.

I don't see how we can stay that long. Uganda is unraveling before our eyes.

'If it doesn't rain soon, they will die by the thousands.' He shrugs.

Crickets have woken up and a few birds are calling each other with a high-pitched trill.

Omony looks at me, his dark brown eyes serious. 'Having long hair like yours is dangerous. It's a sign of wealth. You were probably targeted in the riot.'

'I'm sure I was just in the wrong place at the wrong time. It was reckless to leave the hospital on my own.'

'You can come here anytime you want and use my home if you need more water than they can provide at the French Doctors' hospital.'

'Thank you.'

'Or you could, of course, cut your hair.'

I touch it reflexively. He does make a good point. I'd already started thinking that I should probably shave it like everybody else does here, to avoid attracting attention.

'But maybe you should know that I find your hair very...' he searches for the right word '...provoking.'

An electric shock of desire zigzags in my abdomen as he smiles his predatory smile again.

8

OLIVIA

K *ampala, Uganda, December 2081*

FATHER OPOK SINGS the Hallelujah out of tune and the congregation chant it back with much more fervour than at my usual Chelsea parish. Most of the parishioners are locals but there's a handful of expatriates; one of DeAnn's colleagues is hunched in a pew, her face in her hands, her dusty French Doctors' jacket thrown over tired clothes. I wonder how DeAnn is doing. I hope she's OK. A wave of guilt washes over me again, as acutely as the first day DeAnn and I quarrelled. She still thinks I'm a white supremacist; I haven't found a way to talk to her about anything meaningful or set the record straight yet.

Christ is hanging on the pink wall, mouth open in agony, looking down on me. 'God, please watch over her and let us find a way back to each other,' I pray silently.

Things have become completely untenable in the capital

city. The massive overpopulation was visible when we first arrived, but with 209,000,000 people crammed into a country the size of the UK, something had to give.

People displaced by border skirmishes, famines and droughts drift to Kampala where there's no infrastructure to absorb them. So they cluster in the slums for weeks, months, years, and the situation worsens. The lack of sanitation, rubbish collection and waste management ends up spreading diseases. For the poorest among them, food is becoming hard to come by.

Father Opok likes to hear himself talk and he's still droning on and on, it's been over an hour already for God's sake. 'Examine your souls, brothers and sisters. God will protect the pure of heart. Put your lives in His hands and look within to find what each and every one of you has done to usher in the devil.'

The parishioners are eating this up, listening to him attentively and nodding.

I don't know if it's the devil who's causing this chaos. I'm pretty sure it's small, armed groups ransacking wealthy neighbourhoods. They're not evil, they're just young men, driven by hunger, thirst and hopelessness. Too many people. Not enough food and water. Deadly combination.

So here we are, praying under armed guard. Praying to be sent back to England, praying to survive the day. Praying that our homes won't be attacked. Praying for Colonel Groebler not to kill me. Well, it's probably just me praying for that last one.

I line up to take communion and the priest is placing the host on my tongue when machine-gun fire erupts. Close. Too close.

Tensing up, we all look at the doors. The guards yell something and set off running towards the gates, shouldering their own machine guns. Rubaga Cathedral is on one of Kampala's seven hills; it's supposed to be more defendable. At least I hope so. The other churches have all been raided, looted and burned to the ground. I hold my breath as the host melts on my tongue, forgotten. More gunfire. Then silence. The cathedral is frozen. Somebody whimpers behind me.

One of the armed guards comes back and nods to Father Opok.

The line resumes. I swallow the mushy wafer and stand up. Breaths are released. An infant starts to bawl. The choir resumes their hymn. I walk back to my seat, wiping my palms on my trousers.

'The Mass is ended. Go in peace, glorifying the Lord by your life.'

'Thanks be to God.'

We spill out of the church. The sun is already scorching hot and the parishioners are anxious to get back home to their ACs and ceiling fans. As I prepare to leave, I spot Edigold. Her eyes are red and her composure frazzled.

'Edigold, what's going on? Are the children alright?'

For an answer, she pulls me behind her into Father Opok's office, her hand cold in mine.

'Close the door please.'

Edigold and I stand in front of Father Opok, who ignores us for a while, as he finishes writing a letter and stamps it. Lately, Edigold has been pocketing a few items from the charity stocks to give to her children. I never say anything. Maybe these small thefts are what this is about? Surely not.

'I have asked you both to come here because there have been reports from parishioners that you are both leading women into temptation and sin.'

He folds his hands one on top of the other on his potbelly and stays quiet, observing us.

I frown. 'Sorry, what?'

'Olivia had nothing to do with it. She just came on a walk with me once. She's not involved.'

Father Opok was such a lovely plump man when I arrived. Now he's shrunk and greyed and he's permanently sad these days. But I've never seen him as stern as today.

'Do you have anything to say to me, Edigold?'

He waits for something, staring intently at Edigold. An admission of guilt perhaps. Or pleading for forgiveness? But she stays silent.

The silence stretches and Edigold's hand trembles around mine. Shaking his head, Father Opok sighs.

'Very well. Edigold Murungi, you have committed both a sin and a crime by procuring contraception and abortion pills for your fellow parishioners. This, as you have been warned, carries a penalty. I hereby excommunicate you from the Catholic Church.'

Edigold is straight as a rod, her fists clenched.

'Olivia.' He turns towards me and my breath catches. Oh no.

'Leave her out of this, old man.'

He stops and turns to Edigold. I breathe out and slump with relief as she continues, a bitter note in her voice, 'Can't you see Uganda collapsing around you? Controlling our fertility is the solution, not the problem.'

'Father Opok, there must be a mistake.' I step closer to his desk. 'Edigold has been trying to help these women.'

'Olivia, contraception is not condoned by the Church. You know that very well. We only advise abstinence.'

'But that's ridiculous; no one wants to abstain and no one does, just look at the birth rates in this country,' I say.

'The act of love must always contain the promise of conception; otherwise, it's just lust.' He squirms in his seat.

'Shouldn't the Church adapt its teaching to the current situation? The world is on the brink of collapse because of overpopulation – you must tell people to use contraception and to stop reproducing,' I say.

'No, the Church never adapts. Where would we be if we had had to change our doctrine every time there was a slight difficulty in the last two thousand years? No, we stick to our teachings through thick and thin. That's what the Church is all about, Olivia, we provide an immutable North to guide the flock through the storm.'

'You're wasting your breath, Olivia.' Edigold shakes her head and gestures for us to leave.

'So you approve of people making eight or ten children in the current conditions?' I ask, refusing to believe that this kind man would be so inflexible.

'I'm concerned, of course, but our teachings clearly say that man must multiply and be fruitful.'

'When they can't even feed them and end up holding their dead kids in their arms and begging for food on the streets?' Edigold snaps.

'The Lord giveth and the Lord taketh away. It's not for us to question. We just have to do what the Bible says: have intercourse within the bounds of marriage and bring forth as many children as God will see fit to send.'

Feeling that I need to stand up for my friend, I try reasoning with him. 'The New Testament was written a hundred and fifty years after the death of Jesus mostly by people who hadn't even witnessed his life. The canon of what became the New Testament was only put together in the fourth century. That's not the Word of God, that's just a historical patchwork of texts that suited the political establishment of the day.'

'We believe that God guided their hand and told them which texts to include.'

'So you don't think it's rather convenient that the twenty-seven texts that comprise the New Testament were consolidated by a council of *men* who picked and chose what to include and what to remove? Texts written by women were excluded.'

'Gender doesn't matter, this is the Word of God...'

'Don't make me laugh, Father. Of course it's about gender. Of course it's about power. Do you really think any of these *men* asked the women whether they wanted to have eight kids and spend their lives caring for them? It's effectively removed all women from any position of power in society ever since.'

'*Unto the woman God said, I shall greatly multiply thy sorrow and thy conception; in sorrow thou shalt bring forth children; and thy desire shall be to thy husband, and he shall rule over thee.*' He crosses his arms as if this solved the debate beyond argument.

I can't believe my ears. 'You can't be serious. Eve's curse? It's madness to continue believing this message from antiquity when we're at a junction – twenty centuries later – which could mean life or death for humanity.'

'Surely He doesn't want everyone to die?' Edigold says. 'Why would he ask us to make so many babies that we choke the Earth and kill everyone on it through starvation?'

'How do you know what God wants? That strikes me as very arrogant, Edigold. If this is how He wants his creation to end, then we must accept it.'

Edigold laughs but it comes out like a sob. 'Well, I don't want to die. And I don't want my children to die. So I will continue helping women who want to take control of their bodies and their fates. You can keep your religion.'

The priest rubs his forehead. Edigold takes a shaky breath and I squeeze her hand.

'You should both leave. I'd like you to reflect on the blasphemies you have committed today. Go home.'

Edigold makes a disgusted sound and marches out of the office, her emaciated frame fragile yet still proud. As I watch her walk out, Father Opok's hand lands gently on my shoulder. He's standing next to me, looking gaunt and exhausted.

'I had to do it, Olivia. Her ideas can't be allowed to contaminate the congregation. She can get the sentence lifted. But only if the bishop perceives repentance.'

I wince. 'Not a lot of that, I'm afraid.'

Father Opok's doing the best he can. His grey skin sags and new wrinkles have appeared around his eyes. Maybe he's just a captain going down with his ship. A relic of a bloated age sinking under its own weight. He can't understand what Edigold is trying to accomplish any more than she can understand his steadfast clinging to rules that once defined Good and Evil. And yet humanity must adapt or sink.

I hug him fiercely and take a step back, wiping away a tear. He looks surprised, then his face softens.

'Go in peace, Olivia.'

I walk along the aisle, light a candle for Mary and touch the statue's foot as I say a quick prayer for my two friends. To be fair, even if the Church miraculously started to allow the use of contraception right now, during Advent, in 2081, it would change nothing for the millions about to die. This ship's so brimming with passengers that it's already taking on water. It's all too late. It's such a large societal, economic and cultural problem that you'd have to work on it for generations to arrive at a solution.

It's only when I get out into the bright morning sun that it hits me: I'm a bloody time traveller. We still *do* have generations to tackle the issue and solve it before all these people die of starvation. I must get back to 2016 and find a way to fix this horrific mess.

In front of the church, Anthony is waiting for me by the armoured SUV. In a way he's also a victim of this new world. Who knows what a nice guy like him might have become in a different society? Maybe an architect, a baker, a marketing manager? Instead, here he is: a soldier in a white supremacist army, reduced to killing in order to survive.

I can tell that our conversations are starting to have an effect on him, that he's conflicted yet also unable to imagine another reality, another path because that's just how everyone thinks now: 'me first', 'my country first', 'my race first'. When did it all go so wrong?

9

DEANN

K *ampala, December 2081*

EACH DAY MELTS into the next, with life at the hospital inspiring in turn awe and despair. But I hold on, thanks to my friends and Omony.

Through my relationship with him, I've been introduced into the Ugandan society and charmed by its people and culture. With him, I experience the beautiful side of the country and I live a world away from the poorest and most destitute people who wash up at the hospital's door, day after day.

People treat Omony with deference and when they learn that I'm American and a doctor *and* his guest, they treat me like a queen at his side. I must admit I like the attention and the respect that this grants. It's a heady *mélange* that could go right to my head if I'm not careful.

He invites me to expensive restaurants. Food costs so

much now that we're practically the only ones in the places where he takes me. Or maybe he rents the whole restaurant for the evening, who knows?

He's courting me the old-fashioned way. He's persistent but he hasn't laid a finger on me yet or even made a move. I get flowers, cards, formal invitations to events. He provides the dresses, the rides, the staff to help prepare me. It's all a bit surreal and when I'm back at the hospital, plunged in real life, the evenings with Omony seem like a dream or a guilty indulgence.

I sigh and unclasp the sphygmomanometer, sliding it off my patient's skeletal arm, when Rosebell barges in my consultation room, all excited.

'Doctor Herault needs volunteers to close down an outpost clinic near Kibale. And guess what? We're going.'

'Kibale? That's in the sticks. Are you joking? We've got more urgent...'

She cuts through my complaints. 'I heard a rumor about the outpost manager. She's a *muzungu*. People are saying she's been pestering HQ about her patients' strange symptoms. This could be the same as what we're seeing here. An inexplicable rash of ovarian cancers. It's worth checking out.'

'Not that again, Rosebell,' I snap, annoyed. 'I've told you fifty times. It's probably a statistical fluke. You're obsessing. You need a hobby.'

'I've already told Doctor Herault. I'm going. You're going. We're going. End of story.' She turns on her heel and leaves.

'No, I'm not!' I call after her.

.   .   .

THE NEXT MORNING, I'm waiting by the compound's gate at too-early-o'clock when a khaki van that has seen better days shudders to halt in front of me.

I grip the ceiling handle and climb in. 'What's this monstrosity?'

'Why? Is the style too last season for you, your highness?' Rosebell says. 'It's all I could find on such short notice. My cousin's a safari tour operator and he doesn't need the van this weekend. It doesn't have the French Doctors' logo but it'll have to do.'

Struggling to remove my backpack, I turn around to stuff it behind me and nearly jump out of my skin when Kitsa grabs it.

'What the...'

'Oh yeah, I'm bringing the kid, she needs a change of scenery.'

'No, absolutely not, that's...'

'... a great idea,' Rosebell finishes. 'Oh and by the way, we're staying at my parents' tonight.' Then, seeing my face: 'Just go with it, my friend.'

We set off in the busy Kampala traffic, narrowly avoiding pedestrians who weave oblivious between the cars and matatus crammed full of commuters. Rosebell introduces us to the more colorful side of her swearing palette as boda bodas zigzag around our van, laden with precarious loads of gigantic green banana bunches, trussed-up goats and entire families.

A blanket of yellow smog hangs over the city and there's still not a drop of rain on the horizon. It takes us two hours to extricate ourselves from the jam. But we finally burst out of the suffocating city and take the road. Well, if it can be called that. It's more of a strip of dried red mud with rickety huts on either side of it. In every village, the same three shops, of the same three brands, painted in the same three colors greet us: red, blue, yellow; iMode shop, corner food store and DYI. The rest of the buildings are dilapidated, with a few people listlessly sitting on the beaten dirt out front, some selling food, others just going about their daily activities, washing in buckets, eating, flirting or simply staring at us.

Rosebell stops for gas and while she negotiates with the attendant, I notice again, like everywhere else we stopped, a group of young men doing nothing whatsoever with AK-47s slung around their backs. They sit under a half dead tree, motorcycles parked nearby, chatting and laughing, while a few feet away, an elderly woman, at least eighty years old, plows a field, preparing it for sowing. Not a single one of the thugs even acknowledges her presence, let alone thinks to help her.

I shake my head in disgust and look for the toilets. Toilet is perhaps a misnomer; it's a square hole in the concrete floor. Buzzing flies circle the stains on the edge of it and a t-shirt slung over the door is supposed to be used as toilet paper.

I take one look at the facilities and retreat, holding my sleeve against my face and wiping my fingers against my trousers. I'll hold it.

We set out again. Rosebell tosses a soft drink and a pack of candy to the kid and turns the music on.

'What's wrong with the men here?' I burst out, exasperated, my mood worsened by my bladder pressing against the seat belt. 'They don't do anything. I can't understand it. There's so much to be done in this country. So much that needs fixing. Why don't they do something about it?'

'What? Who?'

'These guys.' I gesture to the loitering group sitting

under a nearby tree, as the van drives away. 'Sitting on their fucking hands while the country falls apart around their ears. It doesn't even occur to them to do something with their days, apparently.'

'Oh, these guys. They're brokers. When you want to buy property around here, you go through them.'

'Mmh. Wouldn't their time be better spent building actual houses or sidewalks or, I don't know, planting fields?'

'Who would pay them to do that? There's no money in it.'

Between forlorn villages, the desolate countryside, ravaged by drought, rolls past our windows. Entire fields of corn bake under the midday sun, trees droop, their leaves fallen a long time ago on the parched ground and animal carcasses dry on the curb.

'So, DeAnn, how do you like our African massage?' Rosebell asks.

I look at her blankly, holding the oh-shit-handle while she maneuvers the huge van like a pro, around potholes and over bumps.

'You know, the roads.' Just then, we fall in a deep rut and I bounce up and down, slamming against the seat. In the back, Kitsa giggles and licks spilled soda off her hands.

'Oh, ha ha.' I wince, stretching.

On the side of the road, we keep passing children as they walk to school, wearing brightly colored uniforms. Each district seems to have a different color: hot pink, bright green, electric blue. As soon as they catch a glimpse of me, they start screaming, '*Muzungu, muzungu!*' and run alongside the van, big grins on their faces.

'Come on, you know you want to,' Rosebell says, smiling as she rolls down my window from her main control panel.

I find myself grinning back and start to wave like

goddamn princess Di on her wedding day. But the kids love it, they cheer and wave and point. I can't help but love these people. Against my better judgment – because what's the point, really? And yet, I do, so I wave some more.

Finally, we arrive at the French Doctors' outpost and park. Rosebell and I stretch and groan; African massage, my ass. More like torture.

The clinic sits at the top of a yellow grass knoll. A dried-up forest surrounds it, the spectral trees looking more like kindling than living wood. We start walking along the long gravel path toward the far-off clinic, slowing down as the slope gets steeper. As we near the building, we realize that the place is teeming with patients. Babies are crying, people are panicking, there's a huge line and no discernable order.

'Are you sure we're supposed to close this place down? What will these patients do?' I ask.

'The instructions are clear. Came directly from HQ. Apparently the leader of this outpost went a bit...' Rosebell twirls her finger around her temple. 'She failed the last several inspections and multiple reports have been coming in about her not following protocols.'

'Great, so we're getting our intel on the ovarian cancer epidemic from Marlon Brando toward the end of *Apocalypse Now*. What could possibly go wrong?'

'You're speaking gibberish again.' I'm about to explain when she frowns and cocks her head. 'Oh, interesting. You should try putting it on,' she says and points to my collar.

My iBubble snaps into place and an image superimposes itself on top of the decrepit building. The trees all around become green again, the shrubs fill with flowers, a gaggle of laughing children emerge from the entrance and I jump out of their way but they go right through me and dissolve in a shower of colorful sparks.

A white woman in her thirties glides through the door of the impeccably kept building and beams at me.

'Welcome, DeAnn. My colleagues and I hope you had a nice journey.' Her Scandinavian accent seems out of place in these surroundings. 'My name is Doctor Eskelin. Is there anything I can do for you today?' She hovers there, smiling vacuously as I figure out what to say to a hologram. The translucent figure pats her blonde bun and adjusts the stethoscope around her shoulders. I wonder if she'll reset? She shuffles from one foot to the other.

Rosebell's speaking to thin air; she must be talking to another interface.

I turn to my *muzungu*-friendly hologram. 'Hi there. I need to contact someone in charge, please.'

'Just a moment.'

A few minutes later, something moves in the real world. Spooked, I collapse the iBubble; the same woman stands in front of me but time has not been kind to her. Now in her seventies, her face has collapsed like a chalk cliff into the sea. Yellowing strands of gray hair hang loose from her bun and her blue eyes are washed out, as if the color and happiness had been bleached from them after one too many cycles.

'Hi, we're from Doctors Without Borders in Kampala...'

'About time! Are you the only ones who came? That won't be enough!' She turns on her heel and walks away, talking to the air. 'Nobody cares... They could all drop dead... I won't let them do this... This is not...'

Rosebell and I exchange a look and follow her inside into the hallway.

Temporarily blinded as our eyes adjust to the gloom, we lose the doctor and have to elbow our way through the long line of protesting patients in order to catch up with her. The locals look like they're all suffering from a similar condition; most have rasping voices, asthmatic breathing and phlegmy coughs. I lift my shirt on my nose as we squeeze through the corridor and follow the doctor through to a dilapidated exam room. Taking in the overflowing garbage can, the cracked windowpane, and the floating smell of sickness, I stand in a corner and try to touch nothing.

Still ignoring us, Dr. Eskelin's taken a seat and rolled her stool closer to a young woman who is wheezing and coughing blood into her cupped hand. Startled by our arrival, the Ugandan girl tries to bolt, but the doctor stops her with a surprisingly soft gesture. She speaks to her patient in rapid, clipped dialect, her voice low and her gestures slow. The young woman calms down and sits back on the examination bed.

The Finnish doctor takes a sample of the woman's bloodied saliva, mumbling under her breath as a few involuntary jerks contract her shoulders.

'You should put some gloves on.' Rosebell is looking around the room, a concerned expression on her face.

'Gloves?' Dr. Eskelin roars with laughter. 'Would you like me to wear a face mask as well and have them fill out an insurance form on their way in?'

Irritated, I say, 'Look, I'll just come right out and say it: we're here from headquarters; we've come to shut down your clinic. We brought a van, so we can take any gear that's still usable and all your personal effects.'

'American.' The old woman glares at me, a bitter slant to her mouth. 'Do you work for them? Have you come to kill me?'

'What? No, of course not.' I glance at Rosebell, eyebrows raised.

Dr. Eskelin weighs my denial, her face twitching. Then

she turns back to the Ugandan woman and speaking to her in urgent, hushed tones, presses a small blister pack into her hand. The young woman gets up and slinks out of the small consultation room, her eyes glued to the floor. I throw a glance at the line of desperate patients outside and wonder if it might be TB.

'Are they all suffering from the same symptoms?' Rosebell asks.

The doctor grunts, stocky frame hunched. 'The villagers still come from miles around, but I'm the only one left now. Soon, I won't have any drugs left to treat them...' She walks away, talking to herself. 'So, that's it, it's over... I guess that's the point.'

Rosebell and I glance at each other.

'Doctor Eskelin?' Rosebell runs after her and places a careful hand on her shoulder. The woman flinches. 'There's nothing left for you here. We're taking you back to Kampala and from there, back home.'

The old doctor looks up, her arthritic hand reaches gently for my friend's, the bones protruding under her age-spotted skin. She pats Rosebell's hand.

'This *is* my home. These are my people. What would I do in Finland?'

'But you can't stay here anymore, Doctor Eskelin. It's over.'

'Tomorrow. Come back tomorrow.'

'Will you come with us then? I have questions I would like to ask you...'

The woman doesn't even bother answering, she walks out of the room and we hear her shuffle off down the hallway.

'Something's definitely wrong with that woman,' I whisper.

Rosebell frowns and nods. I can see she wants to stay and help.

'Come on, we need to go,' I push.

My friend hesitates, then she nods. 'You're right, we have to get to my parents' house before dark. We'll pick her up tomorrow on our way back. That'll give her time to wrap things up and pack.'

I follow my friend out of the clinic, past the silent row of patients, waiting, staring at us with huge, hopeful eyes.

'Kitsa, we're off!' I yell as we get back into the sun-drenched afternoon, temporarily blinded by the sun.

The girl runs down the length of the long gravel path and skids to a halt in front of the car.

'Look!' She beams.

There's a stethoscope around her neck.

'Where did you get that?'

'The crazy old *muzungu* gave it to me when I told her I wanted to study medicine, like Doctor DeAnn.'

I look up at the clinic at the top of the hill and spot the doctor standing in the entrance. It's hard to tell, from this far away but there might be a timid smile wavering on her lips, as if she can't quite remember how to do it. Eskelin lifts a hand and then disappears inside the building, swallowed by the gathering dusk.

Kitsa spends the rest of the trip listening to her own heart and to anything else she can stick the chest-piece on. I can't help but smile.

A couple of hours later, we arrive at Rosebell's parents'. The mother is plump and lovely, and she insists on treating me as if I were her daughter and Kitsa her grandkid. She teaches me how to make katogo, a sort of poor man's stew made with root vegetables, and it turns out to be surprisingly good. Then, we all have dinner on the patio. The air smells of cows and flowers. Crickets put on a serenade for us, and stars shine against the African night's vast backdrop.

Rosebell's father, Asiimwe, makes us laugh all evening. He looks like a sixties intellectual with his collar beard, his glorious white Afro and sharp wit. After dinner, reading glasses perched on his nose, leaning back in his armchair, hands clasped on his belly, he regales us with stories about the Uganda of his youth, a wistful look in his eyes.

Kitsa has finally collapsed after our full day. In the dark, she forms a little ball on the nearby sofa, the cast on her arm protruding like a broken wing, the stethoscope clasped fiercely against her chest.

THE NEXT DAY, Rosebell's father shows us around the Bigodi swamp. We put on rubber boots, long-sleeved shirts and set off for the hike. An hour into the walk, we reach a narrow path where we have to form a single file and when Asiimwe stops, I take advantage to wipe the sweat off my forehead, take a swig of water and adjust my cap in the baking sun.

No noteworthy feature jumps out at me. Nothing that might justify the walk. To the right, fields of corn extend as far as the eye can see, yellow and dry in the unrelenting sun, the stalks just standing there, looking half dead.

I look toward the left, thinking that maybe I've missed a monkey or a bird, but there's nothing there either, just a forlorn thicket of jungle that seems devoid of life. Kitsa's playing in a dried-up stream that's more of a mud trickle at this point.

'This is what I wanted to show you,' Rosebell's father says. 'The demarcation line, you see. Between us and them.'

'Between who and who?' I ask, puzzled.

'The Bakiiga and the Batooro.'

As if that meant anything to me.

'We are Batooro. We used to be hunters and gatherers. We only took what the forest could give, no more. We had few children but those were cherished.' He wraps his arm around Rosebell's shoulders and brings her close. She smiles and looks up at him. Something twinges in my chest. Dad. I hope he's OK.

Asiimwe points to the beaten dirt path under our boots. 'This is where the Bakiiga territory stops... for now.'

Rosebell chimes in, 'they're farmers; they have no respect for the jungle. The government keeps giving them our land. And the Bakiiga keep growing. Their crops, their livestock, their families.'

'We call them Tukaizirua: those who came to stay.' Rosebell's father spits on the ground and walks away.

Soon, we come across two women who are working the fields, hacking at the dead corn with machetes. A few feet away, an elderly woman, looking gaunt and exhausted, is trying to salvage a few green bananas, no doubt hoping to make a meal for the group of children who are gathered around her. There are at least eight of them, ranging in age and height, all sitting on the ground, barefoot and in grubby rags. It doesn't look like there will be enough matoke for all of them.

'There used to be birds here,' Asiimwe says. 'People came from around the world to see them. And monkeys, red colobus, baboons...'

'What happened to them?' I ask.

'The Bakiiga killed them because they ate the crops.'

'But, Dad, they need the corn for their children. Would you rather they let their kids die, to save a few birds?' Rosebell asks.

Asiimwe doesn't answer and just keeps walking. We pass a dog sleeping under a thatched shed and when Kitsa approaches it to play, the mongrel growls and its hackles rise. Four men materialize from behind the straw hut, grabbing their machetes.

'Kitsa, come here.' I clutch the little girl and hold her against me.

Rosebell and her father ignore the men and continue walking along the narrow path, so Kitsa and I hurry after them, feeling the men's stares on our necks.

As the afternoon's shadows start to expand and yawn, we take to the road, reluctantly saying goodbye to Rosebell's parents, promising to come back soon. The drive back to the MSF outpost is dull, each of us wrapped in our own silence. There are no children in bright school uniforms today, no cheering, no waving.

'You OK?' Rosebell asks, eyes on the road.

'Yeah. I just wonder what's wrong with Eskelin's patients. We should report it to headquarters, get a taskforce over to help.'

She snorts.

'What?' I say. 'If we have an epidemic on our hands they'll want to stamp it down before it spreads.'

'You still don't get it, do you?' she says, changing gear. 'They *want* us to die. Even if we reported it, nobody would come; they'd let the disease kill us.'

Queasiness spreads in my gut. 'You're exaggerating.'

Rosebell shakes her head. 'No, I'm not. What my father told you this morning about the Bakiiga tribe taking over the Batooro territory? It's like that, but on a global scale.'

'What does this have to do with—'

In reply, she gestures to a cluster of Mukiiga farmers, trying their best to harvest a field of corn by the side of the road. They barely look up as a cloud of dust engulfs them in our wake.

'The tribe. The tribe, *muzungu*. Now that resources are scarce and it's starting to dawn on humanity that there is no longer enough air for all of us to breathe, enough water to drink and enough food to eat. Guess what?'

'Tribes,' I say.

'Yes!' she says, gloomily. 'The tribes will stick with their own and the strongest tribes will take territory and resources away from the weak. The white tribe has already started. They withhold the drugs that would save us from malaria because there is no malaria in developed countries. They no longer send any help when there is a famine and they will definitely not care about Eskelin's patients.'

Now that she says it out loud, it seems too outrageous to be real. All the same, I've suspected this for a while, but for once, or the millionth time since I've been here, I was hoping I was wrong. 'Are you sure? That's extreme even for the White Man.'

'You know better, my friend,' Rosebell says. 'They saw us as chattel for the slave boats. They saw us as test subjects for their medical experiments. Now they see us as competition for the planet's food and water supplies. And as always, we'll die.'

I feel colder, all of a sudden. 'So what are you saying? That each tribe is now going to fight the others to death for scarce resources?'

'Yes. And Africans will be the first casualties of this war. Whites will wipe us out, like the Bakiiga did the Batooro,' Rosebell says. 'They won't even necessarily kill us outright.

They can just take our land, our food and our water, and the end result will be the same.'

Finally we reach the clinic, as twilight starts to bruise the sky. This time, nobody comes to greet us, so we climb the graveled path to the main building, stretching our sore limbs. At the top of the hill, Kitsa skips off to the back of the building, to look for a baby goat to play with or whatever.

A muddy tarpaulin rustles, making me jump in the eerie silence. The door is wide open and there's no light inside.

'Doctor Eskelin?'

The equipment sits abandoned, old and dusty. The glass doors of the cabinets are smashed and the shelves are empty. It looks like there might have been a break-in. In one of the rooms, dried-up tendrils have forced their way in through a crack in the wall. Maybe it was already this derelict yesterday and I just didn't notice.

Eskelin is nowhere to be found.

I shudder. 'This place is giving me the creeps.'

'Hey, look what I found,' Rosebell calls from somewhere nearby. There's shattered glass under my feet as I go to join her in the neighboring room, where I find her sitting on a three-footed Ugandan stool, leafing through a leather-bound journal. An old-fashioned microscope sits on a desk, along with stacks of hardback medical manuals and piles of papers. A single bed is pushed against the wall and the deep indentation in the mattress seems to call for its missing owner, as the smell of old age and loneliness floats in the dusty air. The bed is unmade but there are suitcases near the door.

'It's weird, why would she keep medical notes on paper? They're impossible to share.' Rosebell frowns and flips through the leather-bound journal. 'And if the villagers had looted the clinic, why would they have left the suitcases? None of this makes sense.'

'Bring the notebooks, Rosebell. Doctor Eskelin will probably want them.' Unsure what to do, I pick up the old woman's suitcase and carry them outside.

Where is the woman at?

We're loading everything in the van when Kitsa skids to a halt next to us.

'Doctor DeAnn, Doctor DeAnn! Come, I found the old *muzungu*.'

Before I can answer, she's off. Cursing under my breath, I run after her, as Rosebell struggles to keep up. When we reach the top of the hill, I walk to the back of the clinic and into the copse behind it. The branches of the dried-up trees cling to my clothes and a smell of baked earth and dried underbrush wafts up as we struggle to find purchase on the crumbling slope.

Why couldn't she just wait and tell me what she found?

'Maybe Dr. Eskelin's hurt and needs help?' Rosebell puffs behind me.

'Kitsa!' I call.

Worried, I survey the forest in the gathering dusk and spot the girl. She's found the old doctor. I exhale and start to slide down the slope toward them when I realize something's wrong. Kitsa and Dr. Eskelin are hiding behind a tree trunk and staring at something at the bottom of the hill.

10

OLIVIA

K*ampala, Uganda, December 2081*

THE FIRST TIME I went to Adroa, the cathedral's orphanage, I stood in the reception area, waiting for the nurse to tell me what to do. She was harassed and uninterested; a *muzungu* who wanted to help, what else was new? The thin, tired Ugandan had no time to show me around and there was a sick baby that needed tending to. So I waited for about an hour, wondering whether to leave. The bag of toys and sweets sat heavy in my hands. Maybe I could just drop it off and go? Anthony remained by the door, checking entrances and exits, hand on his holster, as kids chased each other around the playground.

'Olivia, come on,' he called from outside. 'They don't have time and I don't think they want your help.' He looked like he'd rather be anywhere else.

I hesitated, shifting the bag's weight from arm to arm.

Maybe I wasn't needed. I was still shuffling from left to right, when a baby crawled into the reception area towards me, a determined look on his round face. He stopped at my feet and oscillating back and forth, tipped himself into a sitting position, so he could look up at me. Then he broke into a huge grin and my heart flopped right out of my chest and into his lap.

I put the heavy bag of donations on the floor and swooped him up into my arms, glad to swap the heavy bag for this small bundle, which seemed perfectly moulded to fit into my embrace. He grabbed a handful of my hair and proceeded to eat it. Laughing, I removed as much as I could manage from his mouth and swung him against my hip, just as the nurse returned.

'Oh, I see you've met our little charmer. This is Jonathan – you don't have to carry him, you know.'

'Oh no, it's quite alright, no trouble at all,' I said lightly, pretending not to care. But inside me, a wave of emotion rose like dawn after a cold night, drenching everything in its path in warmth and light.

'You, little man, are going to show me around, OK?' I said to Jonathan as he tried to bite my nose.

The main dormitory was lined with small cots draped in colourful mosquito nets. Mickey Mouse and Donald Duck seem to cheer me on from the decorated walls, as I picked my way across the toy-littered floor, careful not to drop my precious cargo.

Jonathan settled on my left hip, gurgling, as I introduced myself to the Ugandan nurse and to one of the volunteers, Evelyn, an Irish woman who'd been here for three months already and lived in the guest rooms.

'So what should I do?' I asked Evelyn. 'I'm here to help.'

'Nothing.' She shrugged with a smile. 'You just hug them and love them. That's all they want, really.'

I'd never heard anything sound so good. So I sat with my legs extended and tried not to move as one by one the babies started to crawl and climb on my legs, cling to my arms and rummage in my handbag. And I just hugged them and learned their names and wiped a few tears as I breathed in their baby scent. Silas the inquisitive pinched my sunglasses and put them on upside down, Moses the inconsolable cried every time I put him down and Jonathan, the most adorable, used my hands as a teething toy and didn't budge from my lap.

After a while, Anthony wandered in and smiled when he saw me under the heap of children. He sat on a chair, not quite within the babies' reach and looked tentatively at the exit until Suzanne commandeered him. Soon, Anthony was twirling his hands for her and bouncing her up and down on his knee until she squealed with joy.

Anthony and I went back to Adroa after that first visit, of course; the next Sunday we brought more powdered milk, more toys, more food. And the next, and the next.

Anthony and I kind of adopted each other after that first day at the orphanage. He looks after me when I do things I'm not supposed to, like go to the slums to visit Edigold. In exchange, I bake for him when I can find supplies, and we eat the biscuits together and chat about principles and values. It's so interesting to hear his point of view. I get the sense that among all the soldiers at the compound, he's the only one who might understand and come round to my way of thinking. He's so kind to me, I don't want to accept that he's a white supremacist at heart. I can't help but wonder whether he'd have been quite so racist, had he grown up in another era, so it's encouraging to see him playing with the orphans.

Now I volunteer here every week after Mass. Today, Anthony stayed behind at the church, saying he'd come and fetch me later, so I hitched a ride here with the lovely Evelyn.

I'm sitting on a mat, holding baby Jonathan. He's wearing yellow overalls and biting the side of my hand. I don't mind the small scratches and the drool, Jonathan can do anything he wants, he's too cute to say no to. I blow a raspberry on his belly and he babbles happily, his laughter tinkling like a wind chime in the morning sun.

I've just spent an hour bonding with the babies and giving them as much love as I can. So, my dream-life duty done, I put Jonathan on my hip and go help in the kitchen. Today is a special occasion: we've prepared a pre-Christmas treat for the children. Evelyn and I chat happily as we put the finishing touches to the feast; the kids are going to be so happy. There are sweets and cakes in the kitchen and we've got presents for them as well – there's a brand new toy car in my pocket for Jonathan and the rest of the gifts are in the back room.

When the food is ready, the usual mayhem ensues as we chase the little rascals and try to get them to sit down nicely, with a plastic plate in front of each one. The older children are chatting happily and the toddlers babble in their high chairs, all of them lined up against the wall, all clamouring for their meal. But first, it's time for their bottles of milk.

There are hundreds of children to be fed and few volunteers. I keep an eye on Jonathan as I tip a bottle each into his and Suzanne's mouths at the same time, careful not to spill the formula. The next baby clings to my arm, trying to get the bottle for himself, so urgently, so desperately that I choke back tears. He has to wait until I'm done, I only have two arms.

Just as Jonathan and Suzanne finish their bottles, there's a deafening racket in the yard, like firecrackers. I turn around and see a dozen thugs with machine guns sprinting over the playground, towards us.

11

DEANN

K*ampala, Uganda, December 2081*

A BEAM of light sweeps over Kitsa and Dr. Eskelin's heads and I dodge out of the way, pulling Rosebell to the ground with me. The old woman throws a glance at us over her shoulder and holds a finger in front of her lips, then turns back to her surveillance. What the hell? Moving slowly, bent double, Rosebell and I reach their hiding spot and lie down next to them.

Below, in a clearing, white soldiers are positioned around a construction site. There must be twenty of them. Their gray and khaki fatigues blend in with the surrounding forest, their equipment is clearly top notch and their movements seem practiced and professional. An excavator is backing up with beeping sounds, as it moves soil from a mound into a large hole in the ground of the clearing.

Dr. Eskelin looks pale and dishevelled.

'What's going on? We need to go...' I stop mid-sentence. There's something in that hole.

It's a human foot.

Rosebell's fingers close painfully around my arm as she realizes what we're looking at. Dirt tumbles out of the bulldozer's metal teeth, covering dozens of dusty, gray corpses.

I slap a hand over my mouth.

Rosebell pulls on my sleeve and motions for us to go. I'm backtracking slowly when a beam of light catches the old doctor's white coat and torch beams converge on our location.

Several soldiers yell, 'We've got company!'

'Over there!'

A few feet away, a tree explodes in a blast of splinters. They're shooting at us! I grab Kitsa by the hand and, dragging her to her feet, rush across the slope and up toward the clinic.

'Fuck. Catch them!'

The ground next to my feet bursts. Something painful cuts into my calf. I scream and pull Kitsa forward, willing her to run faster as the deafening staccato of machine-gun fire explodes behind our backs. Mouth dry, panic rising, my side is on fire but I can't stop.

I throw a quick glance behind me. Rosebell waddles up the hill, puffing, and Dr. Eskelin is bringing up the rear, when a shot echoes and the old woman's eyes go wide. A look of utter astonishment on her face, she grabs at her chest where a large red stain spreads and then she collapses, face down into the dry underbrush.

'Freeze!'

I hesitate but Rosebell catches up and thrusts me forward. We stumble across the hill crest and slide, half falling down the slope, past the clinic. I trip over a root and sprawl on the ground. Kitsa helps me up as Rosebell runs down the gravel path to the van.

'Don't let them get away!'

Gunshots explode again and something burns a fiery path along my cheek. Shrieking, I hurtle down the hill. My friend yanks the door open and starts the van.

'Fucking stop them!'

Kitsa and I jump in the backseat. The tires skid on the gravel as Rosebell grinds the pedal to the floor. Arms straight, knuckles clamped around the wheel, she drives away and just as I'm slamming the sliding door shut, slugs punch a dozen holes in the metal. I throw myself on top of Kitsa and the window explodes, showering us with shards.

'Hold on!' Rosebell yells.

She changes gear and we fly out of there, faster than I ever though this pile of rust could go. The gunfire continues to explode in the twilight but soon the noise recedes and I lift myself off Kitsa.

'Are you alright?'

Her little face is shocked, as if she's seen a ghost. Remembering how her family died, I check she's not bleeding but find nothing. Exhaling a breath I didn't realize I was holding, I glance at the metal holes punched in the door and the shrapnel planted in the backseat.

Trying to get my heart under control, I stare long and hard at the road behind us but thankfully no one's chasing us. Just then, as darkness swallows the remnants of day, a column of flame erupts above the horizon and smoke starts to billow in the distance. I fasten Kitsa's seatbelt and kiss the top of her head and clamber over into the passenger seat.

'Who the fuck were these guys?'

'No idea.' Rosebell's elbows are trembling but she's holding that wheel tight. 'You OK?'

'Cuts and bruises. You?'

She nods, jaw clenched, eyes on the road. 'This is not good. Not good at all.'

I rub my face and feel a sting. Blood on my fingers. A look in the mirror reveals a thin horizontal cut on my cheek where a bullet grazed me. Fuck. That was much too close.

'Doctor Eskelin?' Rosebell asks.

'Dead.'

She shakes her head. 'It looked like a mass grave.' Her eyes keep darting to the rear-view mirror. 'Yesterday's patients probably.'

'The disease?' I glance at her, alarmed. 'Maybe they're burning everything to avoid a mass contagion.'

She groans with frustration and hits the wheel with the palm of her hand. 'I don't know! Maybe they executed everyone for some other reason. But it sure didn't look like the villagers dropped dead of their own fucking accord.'

A glow of red flickers up into the sky behind us. They're probably burning down to the outpost and it won't be long before the whole copse around it catches fire.

'It looks like they're tying up loose ends too,' Rosebell says.

'We have to tell the police.'

'Are you mad? No, we didn't see anything. We weren't even there.'

'But we need to alert the authorities.'

A humorless laugh bursts out of her. She mumbles '*muzungu*' under her breath, then says, 'You cannot say anything to anyone, DeAnn. Do you hear me? If you do, we are dead.' She throws a quick glance at the kid.

Kitsa's knees are folded against her chest, as she rocks herself, staring out of the shattered window at the pitch-black night. Fragments of glass gleam around her in the moonlight.

'At least they won't know we're MSF,' she adds, eyes on the road.

'Oh. Your cousin's van. Yes. Khaki paint, no logo.' I frown. 'Why you think they'll try to find us?'

She shakes her head. 'I don't know. I don't fucking know.'

Her anxiety is so palpable that I fall quiet. She accelerates and we drive for hours in tense silence.

12

OLIVIA

K ampala, Uganda, December 2081

THE ORPHANAGE DOOR clatters against the wall with a crash. The thugs barge in, firing machine guns at the ceiling. The din is deafening in the small space; the sound booms, reverberating against the walls and inside my skull. Plaster dust fills the room. The intruders yell incomprehensible orders. I scream and gather Jonathan and Suzanne in my arms, as plaster fragments rain down on my back and my hair.

The room erupts into shrieks, the babies are hollering and older children, bawling pitifully, are straining to get out of their chairs but unable to remove their straps. Terrified, they scream and fight the restraints. The sound of hundreds of crying children is unbearable. Fear electrifies the air like a thunderstorm.

Fumbling to release some of the toddlers closest to me from their chairs, I gather a few more children behind me and crouch in an unobtrusive corner. Biting down on my lower lip, I spot Moses and Silas. They're too far away to grab.

As the smell of our attackers' sweat mixes with peppery cordite and dull plaster, it becomes hard to breathe. The thugs lunge at the food, their fingers smeared with mash, their stubbly chins dribbling with milk, as the bottles' rubber nipples lie discarded by their combat boots. I crouch even lower and shuffle backwards, hiding the four children behind me, gripping the two babies tighter in my arms. Jonathan is shrieking in my ear. Suzanne is quiet, I check her and see a wound in her leg. She's staring wide-eyed at the round hole as if it were someone else's leg. Oh God, oh God, oh God.

I try to put Jonathan down but he clutches my arm even harder, his small face bathed in tears, the panic in his screams scaling up a notch, so I do my best to press down on Suzanne's skinny leg with both of them in my arms.

I'm crouching, hiding the children behind me, feeling Suzanne's warm blood leaking through my fingers, my heart beating madly in my chest, eye to eye with the machine guns' muzzles. Just as I look up, the head nurse starts to shout loudly in Luganda. She marches towards the thugs, berating the young men, finger raised. In her anger, some of her remonstrations come out in English: 'Stealing from babies! Is that what your mothers taught you? Shame on you. Shame on all of you...' For a moment I think she's going to scare them away. Most of the intruders are little more than teenagers and they look unsure, hesitating on the threshold, and some start to lower their rifles.

The nurse is getting close to one of the young intruders; she's on tiptoe, incensed, and he's retreating. 'I've seen you before, I know your mother, I'm going to...' Her reprimand is cut short when one of the older thugs shoves her aside. She slams against the wall like a discarded puppet, her head knocking against the plaster with a thunk, then she slides down to the floor as the painted Mickey Mouse looks down at her from his mural with a lurid smile. Her attacker steps over her inert shape and fires his machine gun, spraying bullets in the walls above our heads. The screeches redouble as terror engulfs the room.

I shield the babies behind me, fixing on the muzzle of the machine guns as they pace in front of us, back and forth. The leader bellows, grabbing Moses by the elbow and shaking the child. It looks like he's making a point. "Exhibit A.: scrawny orphan no one cares about." Moses shrieks and wriggles as he's being dangled; then he falls down and his small head slams against the tiled floor. I tighten my grip around Jonathan and Suzanne as I stare at Moses, willing him to move. But his small shape is completely immobile.

The leader yells something, jabbing the muzzle of his machine gun in the chest of the ones who are still staring down at their feet. But most of the young men are egging each other on now, working up their courage.

The leader yells another incomprehensible order and the young thugs snap out of their hesitation. A couple of them yell at us to stay still and not to try anything, while the others are already on the move, ransacking the back rooms. Clattering noises ring in the kitchen. A woman screams. My breath is coming in short panting bursts.

Some of the young men look at Evelyn and me and then chat among themselves, pointing. '*Muzungu, muzungu*' – the word seems so incongruous in their mouths as a threat, after I've heard it said so many times with delight and curiosity. I avert my eyes and hug Jonathan and Suzanne closer.

One of them comes over and pulls me to my feet by my

elbow, yelling and thrusting his AK-47 into my belly. The muzzle is hot and prods painfully against my skin. I can't understand what he's saying. His spittle is flying on my face, he's so close.

Another man pulls me away from the corner and starts frisking me from behind, as I cling on to the toddlers and stay very still. I have nothing on me today, no cash, no food. His hands push and pull at my clothes as I make an effort to close my lips but a whimper still emerges and my nostrils flare with each panicked breath.

He finds the toy car in my pocket and throws it to the ground, then grinds it under his heel, yelling at me. I understand – not the words but the frustration in his eyes. Jonathan's sobs merge with the rest of the children's cries as I squeeze him close and Suzanne starts to go limp against my right shoulder.

Evelyn pleads with the leader in Luganda and he backhands her, then he drags her by the hair to the courtyard. Taking a step towards her, I protest but the thug who searched me grabs me by the arm and starts to pull me out of the building too. The children wail when he wrenches them off me. As he drags me away, I fight and try to hold the door jamb, staring at Jonathan. He's OK. He's OK. A blinding pain in my kidneys. My fingers let go. The orphanage reaches a crescendo of fear and frenzy as they drag us out.

I dig my heels in and fight, but the soldier's hold on my arm is too strong. He seizes a handful of my hair and drags me through the playground to the parking lot, past the guard's shack. The old man's legs are protruding from the entrance, sprawled in a pool of blood. They've already put Evelyn in a van. Her kidnappers slam the door shut and drive away, gravel flying in their wake.

My captor drags me to a jeep, there's only a driver and him remaining now, the rest of the militia having left with Evelyn and the food. I try again to pry the man's fingers off my arm, but they're like a steel vice.

Just as he lets go of my hair and swings his machine gun onto his back, to force me onto the jeep, Anthony emerges from the shack and steps over the guard's corpse, gun trained on the man holding me.

'Let her go.'

The two muggers hesitate and Anthony fires a round in the air, then aims his gun back at the thug's head, both his hands on the grip, looking determined.

The attacker lets go of my arm and jumps in the jeep as it peels out of the driveway. Relief floods over me as my knees buckle and I sit down hard on the ground.

'Are you OK? Are you alright?' He holsters his gun and crouches next to me. 'Olivia, are you OK?'

I nod.

'Come on, get up, we've got to move.' Anthony pulls me roughly to my feet and leads me behind him through the orphanage gates and into the street.

'What are you doing? We have to go back! The babies...'

He ignores me and drags me to his Humvee, parked on the kerb.

'Let me go back. I have to check if the babies are alright!'

Anthony's oblivious, he stuffs me in the car, slams the door and drives like a maniac on the way back home.

We skid to halt in front of the compound and he hauls me bodily out of the SUV, pale and resolute as he drags me towards the building, tugging me by my wrist.

'Anthony, you're hurting me, let me go. Stop.' I plant my feet in the middle of the courtyard and refuse to go further.

He turns to me, livid. 'You could have been abducted or

killed! On my fucking watch.' His lip is trembling. The anger that I sometimes notice in him uncoils like a snake rearing its head. 'You can't mention what happened today to Colonel Groebler, do you hear me, Olivia?'

'Who gives a bloody hoot about Groebler? Anthony, we have to go help the babies. We have to go back.'

He grabs my arms, shaking me. 'Don't you understand what they will do to you if they think you're endangering...' His fingers are gripping the exact same spot where bruises from the attacker are darkening on my arm.

'Let go of me. Let. Go.' I shake him off, angry. 'You only care about me because if I'd been abducted, my chip would have disappeared with me. You think I don't know that, you utter twat? If you won't help me, then I'll go back on my own.'

'Don't be ridiculous, my mission is to keep you alive. There's no way I'm letting you go back there. So help me God, I'll lock you up if I have to.'

'You can't do this.' Tears of rage and powerlessness start to roll down my cheeks. I wipe them away.

'Watch me.' He starts pulling me again towards the building muttering under his breath. 'You bleeding-heart leftists, you're all the same. These charity cases, they're exploiting you, trying to get as much as they can out of you. And you can't even bloody see it.'

'Don't give me that stale act, Anthony – I know you! You played with those children. I saw you. You like them.'

'You don't get it, Olivia. It doesn't fucking matter if I like a handful of kids in an orphanage. They're parasites, the lot of them. Can't you see that these babies will grow up to become just like their parents and the rest of the bloody Ugandans? Look at the fucking mess Africans have made of their own continent, all because they can't be arsed to stop proliferating.'

'That's not fair, and you know it. We've been pillaging and despoiling their continent for centuries—'

'Please, don't make me laugh – how long ago was colonisation? When will they get over it already. If they'd been smart they'd have jumped at the opportunity to improve themselves, instead of whinging about it two centuries later,' he yells, breathing hard.

'I'm not talking about two centuries ago. Right this minute, the corporations I help do business here don't pay even a fraction of the taxes they—'

'That's bullshit, we bring money, opportunities—'

'... should and we don't even let them govern themselves,' I finish, refusing to let him talk over me. 'Any time a government which we don't like takes over in a democratic election, we finance a coup and they fall back into chaos.'

I stop, breathing hard, hands on my waist.

His face is very red. 'This has nothing to do with you. It's their own fault that all this bloody chaos is happening.' He gestures towards the city. 'That's not our mess. Let them deal with it.'

'We have a moral duty to help.'

'No, we do not. We have a duty to protect ourselves and our loved ones.' He glances at my lips as he takes a shaky breath. 'Close your eyes all you want. That won't stop those bastards from proliferating and fucking things up for the rest of us—'

'While we're arguing, the orphans are dying, Anthony. Suzanne was shot. I don't know if she'll make it. Why are we standing here, fighting about politics, when flesh and blood children are dying.'

His jaw clamps shut and I see a shadow of guilt glide over his face.

'You're a better person than you think you are, Anthony.' I take a tentative step closer and lift my hand towards his shoulder but he bats it away.

'Olivia, you're not to go back to that orphanage under any circumstances. You're assigned to residence and you're not going anywhere without an armed escort until further notice. That's final.'

My hand falls at my side as he walks away.

13

DEANN

K ampala, Uganda, December 31, 2081

'YOU'RE GORGEOUS,' the drunk Australian slurs and tries to kiss me, his hands all over me, not very expertly but with the persistence of drunks.

I deflect him easily and escape his lean-in. My colleagues, in various states of inebriation, are dancing and singing out of tune in the Embassy's ballroom. A couple of nurses sing loudly, arm in arm, bent over from laughter while my serious German colleague kisses Amy in the corner, against a wall, his leg thrust between her thighs as her too-short dress hikes up precariously high. They're necking intensely like teenagers, as if kissing were water and they've been in the desert for days.

There's a group dancing hard in the middle of the dance floor, each one lost in a trance of their own, no pretense of daintiness in sight. We came to the hotel before sundown under armed guard and we're spending the night here, partying to forget. There is so much sex. So much sex. We deal with death, violence, exhaustion and we release it all in each other's arms. Sex is life.

We work hard and party harder because Africa gets to you. We see things here that no one should have to see. The mass grave flashes before my mind's eye. The Finnish doctor's surprised face as she fell. The dusty limbs of the corpses as the digger beeped.

The music's throbbing beat dies down and the DJ blasts out a new track. I shudder, plastering a smile on my face. Yeah. Africa gets to you. At least we don't seem to have caught whatever it was that killed the villagers. I thank my lucky stars that we didn't spread it in the capital. It looked like a TB outbreak. Or worse.

I shake my head and glance round the dance floor, sipping a Cuba Libre. These are my colleagues, my brothers and sisters in arms. I've never felt so much a part of anything. I've never belonged before. Here I do.

Rosebell laughs uproariously and I spot her slapping a male nurse's ass; he grins and grabs two handfuls of her, pulls her toward him and they start to grind on the dance floor. I smile despite myself as they sway to the beat and laugh.

It's New Year's Eve so we're taking the night off. We don't stop for the holidays of course, it's just one free evening. The four horsemen of the Apocalypse don't believe in holiday breaks.

My drunk Australian colleague has moved on to a newly-arrived French nurse with blue locks. As he gropes her, I notice her hands fondling his ass through his cargo shorts. I bet she likes his eyebrow piercing and his marijuana breath. He wasn't an option for me. Even before he ran out of deodorant a few months back. Plus, I've got Omony on my mind.

Since I came back from Kibale, I haven't had much time for him. He's invited me on a couple of dates but they keep getting cut short because I can't relax. My mind can't let go of the patients, the bodies in the mass grave, the fear that the soldiers will eventually find Rosebell and me. Most of the time, I end up rushing back to the clinic, or worse, Omony and I speak about politics or the deteriorating situation in the country and the mood fizzles out. It's... frustrating.

So, tonight, I've decided enough is enough. I need a proper break, and it's been too long since I've been with a man, so I've invited Omony to the party. I hope he'll come. I'm ready to progress to the next step. If there is a next step. Lately, I've started to wonder whether he's just interested in me platonically. No man has ever taken so long to fuck me, especially when I have been as willing for as long as I have been with Omony.

He seems genuinely interested in my work as a geneticist and asks me pertinent questions about being a doctor with MSF. He talks about his work too and I'm enjoying our meeting of minds. This is just the type of intellectual intercourse I have longed for with all my boyfriends and never found until now. He's my equal. He might even be more intelligent than me. It's uncanny. It's never happened before. I love it and hate it as well.

I hear peeling laughter and look up, my thoughts snapping back to the party.

Akello had an appendectomy only a week ago but she's dancing, graceful and intense. When the music ends, she collapses on the rattan sofa and orders a drink. She looks happy, or maybe manic.

'Should you be dancing, so soon after your operation? You'll pull your stitches,' I say.

'Nah, I'm fine.' She's tapping her foot as she watches the dancers. 'How about you? Not dancing? What are you doing here all alone – thinking about your dreamy boyfriend?' Akello says too loudly.

'He's not my boyfriend,' I reply, maybe more vigorously than I need to, feeling like a teenager as I bury my nose in the glass.

'Oooh Omony, I looooove you,' she teases.

'Stop it!' I complain with a laugh.

The waiter passes by with a tray of cocktails so I grab a couple, just as Rosebell flops next to us. We make a toast and take a long gulp of the sweet drink. It's really strong.

'Lots of babies are going to be made tonight,' Rosebell says, wriggling her eyebrows with a laugh.

'That's just great. Just what you guys need,' I say, snorting.

But Akello looks at me sideways. 'What, you think the savages shouldn't proliferate, is that it?'

Taken aback by her tone, I start to backtrack and then decide to stand by it. 'Yes. Actually. I'm thinking that the fucking mess outside these doors would have been easily avoided if we'd all managed to prevent overpopulation about fifty years ago with a few education and contraception initiatives.'

'Developed countries are responsible for using up all the Earth's resources in the first place.' The slender woman piles a napkin with canapés and passes it around. Then she turns to me with a thoughtful look on her face.

'Yeah, sure,' I say. 'But don't you think the problem's compounded by overpopulation? That's sucking up resources as well.'

'We don't have an overpopulation issue,' Akello says. I splutter in my drink while she continues, 'The first time I went to Europe, years ago, I was shocked by how crowded the place was. I mean, how can a country like Belgium justify having roughly two million more inhabitants than the Central African Republic, on a territory that is twenty times smaller? They're crammed in like freaking sardines.'

'Belgian sardines,' I laugh, the alcohol starting to go to my head.

'It makes you wonder why the world thinks that there are too many Africans and that the problem is always us,' Akello says. '*We* have enough resources on this continent to thrive. You're the fucking leeches who are sucking the world dry. If you restrained yourselves to the number of people that your barren, polluted continent could *actually* sustain and didn't come to steal *our* resources, I bet you there would be a lot fewer Europeans. You're the ones who should reduce your numbers.' Akello drains her glass.

'But we have.' I tipsily check my iMode for fertility rates. Goddamn it, I need reading glasses, I'm getting old. 'There, look. Belgium has a fertility rate per woman of 1.7 and Uganda is at freaking 5.9. ' I squint, extending my arm to see better. 'And the number of people in the developed world has stayed constant at around one billion since 2010.'

'OK, so congrats, you want a gold star?' Akello retorts.

I laugh, finishing my drink and gesturing to the waiter to bring us another round.

Rosebell laughs drunkenly. 'Fine, so the Noooorth has kept its little shriveled dick in its pants, whereas the South has let its laaaarge member spring free from its breeches, if you ask me, that's a false debate. At the rate you guys consume, what does it matter if there are more of us? You're the ones putting the planet in danger. Take America, the place where you come from, *muzungu*: your country consumes thirty percent of all the world's resources and you're only four percent of the world's population.'

'But this doesn't feel right. I mean, let's bring this back to a thinkable, human scale. Imagine for a minute that continents are families. Let's think of Europe and Africa as families and they both have a budget of one hundred dollars. You have a European family where the dad has kept his...'

'...shriveled little white prick,' Rosebell laughs, holding up her pinky as she drinks some more. Akello collapses in a heap of laughter while I try to keep my train of thought.

I laugh: '... his shriveled little white prick in his pants and the white family have two kids. Then you have the African family and there the dad has been enjoying himself *a lot...*'

'With his glorious, amazing black tower of a member!'

The other revelers are looking at us, amused. I ignore them, trying to focus on my argument before it slips away.

'So, of course, as they both have a budget of one hundred dollars, the European family has a higher quality of life because they only have to feed two kids whereas the African family has to feed six children on the same budget. Isn't it logical to conclude that it's in Africa's best interest to stop making so many children, so they can feed them and develop faster?'

'First off, your example is ridiculous,' Akello says, fanning her face with her clutch, leaning back in the sofa.

'Thank you.' I take a mock bow.

'Second, you're not getting what I'm saying. What I am saying is that the European family is a bunch of thieves who've stolen the African family's budget for centuries. The latest generation of the European family now has a budget of one hundred and eighty dollars and the African family barely survives on twenty dollars.'

'OK, but if that's true, isn't it all the more reason for the African family to restrain themselves, so they become strong enough to get their eighty dollars back? What will be accomplished by starving six kids on a budget of twenty dollars?'

'I say that the European family needs to give back the eighty dollars and Africans should just continue having six kids if they goddamn want to,' Rosebell says, sounding perhaps a smidge drunk.

'That's neither a good long-term strategy nor very realistic, Rosebell. I mean maybe you're right in principle; life's not fair and history's fucked up. But you know, it is what it is. Shouldn't the African family be making plans, given the reality of the world? Not as you want it to be?'

Amy calls us from the dance floor. 'Hey, you coming or what? All that ass ain't gonna tap itself.'

We look at each other and burst out laughing.

We join her and I forget all about tribes, famines and fertility rates for a few hours. The strong, cheap alcohol warms me up, making me laugh louder. My inhibitions fall away and I dance and dance, loving my oddball colleagues, my African sister Rosebell and my unexpected new life.

14

OLIVIA

K ampala, Uganda, 31 December 2082

I TURN the shower handle tentatively, wondering if any water's going to come out. I'm in luck, the hot water smells of wood smoke and it's brown, but at least it's flowing. It only runs at certain times of the day now. I need to be quick.

I've mulled over my quarrel with Anthony obsessively for days, agonising over whether I revealed too much. I think I even said something about the Programme wanting my microchip. Fuckety fuck fuck fuck. I'm so abysmally bad at this cloak and dagger malarkey. I wipe away an angry tear and shower as quickly as I can, to avoid finding myself covered in soap and unable to rinse it off, like the other day. Thankfully, the fuming brown water holds out long enough for me to finish.

I get out of the shower, not feeling much cleaner than before and wrap a towel around my hair and another around my body; it's too short to cover much below my bum, but if I hurry across the hallway to my room, it shouldn't matter. So obviously, I'm halfway down the corridor when Anthony finds me.

'Ah, Olivia, there you are.'

'Hi.' I turn towards him, very aware that I'm barefoot, wearing next to nothing and that I probably have panda eyes from the shower.

'Are you OK?'

'Yes, why wouldn't I be?'

'Just checking on you.'

I haven't really talked to him for the last ten days. I can't forgive him for not going back to the orphanage to help. For not even letting me check on them. Jonathan is alright. I got word from one of the parishioners. But little Suzanne is dead. And so is the head nurse. Evelyn is still missing and Moses is in a coma and hasn't woken up since that day. There's no food left. The cathedral is doing what they can, day to day, to make sure the children get supplies, but there are hundreds of them. I physically ache to go see Jonathan. But I can't. Because of Anthony.

He's considering me, searching my face, his large muscular frame towering over me. I wonder if I can just go. I take a step toward my bedroom, just as he says:

'So, there's a New Year's Eve party tonight, at the Embassy,'

I stop. It looks like I'm going to have to drip on the tiles for a while longer.

'We've got to leave someone here to guard the compound, but I was thinking of letting everyone else off for the night as well. The boys need it. It's been a hard couple of weeks.'

'Good idea,' I say with a fake smile.

The most recent attack took place just a few days ago. A gang of militia tried their luck and found out the hard way that we are very well armed. I bandaged Tom's arm where a bullet grazed him. We escaped relatively unscathed but the permanent tension and the sense of siege are taking their toll on morale.

Tom comes into view, his arm still sporting a large white compress, sees Anthony is talking to me and does a swift U-turn, walking right back out of the corridor.

'So you have a date?'

'Mmmh?' I ask, distracted, as I was trying to lower the towel without uncovering my breasts. 'Oh – yes. Thank you for lifting my house arrest for the night,' I say, thinking about my lacklustre date, that chinless wanker Hugh.

Why would Anthony ask me? Probably to prevent me from going. Or maybe to send someone to watch over the microchip in my arm. In case I do something stupid again.

'Well, good for you.' He looks away and leaves me standing there, puzzled.

I blew it, I'm sure of it. The mere fact that I cared enough to volunteer at the orphanage gave it away. How can I still pretend that I don't mind his white supremacist views if I'm also obviously a Christian? I mean, no matter what colour we are, Jesus was pretty clear about us loving one another. Shit, shit, shit. It didn't even occur to me how it might be perceived to go help at Adroa. I just thought about how much I enjoyed being around the babies, I'm so stupid!

I had been pretty good up to that point, hearing the boys out without objecting. Listening to their arguments and asking for more details to get a sense of their racist ideas: where do they come from? What are they based on? Is it a political view for them? An emotional knee-jerk response to something? Is it a party line that they're forced to adopt because of their work? Are there any theoreticians of this neo-Nazi movement? Authors I should be aware of, so we can put them on a watch list if I ever return to 2016?

I get the sense that this is simply the dominant ideology of this era and that no one bothers to question it. For the longest time, I couldn't tell if they really believed the hate speech they spewed or whether they were just parroting it. But now it's beginning to dawn on me that I'm surrounded by very dangerous soldiers, not just a bunch of kids who don't know any better.

I fret, biting my lower lip anxiously as I get dressed.

What if Anthony's seen through my pretence? Will he lock me up for the rest of the year and kill me at the end? Maybe I should try to talk to him, figure out what he knows? No, that's stupid, Olivia; not everything can be solved by chatting to people over a cuppa. Anguish and bile rise up in my throat. Maybe I should escape now, while I still can? He knows.

I put on makeup, feeling ludicrous. What is there to celebrate?

Colonel Groebler could give the order to kill me and take my microchip away any day now. The line I was walking was really thin and I'm scared that I've crossed it.

A knock on the door startles me.

I check myself in the mirror. I look nice. Thinner. Tanned.

I snort. Stupid, stupid girl.

Jarrod escorts me to the car. It's hot, even at sunset; I'm wearing my favourite perfume, eau de mosquito repellent, and I intensely wish I were home.

All the boys are here tonight. All except Anthony, who's nowhere to be seen. I ride in the back between two soldiers, feeling more like their prisoner than their colleague, as we form a convoy to the Embassy.

Outside, masses of destitute people and refugees drift aimlessly on every street corner, entire families camping on the red ground and watching listlessly as we pass by. Every time we stop, starving men and women stand up and stumble over towards us, their gaunt frames dried up from within. They cling to the windows and peer in at us, their hands shielding the red glare of the setting sun as they beg. A feeling of intense powerlessness engulfs me as the car starts again, leaving a cloud of red dust in its wake and the beggars scatter like a flock of emaciated ghosts.

The Embassy is under heavy guard; a security perimeter has been set up, with sandbags and a barrier that rises only if the sentries let you in. Cars are inspected with care: mirrors under the chassis to check for bombs and all our belongings are X-rayed before we go in. This all rather dampens the mood and so the party starts out pretty civilised, with finger food and some bubbly.

I settle on a bar stool in a corner and observe everyone, sipping on the glass of ersatz champagne I received when I first arrived. I'm not much of a drinker and I'm never too sure of what to do with myself at this sort of event so I usually sit and observe the partygoers, as I don't really know how to mingle. If there were something to do, or organise, I could take charge of that but here I'm just supposed to drink and chat and dance and flirt, and I don't want to do any of these things. So I sit quietly at the bar, wondering about how far I am from everything and everyone I know.

'Happy New Year, here's to 2016!' I said happily to Martin.

I tried to kiss him but he moved his head, preferring to watch the TV instead. He didn't want to go out because apparently, 'New Year is commercial, stupid and it's dangerous to go out on that evening with all the drunks.'

I was starting to realise that maybe this relationship was a mistake. At first, I'd thought Martin was fun, but he was just a killjoy, scared of dreaming big, scared of love and just not interested in me, at least not right then.

Still, I persevered, trying to elicit a response.

'Come on, Bear. You didn't want to go out tonight, you didn't even want to go to the garden to see the fireworks. So I've cooked dinner and now we're watching a movie, just the two of us, like you wanted. Could you at least make an effort and pause the movie now it's midnight? Please wish me a happy New Year and kiss me.'

'I told you I'm not a system-person!' he yelled at me and pushed me away.

I flinched and felt ridiculous for reaching out to kiss him. Stupid me. Why didn't I sense that he was in one of his moods? Now I'd gone and ruined New Year. It was all my fault. If only I'd kept my mouth shut. I should have let midnight come and go without mentioning it at all.

'Can't you see that I don't want to do this?' he yelled. 'I want to go to bed and I don't want to carry on celebrating. You're pushing me. Stop pushing me all the time!'

'You call that celebrating?' I said despondently. 'We've eaten in front of the TV and you didn't say three words to me all evening.' I wondered what I'd done wrong this time.

I should stop expecting so much of him. He was right: New Year was an arbitrary date in a man-made calendar. I'd just hoped for light-hearted evening and maybe a kiss. Stupid, stupid me.

'Why do you ask so much from me?' he continued. 'I want you to leave me alone!'

He stood up, left me there on the sofa and went to bed. Happy New Year to me then. Yay.

A VOICE BRINGS me back to the present.

'I...I...I... see you've made it safely to the party?' Hugh is standing in front of me and I have no idea how long he's been there.

'Oh, hello Hugh.'

'Drink?' He hands me a glass of the drink-pretending-to-be-champagne.

'Why not?'

It's an open bar, so he didn't exactly make a huge effort to get me this. But I appreciate it anyway. I haven't been very charitable with poor old Hugh. Maybe I should listen to my colleague Violet and try it on with him. She's right, I can't be too choosy at my age.

DeAnn and her colleagues are here too. She's made an effort to look nice and she's smiling at something a large Ugandan woman, wearing a very tight white dress, is saying to her. I hope she's alright.

The French medics are a rather rowdy bunch and Anthony's boys soon start to dance with the doctors and nurses. There are a lot of other young idealistic Europeans and Westerners here tonight – NGO workers, Embassy staff, missionaries. Everyone lowers their defences and inhibitions fall away, spurred on by the intensity of the violence outside, the uncertainty about our fate. We're welcoming 2082 tonight and none of us is really sure we'll still be alive when it ends. Couples form in the large ballroom's corners, groping and kissing on gilded event chairs.

Hugh's been saying something. Dear Lord, the man is as boring as a Monday morning meeting about cost cutting. I can't even focus long enough to listen to him for five minutes, how can I even consider dating him? Plus, frankly, it's awful timing, what with the life-threatening situation and all.

'... so, when I'm upset, I just hop on one of my horses and gallop through the night and that usually puts my mind straight.'

'Erm. Right.'

Is this guy for real?

He seems taken aback by my lack of fawning. Maybe I should try harder, bat my eyelashes or something. I just can't muster the interest. He looks dejectedly around for a new target and leaves. He's spotted Violet, who greets him with the appropriate amount of awe-struck girly hair swooshing. Those two will probably be ramming their tongues down each other's throats before the night is out.

Typical. Olivia, the man-whisperer. Oh God, I suck at dating so much.

My eyes are wandering across the room when I notice DeAnn light up as a well-dressed black man strides confidently over to her and whisks her away. DeAnn's friend, the large Ugandan woman, stares after them pensively.

DeAnn's beaming as she leaves. The familiar twinge of guilt squeezes my heart as I realise how long it's been since we last spoke. I should know who this man is. Has the divide grown so large between us already? I resolve to make up with her tomorrow. New year: new start.

Right as DeAnn is leaving, Anthony strides into the ballroom. He hasn't dressed up; he came in the same clothes he wore earlier today, his face is stubbly and his brow furrowed. On her way out, DeAnn stops to greet Anthony and introduces him to her date. What's weird is that I get the sense that it's all a charade and the two men actually know each other. Then the Ugandan man walks out, DeAnn on his arm. Strange.

Across the ballroom, DeAnn's friend has been looking at all this, much as I have, but she seems to understand something I don't. She follows DeAnn and her escort out of the ballroom.

Anthony watches the plump doctor as she hurries after them and his eyes narrow. He walks over to two of the young soldiers under his command and gives them an order. The soldiers follow the large Ugandan woman out of the ballroom.

I lose track of what's happening when the DJ stops the music and everyone cheers, 'Ten, nine, eight, seven, six... five... four... three... two... one! Happy New Year!'

I'm in a crowd but I've never felt so alone in my life.

My iMode beeps.

'GO OUTSIDE. NOW.'

Why would A. ask me to do this? Why now?

I push the questions from my mind, jump off my bar stool and hurry outside just in time to glimpse DeAnn climb into a black sedan. The tall Ugandan man makes sure the car is gone and then he turns towards DeAnn's friend, who's striding over to him.

His face is perfectly composed and he looks like a big cat gauging its prey. Anthony's soldiers are close behind her, but the woman doesn't seem to realise or care; she makes a beeline for DeAnn's date and confronts him.

Feeling foolish and nosy, I follow them as quietly as possible, hiding behind the pillars of the Embassy's entrance, hurrying awkwardly on the unfamiliar strappy heels, as I edge closer to the steps at the front of the mansion.

'I know what you're doing,' the woman says.

The Ugandan man speaks to her in measured tones and his voice is very deep, so I can't hear him. By contrast, the woman is getting increasingly angry and some of what she says drifts over to me.

'How could you... own people? ... reveal who you really are...'

Anthony's two soldiers glance at each other, hands clasped in front of them, standing on the gravel driveway as the tall Ugandan man makes a placating gesture. Saying something reassuring, he takes a step towards her, but she staggers back and raises her hand, making horns with her fingers.

'Cursed be your name and your descendants. Death to you and yours, Omony P'Ladwar.'

She spits at his feet and turns around. Oh no, she's coming towards me, she'll see me.

I hunker down behind the pillar as Omony signals to Jarrod and the young soldier nods and briskly follows the woman. She's reaching the first stone step of the building entrance when he clamps his hand over her mouth from behind. Just as he grabs her, she sees me and her eyes widen above his hand. Her throat moves and she tries to scream, but her cries are muffled.

He can't just arrest her like that. I need to intervene, she has a right to free speech, they can't just manhandle anyone who speaks their mind. I know Jarrod, I can talk to him. I take a breath to speak up and start to come out from behind the pillar, when Jarrod raises his free hand in a sinuous, lightning-fast movement and something glints against her throat. Blood gushes, spraying her face and Jarrod's hand, still clamped over her mouth. I freeze, hidden just out of sight from him, unable to think or move. I can't understand. This can't be happening.

The poor woman stares at me, the whites showing around her eyes and a look of complete incomprehension on her face. She strains towards me, lifts her hand up as if pleading, but Jarrod's arm tightens around her rib cage and he holds her back. I flatten myself against the pillar as my heart beats madly and a scream builds up in my throat, threatening to burst out.

Blood spurts over her white dress and onto the gravel as she fights against the soldier's grip, pawing and scratching weakly. Then she goes limp.

I stay where I am, hands clasped around the smooth stone as the taste of bile and cowardice spreads in my mouth. It takes all my willpower not to peer from behind the pillar; it feels like Jarrod is going to spring out any second and grab me as well. My knees are shaking and I'm terrified I'll fall or make a noise.

Above the sound of blood rushing in my ears, I hear car doors closing and the low rumble of DeAnn's boyfriend talking to the two soldiers. Their answers are curt and short. I can't make any of it out. What if they decide to re-join the party? Then they'll see me and kill me too.

I hear a door close with a low thump, then a car leaving the driveway and gravel screeching under the tyres. My heart feels like an out-of-control clockwork and my head starts to spin. I risk a peek around the pillar. The driveway is empty but her panicked face and her jerky movements are branded into my retinas. My eyes can't help but return to the spot where the woman just died. The dark stain is already barely visible; the gravel has absorbed most of it and the pebbles have started to scatter.

'There you are.'

I jump and yelp, startled. Anthony is standing behind me, staring at me.

'Oh, Anthony, it's you.'

I try to sound jovial while I figure out how long he's been here. Could he have seen me? No, no, I reason. I had my back to the pillar and I was facing the entrance until they drove off. I would have seen anyone coming through the ballroom door into the hallway.

He frowns, stirring his whisky, surveying our surroundings, suspicion etched on his face. The ice cubes clink as they spin around the crystal tumbler.

'Are you alright? Why are you out here on your own?'

He monitors the driveway. No doubt looking for his men.

I swallow. 'Oh, I just needed a bit of air.' His eyes narrow, so I add, 'Too much alcohol, to be honest.'

He scrutinises me a while longer and then smiles. 'You do look very pale.'

His hand reaches for my face and strokes my cheek lightly. Startled, I can't help but flinch. I heave and feel the canapés and the acidic champagne come up. Rushing over to the bushes, I vomit the entire contents of my stomach onto the Ambassador's yellowing topiary.

Anthony approaches behind me. Will he kill me too? Terror rises with a scream that I cannot let loose. He must have seen me.

But he merely holds my hair back as I throw up. The woman's bloodied hand, as she tried to reach for me, flashes before my eyes and I retch some more. The ground feels like it's bucking under my feet and the night sky spins. My knees buckle but Anthony's arm loops around my waist, holding me.

'Woah. I've got you. I've got you.'

I don't think I'm going to survive this trip.

I spit out the bitterness and cough, trying to dislodge the disgusting bits in my nose. Anthony hands me a cocktail napkin from around his glass. Whispering thanks, I disentangle myself from his embrace and wipe my mouth as best I can, feeling idiotic, my throat burning.

'Better out than in, I guess,' he says, laughing.

I chuckle and feel a sob coming on. I push it down and smile.

'Maybe there's still time to get someone in there to kiss me,' I giggle. And that does it. Suspicion turns to condescension, as he completely dismisses me.

'Oh, you're so lovely, Olivia, of course someone will kiss you tonight. Maybe that guy, your date?' he says.

I loop my arm in his and make for the door, back inside where I'll be safer. I figure I might as well lay it on thick.

'Hugh? Oh, no, he's dumped me for that woman over there,' I say, a tremor in my voice.

Who knew that my ability to cry for any bloody reason would one day come in handy? I let the tears well in my eyes and point to Hugh and Violet slobbering all over each other's faces in a corner.

'Well, let's drown your sorrows some more, then.'

'Yes, that sounds wonderful.' I laugh, tears stuck in the back of my throat.

The woman's eyes widen as she collapses in Jarrod's arms again and again, on a loop in my head. The red stain spreads on her white dress, again and again as Anthony holds me close, twirling me around the dance floor.

15

DEANN

K *ampala, Uganda, January 2082*

'QUICK! GRAB HER...' – arterial spray spurts out and douses my face, hot and thick – '... leg!' I yell at the useless nurse. She's standing there aghast, so I put both of my hands inside the gaping wound and press, trying to wipe my eyes with my shoulder. The coppery smell of blood is everywhere. It also smells of pus and shit and gunpowder.

Sweat slides down my spine. The blistering heat is suffocating in this closed room full of unwashed bodies. The din around us is deafening. People are yelling, panicked and angry. My colleagues are issuing commands and outside the staccato of machine guns bursts above the blare of car horns.

The nurse is still standing there with her arms at her sides when someone ties my hair back. Startled, I look over my shoulder. I should have known.

'Kitsa, I told you to stay away from here! You're too young to see this.'

'Too late, Doctor DeAnn.' She screws her face resolutely.

I smile and regret it when I taste the blood and for the umpteenth time wonder whether the AIDS vaccine really works.

'OK, then, make yourself useful. Wipe my face with that compress there.' I point with my elbow. 'Then clean your hands with alcohol like I showed you.'

She does it quickly and well.

'Well done. Now hand me that...'

She's already anticipated what I need and is handing it to me with disinfected and gloved hands.

The kid is remarkable. I yell at the nurse to go fetch the surgeon. I'm out of my depth here and really shouldn't be performing surgery. But the hospital is overwhelmed and I can't just let these people die. I do what I can but I'll feel better when the surgeon takes over or at least checks what I've done.

We patch up the patient as best we can, Kitsa and I. The surgeon comes by and has a cursory look, gives me a nod and is out again.

'What were you thinking, Kitsa? You're too young to be in here,' I say as we wash our hands.

'I want to learn.' She juts her chin forward.

I hug her fiercely and then release her. She looks shocked. I don't blame her. I'm shocked myself. I don't know what came over me. I guess I'm sad; I miss Rosebell's hugs.

Sometime around New Year, my friend disappeared. No one has heard from her or seen her in weeks. I've been looking everywhere for her. I'm so worried. She's my only friend here. My only friend anywhere.

My search, at first, was casual; I assumed she'd met

someone at the party and indulged in a few days of romance. But I started worrying in earnest when she didn't show up for work the following Monday; maybe the soldiers we interrupted at the mass grave found her through her cousin's van. I refuse to let that thought take over.

I've searched for my friend for weeks now, meeting only with shrugs and I-don't-knows. Dr. Herault raised a missing person report with the authorities and reported back to Paris about the disappearance, but Rosebell is a local doctor, not an expat, and we're in a volatile situation. So no one is really looking for her except me.

Kampala has taken a turn for the worse since the New Year. Malnutrition is morphing into famine now. And we're still contending with the waterborne disease outbreak. The elderly are dropping like flies. They give up their rations to feed their families and they get skinnier and skinnier until they can't walk, can't do anything but lie there until they die. The kids are more resilient. If we catch them on time, within ten days they're running around again. But the French Doctors' hospital is usually the last resort and by the time they wash up on our doorstep, it's usually too late.

There's little we can do about hunger as we're a hospital, not a food dispensary. Some people began stockpiling a while back but only those who could afford it. Then rumors spread about who had reserves. And now we're starting to get bleeders.

I'd never admit this to Olivia, of course, but I send some of my patients to her church; it's the only one in the capital that's still collecting and dispensing food.

I wash my hands and sigh. Snow White and I don't talk anymore. We argued again. She came by the hospital a couple of days after Rosebell's disappearance. She had never come by my workplace before. She started talking frantically, spinning some cock and bull story about Rosebell.

I scoffed. That's how ludicrous the story was.

'She followed you out. A black woman. I'd never seen her before.'

'So how do you know it was Rosebell?'

Olivia opened and closed her mouth. 'I saw what I saw.'

I didn't want to think about my friend being hurt, let alone killed. She couldn't be dead. She just couldn't. Olivia had to be wrong.

'I don't know why I'm surprised you can't tell one black person apart from another,' I said, flailing my arms. 'Then again, like you said, you've never seen Rosebell in the first place. So, thanks for the scare. I have patients to attend to.'

'They killed her!' she exclaimed. 'They...'

I walked away from her, my heart slamming against my chest.

'OK!' she shouted at my back. 'Let's say it wasn't Rosebell. You're right, I'm not sure it was her. Can you at least consider that a woman was murdered?'

'What do you want me to do about it? One of your boys probably gets his rocks off by murdering black women. Why don't you ask your Nazi boyfriend, Burke, about it? Not that I'd expect you to care about a random black woman; you're just like them anyway, a bigot.'

'DeAnn, listen to me, please.' She grabbed my shoulders. I *hate* being touched. 'I'm the only partner you have, the only person on your side. We're both in danger, and I need your help—'

'Help you? Why would I help *you*?' I interrupted. The audacity of that little Nazi groupie who never stood up for me once! 'Don't touch me.' I shook her off angrily and spat out, 'You're not in any danger, you're white! They'll never let anyone hurt you.'

'But that's the thing... I'm not safe anymore, and...'

'Well, that's your own fault then. You made your bed, now you better lie in it.' Anger rose and the frustration, built up over the last few months, spilled out: 'You keep hanging out with all these soldiers, hoping one of them will fuck you out of pity. But they don't because you're too old and fat and stupid. Why don't you see if one of them will save you, because I sure as hell don't give a fuck whether you live or die. Now, like I said, I have patients who are in real trouble.'

She looked crestfallen. Her chin wobbled, and she got up and left.

IT WAS weeks ago and we haven't spoken since. Damn Snow White. Of all the partners I could have had, it had to be the most inept one. Maybe she's blown a gasket and turned paranoid. Maybe she should have her head looked at. PTSD brought on by stress or something. Professor McArthur did mention about time travel making people go insane. I've been debating whether to tell Burke about this since it happened.

Maybe I should ask Omony to help me investigate whether a woman was found dead after New Year's Eve. My heart does a backflip when I imagine him locating Rosebell in a morgue somewhere in town. But I push the thought away. She's alive. She has to be.

Omony's been helping me look for my friend already anyway. He's asked his network all over town to keep an eye out for her. Clinging to the reassuring thought, I let myself drift away from fear and worry, deciding to focus on hope instead. I'll find her through Omony's contacts, he knows everyone.

It's starting to dawn on me that there is much more to Omony than the side he's choosing to show me. At first, I didn't realize how respected and powerful he was. I just assumed he had done well; that he had a beautiful house, a successful enterprise and a big retinue of staff. But over time, I've started to think of him as more than just a businessman.

Omony has an aura of power that seems to go further than mere money. He's obviously some sort of regional leader. He has business interests and firms with hundreds of employees. I've guessed between the lines that since the crisis started, he's taken on some sort of public role. Clearly, he's a force for good in the city.

Thank God he's here, to distribute water to the neighborhoods that no longer have access to any other source. His cistern trucks visit Bwaise every day, getting clean water to the people who would otherwise end up with cholera or dysentery, at my clinic or at the morgue. He's saving lives.

I've come to realize that dating someone who has a strong ethos really matters to me. It never did before. Maybe working here has changed me more than I know. I admire him for trying to do something, anything, to help change his country for the better.

I change out of my scrubs and into civilian clothes, shaking off the memory of the conversation with Olivia. Rummaging in my locker, I extract the leather bound notebook from its hiding place and sit on the locker room's bench to leaf through it.

When I looked through all of Rosebell's things, I found the Finnish doctor's journals and read them cover to cover but they didn't make much sense; they were mostly the ramblings of an old recluse and the majority of it was in Finnish anyway. But midway through, Dr. Eskelin's writing stopped and Rosebell took over and started jotting down her own annotations.

I hadn't realized that my friend had continued investigating the ovarian cancers after we came back from Kibale. I guess she must have found something in the old woman's ramblings that was useful after all. But what? And why didn't she tell me? I could have helped. Where are you, damn it, Rosebell? What have you gotten yourself into?

On the last page of notes, Rosebell seems to have uncovered something odd happening in Bwaise. She mentions going to see a woman called Itungo. Well, it's not really the last page. On the last page, incongruously, a naïve painting of a jungle is splashed in blues and greens, like a window to a bygone world. I trace the contours of the yellow moon on the paper, feeling the ridges of dried paint under my fingers wondering, as often these last few weeks, what the image could mean and how it found its way into the notebook.

I've decided to take over my friend's investigation. If I can find what causes the high incidence of cancers, maybe that will be a medical discovery worth bringing back to 2017. But mostly, I just want to find my friend. I stuff the book back in the locker and grab my purse then I turn off the lights in the women's wing, still expecting Rosebell to wave me good night. But Rosebell's gone.

Kitsa and I emerge from the hospital into the fading afternoon light, and as and the driver opens the door for us, he looks the girl up and down as if a street rat had jumped into the pristine leather-seat sedan. I hide a smile as Kitsa enthusiastically presses every button, opens the bar and stares at everything, twittering with excitement.

Once on the road, I sit back and the little girl reaches

over the driver's shoulder and directs him to the commercial center she wants to go to. Acting like she's not even there, he parks the sedan in the underground parking lot and accompanies us, doubling as bodyguard throughout our shopping trip at the luxurious mall.

Dr. Herault got her a couple of old scrubs to wear for her 'shifts' and I found an ancient anatomy book which she studies religiously, every opportunity she gets. I must be doing something right because she's filled out and grown up. So we're off to get her some new clothes today.

A few weeks back, I arranged for Kitsa to sleep in my room at the hospital, as I never used it anyway. So once we're back and she's fed, watered and clothed, I leave her cross-legged on the cot, listening to her own heart with the stethoscope, as she reads the names of the blue and red ventricles from the yellowing pages of her anatomy book.

She's adorable. Something strange is happening to my own heart around her. Instead of feeling annoyance as I usually do around kids, I feel... I'm not sure. I feel like my heart is a bud that's opening up. It's unsettling.

Omony's away on business, so when we're done, I get the driver to drop me off at the Programme's military compound. It's my first time back in weeks. I always feel out of place here nowadays. Olivia tries to connect with me all evening, looking at me like a fucking puppy. I ignore her of course.

I feel like an outsider at the compound. Observing the dynamic here, I notice a few changes. Snow White spends a lot of time with Burke. He's handsome, I'll grant him that. But he's cold, dangerous and racist. Maybe something has developed there, a romance maybe? I guess she must believe in his white supremacist views, otherwise how could it not bother her to interact with him?

Maybe I'd think the same if I were a freckly redhead like her. After all, when you're handed out that much privilege as a birthright and you find yourself in a world where being white is a guarantee of coming out on top, why would you not grab that opportunity with both hands?

She's so naïve and sickly sweet. She probably doesn't see the strand of darkness that I can perceive in Burke. I hope he'll hurt her, so that she learns.

16

OLIVIA

K *ampala, Uganda, January 2082*

ON THE WAY back from the KEW High Commission, Edmand drives defensively, avoiding the withered figures stumbling on the road. Soon we won't be able to use the roads at all. Everyone is packed elbow to elbow and Kampala is fuller than ever, swarming with dusty crowds; a powder keg ready to explode. Young gang members, armed to the teeth, pile into pick-up trucks and drive like maniacs, firing machine guns into the air to scare off pedestrians. But they give us a wide berth; the KEW blazon on the door still evokes a force that they don't feel comfortable challenging – yet.

I'm the last one left in the shuttle; it took longer than usual to drop everybody else off, so it's night already. We're not supposed to be out this late. I can feel the driver's anxiety like static electricity, passing to me, raising the hair on my forearms. He's driving at breakneck speed, skimming corners, honking at pedestrians, who jump out of the way, and sending gravel and dust flying behind us. But when we reach the third makeshift checkpoint, Edmand skids to a halt, his left arm extended in front of my chest to prevent me from hitting the windshield. A giant metal caterpillar, with spikes sticking out of it, lies across the road.

Armed men idle around the blockade, waiting for someone stupid enough to still be driving the roads at night. Thankfully, they're wearing white uniforms, so they're official. In theory.

In the darkness, the policemen look like sharks, prowling deep waters in search of prey. One of the officers takes his time coming over to our window, letting the tension build. Is he really still working for the Ugandan state? Who knows? Maybe he's just a thug who stole a uniform. I grind my teeth and we wait until the knock on the driver's side makes us both flinch.

Edmand rolls down the window and gives the paperwork to the officer without a word, eyes fixed on the road ahead. Trying to look as innocuous as possible, I rummage in the glove box, keeping my head down. The officer pretends to have a look at the paperwork but stares at me instead, then speaks to the driver in a fast and intense whisper, in Luganda.

Increasingly worked up, Edmand protests and then with slow, placating gestures, he pulls out a very large wad of banknotes from his pocket and holds it out. Nothing happens for a few moments. The scene seems to freeze and fear spreads like ice cold water down my back.

The policeman stares at me. Without looking at Edmand or the money, he swipes the bills and reluctantly gives back the papers with a leer on his face. He taps the door twice, then raises his arm up in the air and his associates remove the roadblock.

Everything seems to move again as I exhale deeply and Edmand fumbles with the clutch.

'Thank you, Edmand,' I whisper. That was his own money, I'm sure.

'You've always been kind to me Miss Olivia. I would never let anything bad happen to you.' He wipes his forehead with his sleeve and, eyes still fixed on the road, gets us back to the compound.

As he leaves, I ring the bell, feeling very exposed. Night falls early here and as soon as it's fallen, the darkness is complete. Dogs are barking in the distance and the rat-a-tat-tat of machine guns is getting louder, so they're probably close. Come on, come on, come on – open the bloody gates.

Finally the gates open and I dash inside, before they close automatically behind me. Tom tips his cap from his post on top of the watchtower and I wave back with a fake smile.

I've been stuck in the military compound for weeks now; when I'm not at work, I'm here, always under guard. The jaws of a bear trap are closing around me. I used to be able to talk to people, go see Edigold or volunteer at the orphanage. I could go to church wherever I pleased. Now I'm always under watch, always indoors, always imprisoned.

The soldiers don't feel like my Lost Boys anymore at all. They're tense and aggressive, on the alert and waiting for the next attack from desperate locals. They only watch over me because I'm an asset and because they have orders to keep my chip within reach, but I'm no longer under any delusions that they care about me in any way whatsoever. They'd kill me in a heartbeat if they received the order. I'm controlling myself all the time, minding my facial expressions, conscious of every word, careful not to betray myself.

Jarrod makes my skin crawl and I avoid him because I can't hide my fear and disgust. How can he act normal when he killed that poor woman in front of me? I observe him when we're trapped in the same room and he hasn't changed at all. Same jokes, same face, same tastes in food, movies, same routine. I don't know why I expected anything else. Why would he change? This is his job. Obey orders without question. Kill for a living. He's a soldier.

I can't sleep anymore. I have terrible nightmares where Jarrod slits my throat while Rosebell is watching behind the pillar. Sometimes it's DeAnn watching and she laughs. His blade slices through my flesh and I wake up screaming, my heart bouncing against my ribs like a pinball. I hope I don't talk in my sleep. I try to avoid sleeping now, until I'm too exhausted not to, hoping to ward the nightmares away. Afraid to reveal too much.

I don't know what to do anymore. I'm all alone. The Resistance keeps asking me for more intel every day; more intel, more, more. But they never answer when I ask for assurances that they'll get DeAnn and me out of here safely. I'm starting to think that they don't care if we live or die either. They just want our microchips, like the Programme.

So after Edmand drops me off I don't linger, I go straight to my room; I need to think. My stomach growls painfully and the room spins around me. Most of the time I don't even register the cramps anymore. Hunger's become my constant companion.

Just as I close my bedroom door, my iMode pings; it must be A. I pull back my sleeve to look at the plastic bracelet.

'Will arrange exit strategy as soon as you have info on the

Programme's purpose in Uganda. Get the intel or no evacuation.'

Anxiety floods in, threatening to drown me. How on earth am I going to get what they're asking for? Unsure what to answer, I toss the iMode on my bed and start to pace, just as a bang on the door scares the living daylights out of me. I don't have time to say, 'Enter'; the door is already swinging open and Colonel Groebler barges in.

Frozen with surprise, all I can do is glance at my iMode, hoping he can't read the latest messages on it.

'Colonel Groebler, what are you doing here?' I say as graciously as I can, forcing my eyes away from the bracelet. We've barely seen him at all for the last three and a half months, so his presence here doesn't bode well.

'Come to wrap things up, hopefully.' He means something by it, but I'm too aflutter to figure out what. Things are speeding up a tad too much for my taste.

'Well, it's great to see you again, Colonel. Welcome to Kampala.' I grab my iMode, snap it on my wrist and say, 'I'll go make dinner, then.'

But he doesn't budge from the threshold. He stares at me, expressionless, so I plaster another smile on my face, feeling like an insect pinned under his gaze.

His eyes dip below my face. Ah, typical. Staring at my breasts. Wouldn't be the first time these last few months that a soldier has made no mystery of liking my curves.

But something's off, that's not the Colonel's style. I follow his gaze and realise that he's looking at the scar on my forearm. The one where my microchip was inserted.

17

OLIVIA

K *ampala, Uganda, January 2082*

DINNER IS QUITE SUBDUED. Everyone is behaving in front of Groebler.

'So, Olivia, Captain Burke tells me that you've done quite well these last few months.'

'Olivia has been getting along really well with everyone,' Anthony says, with a sideways glance to Groebler. Could it be? Have I really fooled Anthony into believing that I'm one of them?

'Oh, yes, the boys are lovely.' I try to remember how I felt about them before New Year.

'I hear there was an incident at Christmas.'

Shit. The orphanage. The one thing that could unmask me.

'Oh yes, I'm really ashamed of that. I used to help after Mass at my church in Chelsea, so I did it here without even thinking of the consequences.' I put a hand on Anthony's thigh and lean towards Groebler. 'I'm so sorry about the worry I caused.' The Colonel narrows his eyes.

I continue as innocuously as possible, feeling Anthony's leg rises to meet my palm. 'We were attacked... by the... the gangs.' I should use a racial slur. Swallowing my distaste, I raise a hand to my chest. 'I never thought the negroes could be so ungrateful and violent.'

Colonel Groebler's watches me, then his face smoothens as he plants his fork in a potato. 'Well, I'm glad to hear that. Part of the reason we sent you to Uganda was to open your eyes to the current situation.'

'I realise that now and I'm grateful for it Colonel. I'm also keen to move on to the next assignment.'

'Ah yes, we're nearly ready for your... transition.' An unpleasant smile stretches on Groebler's face. 'Soon, I should think.'

My next assignment is supposed to be in India for the next six months. I'm ready to bet money that instead it will be a morgue slab.

'Excellent!' Anthony says, jaw clenched in a fake grin. 'Well, that's settled then, Olivia – we'll make sure you're sent safe and sound on to your next mission.'

'Oh, brilliant,' I titter. 'You have no idea how much I've been looking forwards to leaving this awful place.'

Halfway through dinner, DeAnn arrives looking exhausted and dirty from work. The whole table tenses up when she walks in, but she seems oblivious. She eats quickly and locks herself in her room, as she always does the few times she spends the night here.

Dinner ends, Colonel Groebler and Anthony disappear and the boys all go upstairs to watch a movie. Oh God, I don't want to die. I wonder how they'll execute me. Probably a bullet to the head as soon as we're back in London. My hand shoots up to my temple, my fingers trembling. Or maybe Jarrod will slit my throat in my sleep and then there'll be no need to lug me anywhere.

I need to warn DeAnn. The time for secrets is over. I can't wait any longer to reconcile myself with her. I've been trying frantically to connect with the bloody woman since the debacle of our post-New Year fight. But she's ignored me every time I've tried. I play back the conversation in my head and wonder how it went so wrong. I just wanted to tell her about Rosebell's murder. Instead we argued. Why? This is all my fault. I was tactless. I have to try again.

I can't do it inside the compound, though; I'm pretty sure there are microphones. So in order to have a quiet conversation with DeAnn, she'd have to be willing to come with me somewhere – and that seems pretty unlikely as she thinks I'm a white supremacist. I didn't even get to tell her about her date's involvement in Rosebell's murder. DeAnn is in so much danger and I'm not even capable of warning her. I need to find a way.

I've been looking for more information on Omony P'Ladwar. He's a frightening man. I get the sense that he's a warlord or perhaps a mobster. Since the state's complete collapse, anyone who appears to be maintaining order in the streets is doing so by force and not for altruistic purposes. I've been told that he controls about half of the city. I'm gathering rumours about him and it seems that he's making money by selling water to desperate slum residents for extortionate amounts of money. But that doesn't explain why people are terrified of him. I tried to ask the parishioners but they clammed up when I said his name and made hand signs to ward off evil.

I tiptoe down the corridor to DeAnn's room, knock on

her door and ask to speak with her, but as usual she declines. I can't make her to talk to me here and she won't come with me to the garden. If I force it, we'll raise our voices and attract attention to ourselves.

Stifling a scream of frustration, I go back to the kitchen, stomach churning and my palms tingling. I'm alone. I'm surrounded by people who want to kill me and the only person who could be on my side is not. It's all my fault, of course. I left her on her own for too long and we lost the tenuous bond we barely had in 2016. I should have done more to keep her in the loop.

Oh God, oh God, oh God, please let us survive this.

Holding back hysteria, I wash the dishes and clean every surface, every appliance, until the kitchen is immaculate. Then, biting my lip, I start to pace. The only way the Resistance will help us is if I find out what the Programme are doing here. I have no idea where Groebler is stationed. Somewhere far. But if I can at least find out what Anthony's team is doing in Kampala, that should be enough of a trading token to get DeAnn and me out of here.

Anthony and the Colonel are having a long one-to-one in the basement. There's no way I can get in there. I've been trying for three months, in vain. And then, I figure it out. Getting down on all fours, I rummage under the sink, pushing past the cleaning products until I find it: the dusty bottle of brandy I hid there months ago for a special occasion. Wiping sludge off my fingers, I clean up the bottle until it shines, then snap a photo of it and send it to Anthony.

'Nightcap?' I text.

Then I wait.

Finally, my bracelet buzzes.

'Where on earth did you find that? You're magic,' he texts back.

'My magic can't go through locked doors yet,' I answer, leaning forwards, hands on the kitchen counter, my foot tapping a frantic beat.

I wait.

Nothing.

'Oh, right. All sorted. Come on down.'

My iMode flashes blue and I release a long breath.

I quickly grab two tumblers and balancing everything on a tray, I approach the basement door, my intestines squirming. I'm an idiot, what am I doing? My hands shake and the glasses tinkle softly as I walk down the stairs into the darkened basement.

I stop in front of the black door, wipe my palm on my leg and, inhaling deeply, I go in as soon as I've knocked, hoping to catch a fragment of their conversation.

'There she is,' Anthony says with a laugh. 'Our magician.' He's clutching a remote control and there's a blank screen on the wall. Shit, he turned it off.

All isn't lost. There are diagrams visible on the screens that are still spread out on the table. Hands trembling, I move the tablets as I deposit the tray on the table and throw a glance: it's a map of Kampala. Two clusters of red dots are scattered loosely around Kisenyi and Bwaise. Careful to keep my face blank, I pour two large brandies and turn to Anthony.

He takes the two glasses, offers one to his commanding officer and then, looping his arm around my shoulders, raises his glass and says, 'To our next assignment.' His smile looks forced as he squeezes my shoulder discreetly.

Groebler looks at me, rolling the tumbler in his hand. He's sitting on the edge of Anthony's desk, immobile, reptilian. He says nothing, he just stares at me.

Deeply uncomfortable, I say 'Anyway, I'd better let you

get on with it,' and excuse myself with a smile, closing the door behind me.

Standing in the murky basement, feeling frantic, I look to my right, towards the top of the stairs and the light seeping through the bottom of the door. I could go back up, that's the sensible thing to do. What are the chances I might find what the Resistance wants in the next few minutes? This is ridiculous. And much too risky. Yes, the sensible thing is to go right, towards the safety of my room.

On the left, the corridor seems to extend forever, dark and deserted. I didn't find out anything worthwhile. I already knew that Anthony's unit was working in Bwaise. That won't be enough. I need to dig up more intel if we're going to survive.

Biting my lip, I rub the iMode bracelet against my wrist and go left.

Fuckety, fuck, fuck fuck. What am I doing?

I creep along the gloomy basement corridor and try the first door but nothing happens. What if Anthony only gave me access to one door and the rest stay locked? The hairs on my neck rise up of their own accord as darkness grows behind me and I walk deeper into the bowels of the building. Another four doors in front of me.

A gym.

The smell of sweat and linoleum wafts cloyingly as the door closes.

An armoury.

Maybe I could... no. They'll know I was here if a weapon goes missing.

I struggle to open the next one, frantically shaking the knob until the door swings open, revealing a server room.

Bugger. Bugger. Bugger.

Nothing.

Looking back over my shoulder, I start to hyperventilate as the shadows move and grow and childhood fears resurface. I keep going down the darkened hallway, whispering to myself, 'It's OK, everything is OK, it's only an empty corridor.'

The Resistance will never evacuate us if I don't give them something worth the effort.

I reach the end of the corridor. Oh God. What if Groebler finds me? The two men who want me dead are just a few metres away, they just need to open their door to find me snooping around, and... I nearly jump out of my skin when my iMode flashes blue in the darkness.

The last door opens with a sharp click. There's no handle. No sign to indicate what's inside. Throwing a glance over my shoulder, I sneak in, not daring to turn on the light.

In the dimness, the shapes of hundreds of plastic blue barrels emerge, like the egg cave in bloody *Aliens*. Winding through the barrels, I advance carefully, holding the iMode bracelet up, so I can see by the light of its glow and make out the shape of machinery. Equipment of some sort but none of it looks like armament; it makes no sense. I need to find the weapon that Anthony's team is building. Maybe there's another room. I hurry back to the door when a noise makes me flinch and the door clicks open.

A shiver shimmies down my spine as I hunker down behind a barrel. Overhead fluorescent lights blink slowly to life, as Anthony and Colonel Groebler walk into the room.

'... made excellent progress these last few weeks. The tests are conclusive and we're ready to repatriate,' Anthony says.

I sneak a glance around the barrel, my palms tingling with sweat.

Anthony's jaw is clamped shut as he slides his arms

behind his back, feet apart. Next to him, Colonel Groebler is surveying the room. '...and you're sure about the results?'

'We'll need confirmation from St Louis. But that's affirmative, sir. We've managed to obtain the required result on a small scale.'

'Over the next month, you should be able to replicate that in a much wider perimeter, now that you've received the stock,' Groebler says. 'Let's wrap this up as soon as you can demonstrate success.'

'Yes, sir.' Anthony shuffles from foot to foot and seems to pluck up his courage as Groebler starts back towards the exit. 'Sir, about Olivia...'

Colonel Groebler interrupts him. 'Look, I don't give a flying fuck whether she's spectacular in the kitchen or in your goddam bed, Burke. This ends as soon as your project is done. Your plan has been voted down, we're proceeding as...'

The door closes and darkness engulfs me.

18

DEANN

K *ampala, Uganda, February 13, 2082*

KITSA WAS adamant that she could find the woman mentioned in Rosebell's leather notebook, Itungo. It seemed far-fetched. A first name is not enough to go on and Bwaise is a huge slum. I'd given up hope when Kitsa came to see me last evening, all excited to have found the woman. So we're going on an expedition today.

Kitsa pulls me through the maze of muddy streets, looking back over her shoulder and smiling encouragingly from time to time.

We turn a narrow corner and find ourselves in the local red light district. As I squeeze past the women and one of them claps me on the ass and the rest howl with laughter, catcalling and mocking me. Startled, I yelp and look around, furious. She gets up, hands on hips, and as I walk on, following Kitsa, the prostitute's cackles ring out behind me.

That slap could have been a stab and this little adventure could turn out to be a very stupid decision.

The packed alleyways are filthy, reeking of urine and garbage, littered with plastic bottles and animal carcasses. I didn't realize things had gotten quite so bad here. The girl takes me to a hut made of mismatched metal sheets, straw and mud. She enters without knocking. Probably because there is no door. I hesitate and then follow the child in.

Inside, an older woman is sitting on the beaten dirt floor. She starts to make happy noises when she sees Kitsa but falters when I stoop through the threshold. The child speaks to her in a fast, clipped chatter and I can't understand anything they're saying but gradually, a grin blooms on the old woman's face. She nods several times appreciatively, then grabs my cheeks and pulls me down to her level, looking deep into my eyes. We stay like that for a good ten seconds, her thin hands warm and dry on my cheeks, her eyes boring into my soul.

Finally, she releases me and as I sit down on the beaten dirt, my eyes adapt to the dim interior and I glance around while Kitsa resumes the incomprehensible conversation with the elderly woman.

There are no windows and the room is bare; there are only a few planks of wood and rags in a corner, to make a bed. But the walls are another story. Paintings of fantastical scenes cover the entire shed; long-dried lakes and rivers flow in the shadows, extinct wild animals glare at us from behind clusters of dewy leaves, luxuriant forests bloom with purple nocturnal flowers. The room seems to rustle with the warm breath of night prowlers and the green heartbeat of the jungle.

With trepidation, I recognize the painting in Rosebell's leather notebook. Pulling it out of my satchel, I open it at the familiar page and run my fingers on the paint as I compare it to the landscapes adorning the walls. The small painting in my hands is identical to the ones on the wall.

'Kitsa, ask her why her painting is in the notebook?'

'It's because her husband paint it there while Rosebell speak with Itungo. I recognize it, that's why I bring you here, Doctor DeAnn.'

Pride unexpectedly swells in my chest, as I glance at Kitsa, chatting and laughing with the elderly woman. Pushing it away, I dig out a pen and flip to the last page of my own notes.

'What is she saying?'

'Auntie Itungo says you are not as stupid as other *muzungus*. You find truth.'

'I'm not white...' I start, but Kitsa just bats my comment away and I sigh, asking instead, 'Does she know what happened to Rosebell? When was she last here?'

They speak rapidly in their dialect, then Kitsa looks seriously at me.

'She says she came here just before New Year. Doctor Rosebell ask about people who became sick here.' She gestures around her midsection waving little circles. 'Auntie Itungo told her it happen for years. At first in Kisenyi, now Bwaise too.'

'Dysentery, cholera?'

'No, dying cancer.' Kitsa tries to explain. 'Auntie Itungo told Rosebell where cancers happen.'

'It's localized?' My mind reels. But cancer isn't contagious. What could cause a geographically circumscribed epidemic? Asbestos or some other external trigger? None of this makes much sense.

Kitsa talks to the old woman but she doesn't seem too keen to tell us anymore.

'She afraid, Doctor DeAnn. She says she showed Doctor Rosebell and now she dead.'

My stomach plummets. 'What? How could she possibly know that? Ask her where Rosebell is.'

The old woman looks at me with pity and pats my cheek. A cannula is jabbed in the back of her bony hand, held in place by a hospital Band-Aid. My heart yanks me back to the Miami hospital and my dad. I push away the thought.

'Rosebell. I'm here to find my friend Rosebell.' I say slowly and loudly. Something jagged lodges itself in my throat. I try to swallow but I only manage to make my eyes well up.

'Rosebell gone,' the old woman says in English.

A tear rolls down my cheek and I wipe it angrily.

'I show. Mazzi. Come.' She gets up with difficulty, groaning as she bends to dusts off her skirt.

THE DIRT PATH snakes down through Bwaise, plunging at a steep angle toward the less savory bowels of the shantytown. Dust covers everything in a fine layer of red, even people as they sit slumped on their thresholds, life leaking out of them like sewage. Half-finished shacks list on either side of the trail, crooked and flimsy. They can't be called houses, just three walls and a corrugated steel roof, really.

As we pass by, a toddler stands up, gripping the side of his mud hut, small body naked under a grimy, ripped t-shirt. My eyes cling to his small form, bobbing up and down excitedly, as we pass him by. On every corner, mounds of garbage exhale their putrid odor. Some, set on fire, belch up acrid smoke. I pull my t-shirt up to cover my nose, as gray plumes billow toward the mercilessly blue sky.

I wipe my forehead and stop. Throwing a glance backward, I notice groups of men loitering a few blocks away, fondling the wooden handle of their AK-47s.

Such a bad fucking idea, DeAnn.

I tug on my hood, lower my head and ask, 'How much farther?'

Kitsa pulls on Itungo's sleeve and talks with her in Luganda, then she turns toward me. 'Not far now. You follow.'

Sensing my hesitation the old woman points to the bottom of the street and says, 'Mazzi. Mazzi.'

Repressing a sigh, I start walking again, careful not to twist an ankle on the potholes and rocks. I might as well go through with it now; we're nearly there.

Soon we arrive at a canal that runs through the shantytown. Children play in this open sewer with cries of glee as they chase each other, filthy water splashing against their shins.

Itungo points at a high wall topped with broken glass and barbed wire. A red and white sign says: 'RESTRICTED AREA – KEEP OUT – AUTHORIZED PERSONNEL ONLY.' She pushes aside the dusty branches of a shrub that's growing against the wall and a crack about twenty inches wide appears at knee height. The rebars look like exposed ligaments in a wound of crumbling cement flesh. I kneel next to the opening and, slipping my head gingerly through, glance inside.

We're about six feet above a courtyard dotted with drab buildings. Puzzled, I look back at the street and realize that the industrial site is at the bottom of the hill we just traipsed down, which is why it's much lower than us. The canal seems to disappear underground on the street side and a connecting pipe emerges on the inside of the wall, leading into the facility.

As Kitsa crouches next to me, I whisper, 'Are you sure this is where she took Rosebell?'

'Yes.' Her small face scrunches with resolve. 'Come, Doctor DeAnn, maybe we find Rosebell?'

'Wait... what are you doing? No!' I splutter as Kitsa squeezes through the opening, swings her scrawny legs effortlessly and lands in the courtyard. 'Damn it, Kitsa, come back here!' I whisper.

But she darts along the wall and disappears inside the main building.

Itungo's face has gone slack with terror. She holds my wrist, shaking her head violently, but I can't let the kid take this risk alone. I gently remove the old woman's hand and shimmy through the hole feet first, wincing as the concrete rips a hole in my leggings and scrapes my hip. Fingers clutching the ridged metal rods, I dangle there for a few seconds, wondering if I've miscalculated the drop. The ragged stones jutting out scratch my arms as I let go and land awkwardly on the other side. Rubbing my limbs and wincing, I hide behind a pile of abandoned wheels and rusting truck parts. Where is that child?

Cursing under my breath, I bend at the waist and skirt the wall until I reach the hangar bay where Kitsa is hiding behind a stack of blue barrels. The odor of mildew, shit and chemicals grabs me by the throat as I crouch next to her. Holding my cupped palm against my nose, I whisper, 'Kitsa! What on earth are you doing?'

I start to pull her back toward the exit but she yanks her hand out of mine. 'Look.'

A local man in gray overalls, his back turned to us, is

working near the top of a huge tank. Metal pipes run to and from it toward a reservoir. Thankfully the guy hasn't seen us. He's busy wheeling something heavy along a hanging metal walkway. When he reaches the top of the large cistern, we hear him groan as he strains to move the object off the trolley. It's a blue plastic barrel. Snapping the clasps open on either side of the barrel, he carefully removes the top and dips his hand in.

Kitsa makes a noise and I glare at her, eyebrows raised.

'Sorry.' She mouths as I wrench my head back up.

Thankfully, the man didn't hear anything. He lifts his hand out of the barrel and a handful of white powder slides through his gloved fingers like sand. Panting with effort, the man positions the blue barrel above the opening and pours its contents into the metal tank.

There's nothing to see here. This was all a waste of time.

'Poison?' Kitsa whispers.

'No. It's chlorine. To make the water drinkable. Come on, we have to go now.' I'm pulling her to her feet and starting to drag her back when the gates of the facility open automatically and a truck rides in. The hangar bay was just a few yards away. We could have made it, I should have pulled her away faster.

The truck maneuvers and then backs up toward our hangar bay, with ear-splitting beeps. Unsure about how the new comers would react to an intrusion, I make sure we stay hidden behind the stacks of barrels.

'Come on guys. Get these barrels loaded! On the double,' a man's voice shouts. The sound of heavy thumping boots reaches us. At least a dozen. Probably soldiers.

'Damn it.' I look frantically around for a better place to hide.

19

OLIVIA

 ampala, Uganda, 13 February 2082

ANXIETY CIRCLES around me like a vulture as I make my way to the shuttle mulling over how I can convince A. to give her go-ahead for the exit plan before Colonel Groebler executes me. Ideas go round and round in my mind but no solution presents itself. Things aren't looking good; DeAnn won't talk to me, I haven't anything new about Anthony's operation in Kampala since my escapade in the basement a few weeks ago and to top it all off, tomorrow is my least favourite day of the year. The unhappy reminder that I'm single and forty-two. This year, I'm spending Valentine's Day in hell. Yay. Things are looking up. Oh wait. No, they're not.

The shuttle drives through the stringent security checks and, once through, the doors open and we spill out, each plunged into our own brand of dark thoughts. We trudge to our desks like they're gallows.

A climate of frenzy and fear has pervaded the KEW High Commission these last few weeks. We're all hoping that we're about to evacuate, but there's no word yet. We've been shredding papers and closing down operations, as we wait for our transfers back to London, any day now. Any day.

I make my way to the archives, thinking about whether I could ask for help from the High Commissioner. But what good would it do? He's a civil servant, he'd have to report me to the authorities and the government pulls the Programme's strings. The High Commissioner wouldn't be able to help even if he wanted to; he's just a cog in the system.

I'm so desperate that I've started wondering whether Anthony might help me. I get the sense that he doesn't want to kill me. I know he's different to the others. There's good in him. He wants to do the right thing. I just know it.

I moan and open the umpteenth box from the archives; I've been asked to triage paperwork and check what should go with us and what should be destroyed. Thanks to this newfound access to classified records, I've learned more than I ever wanted to know about the corporations here. My days are spent getting an education in the ruthlessness of large, faceless multinationals. From lawsuits for the illegal export of wild game trophies to elaborate schemes designed to pilfer natural resources while evading corporate tax and everything in between. KEW corporations are basically treating this country like their very own twisted playground.

All around me, my colleagues are opening boxes of their own and reading quickly, then shredding a few wads of paper. It seems paper hasn't seen its last day in Uganda and this is what eighty years of archives looks like. I sigh and plough on.

What's this one about? I read it cursorily, ready to shred it and move on, but something snags so I read it again, more slowly.

It's a form, filled out by a law firm, Carapadre & Dergrin, to obtain the authorisation for their client, GeneX, to do business in Uganda. I read on, feeling a shiver of foreboding slink down my spine. The memo shows that the pharmaceutical company has submitted a request to test a drug of some sort, on locals, here, in Uganda. This is not good, not good at all.

A colleague passes by and I cover the memo with an innocuous invoice, then resume reading when he's moved past me.

I re-read the memo three times to be sure. This is definitely not something I should have seen but in the rush, the box of papers has landed on my desk. I flip the paper over. There's a stapled addendum. They started out in Kisenyi and then got a subsequent authorisation about four months ago to expand their operations in Bwaise.

Bwaise again.

There's an address.

I snap the iMode off my wrist and expand the corners until it's the size of a tablet then locate the address on the map. Mmmh. It looks like a big empty quadrant. No streets, no nothing. False address? I switch to satellite view. Ah, of course, the streets aren't on the map because the area is on the outskirts of the shantytown. There's a canal, a few hangars and buildings. I zoom in on the brands, the signs. Famase Depot, Mazzi water treatment plant, Kyenvu self-storage place, Muti – looks like maybe a timber factory. It's a typical industrial zone. Something chimes in the back of my mind but the connection refuses to click.

Troubled, I take a photo of the memo discreetly and

send it to A. Then I fold the piece of paper and slip it in my pocket. I keep going through the box, reading everything in detail, but I don't find anything else.

A drug? Were the subjects aware and consenting? I wonder if it's at least something for Uganda's greater good; hopefully a cure for malaria or something. The reassuring thought fails to silence the disquiet I feel.

I remember about three weeks after I arrived that my colleagues were horrified when I said I was visiting Bwaise with a friend from church. Violet came by to whisper a tall tale about locals going sick and dying from some sort of disease in the slums. I just dismissed it, thinking it was an urban legend or that she was trying to scare me; hazing for the newbie. But now that I've read the memo, her story takes on a new, more sinister cast.

I wrap up in the archives and go in search of Violet.

'Ah, Violet, here you are.' I find her in her manager's office, ostensibly putting away his files but more likely enjoying the fan on his desk. She's looking impeccable, her hair held back by a headband, hefty thighs encased in tartan-patterned leggings.

'Olivia, erm... hello?...' She clutches her fake pearl necklace and starts playing with it. 'Now, listen... I know it's Valentine's Day tomorrow, but you have to know, I didn't plan for this to happen.'

What is the woman on about? Oh, she must mean Hugh.

'Hugh and I are very happy together and—'

'Listen, Violet, good for you, I'm sure. But that's not what I'm here about.'

Taken aback, she twists her lips dubiously and then seeing that I really don't care, she breaks into a relieved smile.

'Oh, I'm so glad, Olivia. I've been driving myself sick

with worry about what you might think after I stole him from you. You were such an item and to break the two of you up was—'

'I beg your pardon?' I interrupt her. 'No, there must be a mistake; Hugh and I never went out together.'

She makes a face that says 'yeah, right'. Oh, the woman can't be serious! It's like she's me, six months ago. The whole bloody country is falling apart and what she worries about is a *bloke*? She's welcome to the chinless milksop.

'Look, Violet, I'm so sorry, I'm in a bit of a hurry.' I don't add, *Because Kampala is crumbling around our ears, in case you hadn't noticed, you daft woman.* 'I truly am happy for you both.'

'Oh bless, that's mighty big of you.'

Blimey, sarcasm. What a cow.

'Anyway, could you remind me of that story about those locals in the slums who fell ill and died mysteriously?'

She wasn't expecting that. It takes her a minute to adjust. 'I'll say, you have a good memory, love. I told you that because you said you drank something in the slums. It just reminded me of a rumour I'd heard about strange goings-on in Bwaise.'

'About soldiers?' I prompt, hoping she'll finally tell me where Anthony's soldiers have been going and what type of weapon they've been building there.

'What? No, no. Soldiers?' She frowns. 'Not at all. The rumour was that the water coming from that water plant in Bwaise...' – she snaps her fingers, trying to remember – 'Lassie, Daisy, Maisy?'

'The Mazzi water treatment plant?'

'Yes, that one. People were getting sick and dying after drinking the water, that's all.'

'You mean the pumping station wasn't treating the water properly?'

She shrugs. 'I suppose. Who knows?' She means 'who cares?'

'Right.'

'It's not the first time. God only knows what's in the water in this bloody shithole of a country. There's always something else. A few years back, I remember the same stories were circulating in the local paper about Kisenyi. That was maybe two years ago? They said you could get cancer from drinking the water.' She barks a laugh. 'I mean they were probably dying from diarrhoea... It's not exactly BBC-level reporting we're talking about, is it?'

'So since then nothing?'

'No. Well, apart from the, you know...' – she gestures towards the boarded window – '...the situation.'

I mull things over. It matches. First Kisenyi in 2080 and now Bwaise.

'Sorry, I can't even remember why I said anything, you're obviously fine.' She waves the whole thing away. 'Oh, by the way, Olivia, did you hear yet?'

'Hear about what?'

'We're being evacuated on Monday.'

A flutter of hope soars in my chest. 'Oh, thank God!'

Maybe I could just omit to tell Anthony about it and arrange to be airlifted out with the rest of the KEW personnel? I wouldn't have to reveal my cover to the High Commissioner and in the kerfuffle, I could get DeAnn on board the plane. Chewing my lower lip, I weigh the option. I think it could work. I have to try.

'Just one more day in this stinking hellhole and we're out!' she says as I run out of the office and back to the archives. If this works, we won't have to depend on the

Resistance to escape. We could find a way to survive unde-tected in London for a few months and we'd have time to come up with a plan together for going back to 2017.

Somewhere inside my head, the vultures stop circling and my singsong voice starts chirping, *Oh, gosh, maybe every-thing will be OK!*

20

DEANN

K *ampala, Uganda, February 13, 2082*

GAGGING on the mouldy smell of stagnating water, I pull Kitsa behind me. We backtrack slowly over pipes and rails, and manage to sneak behind one of the tanks and conceal ourselves in the shadows. We can't see anything from here but the men who are loading the barrels in the truck are clearly soldiers.

A loud thump startles me as Kitsa squeaks and we both freeze.

'For fuck's sake! Be careful!' one of the men shouts.

'The seal is broken,' another one says, sounding annoyed. 'OK, take it anyway, we can't leave any evidence behind.'

'Bloody hell, Crash, you hungover or what?'

'Sorry, sorry.'

Kitsa and I shrink back into the shadows, flinching

when something moves behind us, but it's only cockroaches, scurrying away.

At last, the soldiers load the last barrel. The Ugandan custodian talks to them as the truck roars to life, belching a cloud of exhaust. I hold back a cough and squeeze Kitsa's hand. Nearly there. Then we can escape.

Risking a step forward, I catch a glimpse of the old man, as he chats with the soldier; I can't see much, just a small part of the caretaker's back and elbow.

Just as I'm starting to relax, the old man makes an odd movement and there's a choking sound. His spasms as he's lifted up, legs dangling above the ground. My heart beats so hard that it feels like it's in my mouth. Backtracking toward the dark corner, I pull Kitsa with me, eyes fixed on the jerking legs. The metal pipes seem to slither between our feet in the reeking corner. Kitsa grips my hand fiercely, exhaling little panicked pants. I slide my hand over her mouth and keep moving backwards.

There's a sickening crack and the body thumps to the floor.

'Hey, Boomer, come the fuck on. We don't have all day.'

'Just give me a sec.'

In the distance, the gate groans open. The truck hisses and rumbles out. We hear the gates being pulled closed and the sound of the lock clinking against the metal. Then silence.

Knees creaking, I release Kitsa and steal out of our hiding spot to look around. The place is deserted and the sky is darkening. I walk over to the old man, to check his vitals and help. But there's no point; he's sprawled on the floor and his eyes are open but he's staring at nothing, a look of pure surprise painted on his features.

Careful not to touch anything, I step around the poor man. 'Let's go.'

But the slender child darts away, eyes fixed on something on the floor. She bends down to look at a small pile of white powder.

'Don't touch that. Chlorine is toxic.'

As usual, Kitsa doesn't listen. Fishing a rubber glove out of her scrubs, she puts it on and touches the powder tentatively with her finger. I'm already walking across the hangar bay.

'Come on, Kitsa, they could come back.'

I glance over my shoulder and see her grab a handful of white powder. Then she flips the glove around and ties it into a makeshift bag. Clever girl. She catches up with me in the yard and hands me the glove. I put it in my bag and help her climb over the pile of rubble and rusty spare parts. We struggle to squeeze back through the opening and find Itungo there, sitting by the bush, half out of her mind with worry.

Time to go. We can't be walking around Bwaise after dark.

'That was so fucking stupid, Kitsa!' I whisper as we climb back up the slope. 'What would have happened if they'd seen you?'

She has the good grace to look sheepish.

'Don't ever do that again. Do you hear me?'

It comes out more sternly than needed.

She looks hurt but continues to walk without another word. I watch her bony silhouette walking resolutely and feel an unexpected swell of love.

It will do her good to have limits. She can't just keep doing this sort of shit. She'll get killed. We drop Itungo off at her shack and finally climb back up to the city streets. The sunset is setting the sky on fire, as we hop on a boda boda and zoom through traffic, back to the French Doctors' hospital.

We get off and pay, then start walking back inside when a large man steps in my path, his shape dark against the brightness of the setting sun. For a second, I think that the soldiers followed us here. I pull Kitsa behind me and start to backtrack when the man says, 'Where were you?' His deep rumbling voice is familiar.

'Oh, Omony, it's you. You scared the bejesus out of me.'

I take in his tall, muscular, clean-cut presence and my heart does that blooming thing in my chest. Shit. I quash the feeling quickly and take a step toward him, conscious that Kitsa and I look like we've been up to no good.

'Are you hurt?' he says, sliding his hand along my forearm and lifting it up to examine the scratches.

'Oh no, it's nothing. Just a scrape from the boda boda.'

I turn to Kitsa. 'See you tomorrow morning, kiddo. We'll talk then, OK?' I widen my eyes and she nods, looking serious. I kiss the top of her head and she scampers.

'Where did you go?' he asks, strain in his voice.

I nearly tell him but then realize he'd be worried and angry. It was a pretty stupid risk to take. I smile instead. 'Nowhere. Let's get out of here. I can't wait to get to your place and take a shower.'

'I have a surprise for you.'

Come to think of it, Omony has never collected me in person before, it's usually his driver who ferries me around town.

'I hate surprises.'

'I know.' There's a hint of smugness in his smile.

He holds the door open for me and I climb in.

21

OLIVIA

K ampala, Uganda, 13 February 2082

MY COLLEAGUES ARE all delirious with relief. News of the Monday morning evacuation spread like wildfire and there's an air of giddiness around the whole place, a frenzied antici-pation before the long-expected journey. People are laugh-ing, hurrying around, chatting animatedly.

I'm the only one who's worried. I can't just leave. I need to find DeAnn and make sure she's with me on the first KEW plane out of here in two days' time.

Finally, the day ends and I run out of the building to talk to the kind shuttle driver.

'Please could you drive me to the French Doctors' hospital today, before you drop me off at home?'

He looks uncomfortable. 'I don't know, Miss Olivia.'

'Edmand, please, it's a matter of life and death. I've seen

you at Rubaga Cathedral. You're a man of faith, aren't you? Please do this for me, in the name of God.'

He hesitates and then nods. Everyone gets dropped off and when it's only me left in the shuttle, he drives me to the hospital.

'Thank you, Edmand, you're a good man. You're saving a life today. Please wait for me, I'll be just a few minutes.'

I jump out of the van, run inside the hospital and then through the corridors, trying to find DeAnn. Unable to locate her, I get more and more frantic until I come across a nurse who directs me to her room.

I sprint down the corridor and burst in, expecting to find my partner there, but instead there's a slender child on her bed, wearing pink scrubs and reading an anatomy book.

'Sorry, sweetie, do you know where DeAnn – Doctor Carpenter – is?' I stick my head out in the hall, trying to find a nameplate. I don't understand, it does says DeAnn on the door. 'I was told that this is her room?'

'Oh yes, this is Doctor DeAnn's room.' The child hops off the bed and smiles at me. 'I am Kitsa.'

'Hello there, Kitsa. Listen, sweetheart, I'm in a big hurry and I need to find DeAnn. It's very important, do you know where she is?'

'She left ten minutes ago, you just missed her.'

I could scream right now. Has she already been captured? Am I too late? I can't just abandon DeAnn to her fate, I must find her before Monday morning. Can I entrust the little girl with a message? She looks so earnest and good with that antique stethoscope around her neck. She must be twelve at most. It's evident that the child has been staying in DeAnn's room for a while. She should be able to give her a message as soon as she comes back. I have to risk it.

'Alright, listen carefully, Kitsa. I want you to give a

message to Doctor DeAnn, OK?' I pat myself down, looking for a piece of paper, and find the memo that I stole this afternoon. The GeneX thing seems to have happened a century ago. It doesn't matter anymore anyway. It's unrelated to the Programme operations in Kampala and there's nothing I can do to stop it. I might as well have shredded it. I feel a twinge of guilt and amend that silently. No, I can always look into it, once DeAnn and I are evacuated with the diplomatic staff and out of the Programme's deadly reach. But first things first: we need to survive Uganda and be on that plane on Monday.

'Do you have a pen?'

The child hands me one, head cocked to the side, looking at me curiously while I write on the back of the sheets.

I summarise the situation, the danger we're in, my plan to get us evacuated with the High Commission staff and where she needs to be on Monday.

'Hide this piece of paper and only give it to DeAnn as soon as you see her. Tell her to go back without me if I'm not at the rendezvous point at the High Commission on Monday at five a.m. Do you understand?'

She frowns as she takes the folded memo and slips it in her pocket.

'Go back where?'

'Where we came from.'

'But—'

'Miss Olivia? Miss Olivia?' Edmand's voice rings in the hallway. It sounds like he's running. Bugger, he's not going to wait much longer for me.

'I need to go. Just tell DeAnn, OK? This paper will save her life.'

She juts her little chin forwards and nods.

'Miss Olivia?' There's panic in Edmand's voice now and his footsteps recede.

I close the door behind me and sprint towards the exit, hoping he hasn't left me behind.

'There you are, Miss Olivia.' His kind face is etched with worry and fear. 'We have to go. There is an announcement on the radio. A new curfew takes effect tonight. We have to go now!'

22

DEANN

K *ampala, Uganda, February 13, 2082*

WE DRIVE IN SILENCE, Omony sealed in his iBubble and the driver focusing intently on the road. We pass Nsandi, Katende and Mpigi. So we're leaving town, then.

For a moment, the image of the old man's neck, bent at an unnatural angle, flashes before my eyes. The killer was so strong that he lifted the caretaker right off his feet as he strangled him. Who could have done this? I never saw the soldiers. They could have been anyone. Ugandans are famous mercenaries, hired by private army contractors as cheap muscle in countless conflicts, even in my time period. Some of these men certainly would have the expertise to organize into militias.

But why were they removing the chlorine from the plant, instead of delivering it? It makes no sense. And why kill the custodian? He was no threat, there was no food in this facility, there was no reason for them to steal or murder.

I puzzle over this, probing the problem from all angles, unable to let go. Something about this doesn't make sense.

Omony's absorbed in a conversation inside his iBubble, but he smiles through the glass, clearly enjoying my annoyance. Throngs of thin, dusty, shuffling people part to let us through. There are very few children left, just withered adults who look desperate and exhausted.

The car bounces over deep potholes as we pass an overturned tractor by the side of the road and, a few miles later, a dead cyclist. Nobody seems to care or plan to do anything about the bodies that lie strewn in the ditches.

We drive for hours and I doze off until my sleep is interrupted by angry voices and I wake up with a start. For a confused moment, I wonder who shouted; we're still on the road and there is no one there. Then I realize it's the radio. In a sleep-muddled corner of my mind, a small voice is murmuring with disquiet. Omony is whisking me away me to an unknown location in the middle of the night. I don't know him all that well and the country's falling apart before our eyes.

The excited chatter is incomprehensible and then a frenzied news anchor announces that Congolese armies have clashed with armed forces at the border, over the remaining water in Lake Edward. Omony and the driver exchange a look, but Omony lowers his head again and resumes his conversation, so this must not affect our route. I hate surprises.

'What's happening?' I ask the driver.

The driver doesn't answer. I don't think he speaks English.

Just then, Omony's finishes his business call and collapses his iBubble.

'They're whipping up nationalistic sentiment and pushing people to invade Congo. The broadcast is a debate.' He listens for a moment. 'This one is saying that the RDC has a lot of space for us to live, for us to harvest, fish and hunt and that we should just take what we need.' He listens on and adds, 'The other man is arguing that this is a declaration of war and that the Congolese army is poised at the border, ready to mow down any trespassers with machine guns and tanks.' He listens a little longer and shakes his head. 'The first man says we should keep sending our masses and that they can't kill us all. That we should take our machetes and kill them when their ammunition runs out.'

He gestures abruptly to the driver and the silent, tall man switches off the radio.

'Is this really about to happen? War with Congo?'

'Uganda is one of the ten most populated countries on Earth, somewhere behind China, India, the US... but we're also by far the smallest of the ten, geographically. The DRC is ten times as big as Uganda and they're nearly empty by comparison.' He shrugs. 'It would make sense for us to expand there. These borders are artificial anyway, they were made by the colonists and it's time for a change.'

'Isn't it dangerous to leave Kampala, then?' I ask him crossly. 'Where are you taking me?'

'You'll see.' Infuriatingly, he pats my knee.

We branch off and take an interminable dirt road. Desiccated trees stand guard on either side of the track and bugs dance for a split second in the headlights before being swallowed by the black night.

Finally the driver stops and we get out, but I can't see

where we are. Night is always so much darker here. The air smells of hay and something deeper, more pungent as well.

'Where are we?' I ask, looking around, worried now.

'We're in Lake Mburo National Park.' He smiles. 'Happy Valentine's Day.'

'Oh.'

I didn't expect that.

I never cared for the stupid commercial holiday and I didn't take him for the romantic type either.

We walk up a paved staircase winding between trees and bushes to a gorgeous terracotta lodge with a thatched roof. As usual, we're the only ones here. I guess no local can afford it anymore and foreigners have better sense than to come to this country during these troubled times.

We're greeted by an affable British manager and shown to a luxurious room-tent hybrid. While Omony dismisses the manager, I discover a large wooden canopy bed positioned in the middle of the room, with a mosquito net draped around it, the pristine white sheets pressed and turned. There is only one room, only one bed. A lightning rod of desire strikes, burning a path through my abdomen.

I hurry into the bathroom and impatiently shed all my clothes, with a sudden need to be naked and clean. I yank off the ripped leggings, taking stock of the new scratches on my hip, wrestle off the sweaty socks, pull the t-shirt above my head and throw it in a corner, no longer able to bear any of it – the grime, the death, the constriction.

I shake my hair loose, step into the vast shower and wash it all away. I just want to enjoy this unexpected treat, even if it's only for a moment. I lather the fragrant soap all over me and think about Omony, unsure about him. He hasn't even kissed me yet. He hasn't made any move at all. But he behaves like he owns me. I don't know what to make of it.

As usual, Omony's staff has thought of everything, they must have driven here ahead of us. When I come out of the shower, my hairbrush and all my toiletries are arrayed on the counter already.

By the time I pat barefoot to the bedroom, wrapped in a towel, Omony's gone, but someone has laid a brand new white dress on the canopy bed. It's a fit and flare wrap in flimsy transparent linen. My mind flashes to the white dress Rosebell was wearing the last night I saw her, but I grit my teeth and shove the memory away.

One weekend away from it all. Just for this evening I want to feel solace instead of dread.

I can't find underwear anywhere, so I pull on the dress, grab a torch and walk out barefoot, my feet still wet, leaving prints on the glimmering granite rocks that form a path toward the main part of the lodge.

I walk along the darkened path and it reminds me of the first day I met Omony, after the water riot. I remember walking through his living room, looking for him, feeling vulnerable as I do now. My long wet hair is soaking the back of the dress as it rhythmically slaps against my shoulders, swaying with each step I take. It seems that I'm still walking in the dark, in a way. I'm still at his mercy and trying to find him.

It's at least 2 a.m. by now and the staff have gone. Candles burn at regular intervals along the path, perfuming the air with lemongrass, but behind it, surrounding us, the African night is breathing, its hot, rich smell pervading everything; warmer, earthier and untamed.

Finally, I see him; he's absorbed in his own thoughts, arms on the far edge of the infinity pool overlooking the savannah. Everything is plunged in darkness, only a few candles dabble his skin in a golden glow. Large moths circle the flickering flames as if in slow motion, their wings rippling woozily in the night.

When I reach the edge of the pool, Omony turns. He doesn't say anything but I physically feel his stare travelling over the expanse of water and taking in my cold feet, moving up my legs and detailing every inch of me, until he reaches my breasts, my neck, my face.

I shiver, and in the velvet night's silence, I become acutely aware that I'm naked under the loose wrap. Belatedly I realize that there's a candle behind me and that the white dress must be completely transparent. My nipples harden and I feel the warm burn of lust as I sit on the swimming pool's edge, letting my legs sway in the warm water.

'Omony, what are we doing here? I have work to do.'

'Not tonight and not until Sunday.' His tone does not brook any argument.

Soaking in the night's primal intensity, I allow myself to go with the flow tonight. Maybe there's another tent somewhere in the lodge where he's planning to stay the night. He's made absolutely no moves since we first met. Every time we get together we talk about work or have intellectual debates. Maybe I'm reading more into this than there is.

'I like to come here whenever I can,' he starts in a low, deep voice. His eyes are nearly slanted, his heavy eyelids lending intensity to his serious face. His cheekbones are high and sharp. I can only see his neck and the start of his chest, above the water. He looks like an Easter Island statue, larger than life, his features carved as if out of obsidian.

'When I'm here I feel closer to my roots. Sometimes it's easy to forget who I am.'

'How do you mean?'

'I was raised abroad. Boarding school in England.' He's

lost in his memories, he doesn't look at me, his eyes are tracking a faraway point in the night. 'My father was an important man. He wanted the best for me and I did get it, in the end. But at a cost higher than I was prepared to pay.' He's still leaning on the pool's far edge but his voice carries on the water, a deep low rumble, like a storm approaching. 'We were taught to excel in sports, to learn little and to feel nothing.'

I try to imagine what it must have been like to grow up in such a cold environment, never to get a hug, never to feel loved. At least in my family, I did get some love from my father.

He continues, 'It makes you wonder, doesn't it? To be part of this elite, you have to keep your mouth shut about how the rich and powerful are paying to have their heirs abused and stunted.

'When I first arrived, I thought the other children were nice enough, their politeness seemed like kindness, because I didn't know any better. They're hypocrites, the English,' he spits out. 'They're so skilled at saying one thing and meaning quite another.' His cultured, elegant accent contrasts oddly with his words, as he sounds so quintessentially English to me.

'Slowly, I started to realize that they were spreading rumors about me, denouncing me to the teachers, ganging up against me because I was black. Nobody stood up for me. I was told I was ugly, dirty, smelly. I was pushed, punched, beaten up. Teachers turned a blind eye – or maybe they'd suggested it, for all I know.'

I try to imagine him as a child and fail. It's so hard to evoke any vulnerability in him. He looks so strong.

'But in the end, despite their rejection, I learned how to be like them, how to belong. I hate this about me, but I'm

British, in a way. I've become a product of the system that molded me. That's why I come here as often as I can.' We hear big cats roar in the distance and he closes his eyes, breathing in the night. 'To feel this... around us. To reconnect with my land, my roots. To remind myself that I'm still Ugandan under the veneer. Still African.'

His gaze is trained on the darkest point in the night. Then he shakes himself out of his reverie and his deep brown eyes focus on me. I feel like prey; paralyzed and hypnotized, unable to breathe.

'That's who I am, DeAnn.' He rarely uses my name and in his mouth it sounds unfamiliar and startling. 'I'd never touch you if you were English. But I have respect for you; you're a long lost sister. African by blood, American by culture. Similar to me in so many ways.' My heart sinks at his choice of words. His *sister*.

He continues, 'You, especially, are undaunted and fierce. There is a fire within you and I see you clearly.' His eyes once again detail me, lingering on the dark recess between my legs that the short dress fails to cover.

He detaches himself from the ledge and swims toward me, slowly. Insects flitter in and out of the shadows and a loud birdcall startles me. The flickering light illuminates a small monkey as it jumps from one tree to the next, the branches rustling under its weight.

Omony reaches my side of the pool and as he grabs the ledge, a few drops of water land on my thighs.

'May I show you something?' There is something raw about him that matches the night, the heat. Something in him that makes my breath shorter.

He rises slowly out of the water, his movements fluid. I'm mesmerized by the shifting of his muscles under his dark skin, his chiseled chest, his dangerous sleekness. Water drops speckle him with light as they glide down his hard, taut body.

He offers me his hand and I stand as well, relishing the excuse to touch any part of him. His hand feels huge and leathery as it engulfs mine, the skin ridged and hardened on his palm.

He guides me down the stairs into the garden and we walk in silence. The grass and rock prickle my bare feet as the light dress ripples around me with each gust of the evening breeze. The garden is a riot of plants; acacia spring out of their beds of thorns, trailing branches that caress my shoulders as I duck to follow him in the dark, his hand holding mine, pulling me forward.

Finally he stops in front of a small tree and I wonder whether the animals we heard earlier are perhaps all around us now, in the pooling dark. I can't see much at all in the night. Goosebumps erupt on my neck when his breath caresses my skin, as he leans to show me an animal, scurrying away in the night, its name sounding like poetry. I feel him standing behind me, his body warm through the flimsy fabric.

'This tree isn't much to look at by day,' he starts in a low, hoarse whisper, pointing toward the small cactus tree that shoots up its long fleshy branches in front of us. 'But once a year, at night...'

The floral smell intensifies, sweetly pungent in the humid air. Crickets chirp, rhythmically calling to each other. His hand alights on my shoulder.

One of the tree's appendages opens and an enormous white flower unfurls, spreading its orange corolla as it spills a heady scent into the night air. A dozen other flowers start to stir and soon they explode into white and orange fireworks, their petals like sparks against the night's backdrop.

It's a mesmerizing sight. Behind me, Omony caresses my shoulders, the touch of his palms against my skin sending shivers throughout my body. He takes a step forward and the warmth of him seeps through the flimsy linen, as my blood starts to pound like a drumbeat, awakening my body. I open up, like a flower, pulsing in the thickening night.

I lean back, feeling his hard, warm body against me. He inhales deeply, face buried in my hair, and then smoothly moves my hair aside and kisses my neck. He holds me firmly against him. I can feel him hardening, his growing bulge nested against the softest part of me, as he holds us pressed against one another.

I want to turn, to kiss him, but he holds me, locked in his embrace. He caresses my shoulders and the dress's thin straps fall away. My breath catches as his fingers clench around my breast, kneading it roughly and then twisting my nipple.

My body is on fire. One of his arms is pinning my body against his like a dark knotted branch and my breast is crushed in his hand as he squeezes harder, mixing pain with pleasure. His hips press against my back as he undresses, springing free from the swimsuit, and I feel him, hard and warm, between my buttocks, seeking his way toward my warmth, my wetness. He bends me forward, his right hand now grabbing my neck, pushing down to bend me over then he drives his entire length into me in one hard thrust and I cry out in the night.

He's burning his way through my cunt as I swell and pulse around him and a handful of my hair is trapped in his grip and he pounds into me.

I scream with abandon, pleasure and pain, all of it mixing together confusingly. He's still grabbing my hip with his left hand and impressing a hard rhythm, holding me close as he comes; his deep groan overpowering my own. Our voices blend with the raucous chatter of the night around us. He slows down and shudders inside me, his thighs against mine, his hands releasing their iron grip slowly.

As I slide onto the dry grass, the night around us is as soft as velvet; soft, enveloping. A bird calls repetitively to its mate and the grass feels rough against my back. He kneels in front of me and slowly, looking deep into my eyes, he opens my legs, pushing me backwards on the grass, so that I'm now lying down, my legs bent, knees still trembling. Lying down on his belly in the grass in front of me, he buries his dark gorgeous lips in me, lapping his own essence and mine, sucking on my clitoris, his fingers inside of me until I convulse with pleasure, surrendering completely to him as I come again, my mind blinded by a flash of white light, soaring.

A minute or an eternity passes. I feel renewed, washed clean by the light. I open my eyes and see him staring at me. He licks his upper lip with a satisfied and proprietary look and lies down next to me.

We soak in the night, taking in the myriad of stars, the insects' chirping and the heady smell of the white blooms above us as we lie side by side, both exhausted and released.

23

OLIVIA

 ampala, Uganda, 13 February 2082

I WAKE UP WITH A START, tangled in my clammy bed sheets, my pyjamas drenched with sweat. Flopping back on the mattress, I stare at the ceiling as the fan's blades turn hypnotically in the suffocating night. Somewhere a mosquito buzzes. I re-arrange the net to close a gap and lie back down. I know that sleep will elude me now, like every night, playing its pointless game of cat and mouse.

My hand slides under the pillow and clutches the Swiss Army knife that Anthony gave me, after the orphanage near miss. He came to my room that day and pressed his hands around both of mine, nestling the small tool in my palm. 'You must always have it with you, Olivia.'

It was so incongruous in its benign red childishness that I laughed. 'Don't be ridiculous, I'm more likely to slash my wrist open just trying to get the nail file.'

'I'll try to get you a gun but that's harder. Just hold on to this in the meantime, OK?'

Fear still coursing through my veins, from that morning's attack, I relented. Any weapon, no matter how inadequate, was better than none.

Now the pocketknife has become the companion of my insomnia, its weight and shape reassuring in my palm.

I so want to go home.

I've had enough of the heat, the dust, the sweat, the smell of mosquito repellent, the violence and the death, enough with all of it. I stroke the scar on my forearm absentmindedly, like I do every time I dream of somehow activating my chip ahead of schedule and going home this week, tomorrow, now.

My mouth feels unbearably dry. I reach for the bottle, usually on the bedside, and remember: we now have rations. Two litres of water a day for everyone and I've already drunk mine. I try to salivate instead, to moisten my tongue. Moderate success. I fantasise about drinking the pure well water that I tasted once as a child during a hike with my family. My mind conjures the ice-cold crystalline liquid and I try to remember what it felt like to have enough.

There is very little water left. Even for us. We get our water by special truck delivery every Monday and we have to make it last the week. The men work hard for hours in the sun, patrolling, loading trucks, repairing any damage to the compound's walls. A couple of the soldiers started stumbling, slurring and getting headaches. After that, Anthony got more careful, dividing the day into shifts and making sure the men worked at night or when the sun wasn't at its highest.

I never thought I'd experience thirst. It's uncanny. I used to think that water was in infinite supply, readily available at the flick of a tap. I snort, remembering my idiotic naiveté. Apparently, the drinkable water shortage is everywhere. In China, the Yangtze River diversion project has failed and Peking is on strict water rations. Lima's glacier water melted and evaporated, and now Peru's capital is a ghost city, its people evacuated. It's happening all over the world. But there is no contingency plan in Uganda and people are dying from thirst in the streets of Kampala.

It's horrible to witness it and not to be able to do anything about it. Spectral figures stumble through the streets, their skin dry and flaking, their tongues swollen, unable to speak. People don't even try to help them anymore. Once they reach that stage, their kidneys stop working and they're days away from death's embrace.

Fortunately, or maybe unfortunately, I've become anesthetised to it all. Something still pierces through the fog sometimes. Like the mother the other day who was holding her dead infant, howling silently at the sky. All her tears spent. Her voice gone. Or the attack on the market that I saw from the armoured car as I was being driven back to the compound. People killing each other with machetes over tinned food and a handful of water bottles.

The lack of hope is terrible and terrifying. People will do anything when hope is gone. I wonder what is happening to baby Jonathan, I haven't had any news of the orphanage in weeks. I lie in the dark, listening to the crickets as a tear trickles from the corner of my eye to the pillow. All I can think is what a stupid waste of water it is to cry.

A huge explosion shatters the night's silence. A tremor shakes the floor and the walls shudder, as paint chips and dust fall to the floor. For a few seconds I stay frozen in my bed, listening to the absolute silence. Then a clamour roars in the night as a hundred voices rise in unison.

I grab my Swiss Army knife from under my pillow, jump out of bed and run to the window. There's a gaping hole in the wall surrounding the compound, a cloud of dust surrounds the breach and blocks of cinder are strewn about the courtyard as the militia attackers charge into the breach, their shouts laced with rage and despair. One of them looks up at me and takes aim with his AK-47. Before I have time to react, there's a shockingly loud noise to my left and little chips of stone hit my cheek. I squeak and jump out of sight, back against the wall. My heart is hammering against my ribs and I can't think.

I need to get out of here.

I run to the door of my room, remove the chair wedged against the handle and crack the door open. Anthony's men are running, half dressed, putting on their gear as they go. Jarrod hurries past my door, checking the magazine clip of his machine gun. I don't know what to do. Should I stay here or hide somewhere else?

I open the door and slink into the corridor, trying to stay out of the men's way as they run towards the commotion.

Screams of rage and pain are mixing with the deafening cough of machine guns. Plugging my ears, I crouch down and staying low, peek out of an open window. The intruders pouring in through the jagged gap in the outer wall are armed with machetes for the most part, as well as a few machine guns. Their weapons are crude compared to ours, but they're desperate and they keep charging in with no end in sight. How many are there?

There's only a dozen soldiers in the courtyard and they're barricaded behind the main building's entrance, returning fire and trying to hold off the onslaught. A shower of shiny brass flickers in the night and some of the assailants fall but most keep rushing towards our defences, like an unstoppable wave. Bodies are sprawled out in the courtyard and a few of Anthony's men are wounded; they're slumped against the wall of our main building and, in the moonlight, splatters darken the white plaster behind their prostrated forms.

This Swiss Army knife isn't going to do at all. I hurry to the basement door and find it wide open so I sneak in, unsure about whether I should, but I know there's an armoury down there. So I run down the steps and rush to the room, relieved to find it open. I step on a bullet and yelp. After that, I pick my way around the scattered cylinders, feeling the cold floor beneath my bare feet. I shudder and wrap my arms around me, wishing I'd thought to dress more appropriately. Pink pyjama bottoms and a tank top. Seriously? Anyway, that doesn't matter right now. Sighing with frustration, I rush to the shelf and pick a small handgun. I recognise the model; it's the one that requires fingerprint recognition, so I won't be able to use it. I groan with frustration and scan the rest of the racks, but there is nothing. Nothing I can use.

I'm rummaging through a drawer when another loud explosion rocks the building. Destabilised, I grab the shelf, as the tremor shudders along the walls and a crack opens along its path. I stay very still, knuckles white, fingers clasped around the sharp edge of the metal post while a fine white powder rains from the ceiling and the lamps swing wildly, projecting shadows and light across the room. I freeze, listening intently but nothing else stirs except... the suffocating smell of smoke.

Fire!

Feeling my intestines liquefy, I leave the armoury still only clutching the small blade in my sweaty hand. I climb the steps two by two and start to run towards the entrance, but skid to halt in the deserted hallway. I can't go out that way. That's where the attacker's offensive is concentrating. We're trapped inside.

The fire's on this floor. I can't get out, I can't stay here either. Holding my t-shirt in front of my nose, I cough out the smoke and try to breathe and think, but adrenaline is making everything frantic and my singsong voice is wailing for me to *Run!*

There's a heart-stopping thunderclap of machine-gun fire somewhere nearby. Then the incoherent roar of battle cries. Close. Very close.

Somebody yells, 'They're in!'

'Fall back, fall back!'

I make a U-turn and sprint down the corridor but soon I reach a dead end. Tongues of roaring fire lick the walls where an explosion has ripped open the building. No way through. Oh God, oh God, oh God.

Bullets hit the wall next to me with a deafening crack, just as a group of Anthony's men emerges from the smoke. They're cornered and backing towards me along the corridor. They don't see me, they're too busy defending themselves and firing at a group of raging intruders running towards us, yelling and shooting.

I scrabble away as quickly as I can and fall backwards. Retreating on my bum and hands, I try to get up but slip in a pool of blood. The attackers rush towards us, screaming at the top of their lungs. They're so close now that I can see their individual faces, gaunt and desperate, drenched in sweat. Most are wielding blood-stained machetes, but the few who have machine guns are spraying bullets haphazardly as they run.

Whimpering, I finally manage to get up, half stumbling on the debris and I take the only path left: up the staircase.

When I make it to the first landing, I try to get back to my room, but the smoke here is too thick and I feel the hot breath of the fire on my face. So, I clamber up the stairs, out of breath. A bullet will hit me in the back any second. The hair on the back of my neck is standing on end and a small, thin scream escapes my lips, which I'm powerless to stop. I run, not caring about my bare feet anymore, the small knife useless in my hand.

I climb the steps two by two, sensing someone running behind me. Faster, faster. Smoke is already prickling my nostrils, stinking of melting plastic and cordite. I run up the stairs, panic eating away at my insides, up to the top-floor movie room.

Breathless, I lock the door behind me and back away, holding the tiny blade in front of me. I can feel the thread-bare carpet under my feet and the room swirls with shadows and strange noises.

A crash against the door makes me jump out of my skin. It's soon followed by another. I press a hand to my mouth, willing myself to be quiet but a sob comes out through my fingers. I can't move. My legs feel like jelly. Someone followed me here. Someone saw me.

The doors shake, the wood and lock are starting to creak and splinter. The Swiss Army knife, slick with sweat, threatens to slip out of my grip, so I wrap both hands around it. My knees wobble and the room starts to swim all around me. Panting, I backtrack until I bump against the wall and slide to the floor, trying to fold myself into a ball as small as possible. *Help. Somebody, help.*

With a crash, the doors burst open and a man barges in with a triumphant yell, his face hidden in the darkness. As he searches for me, he steps into a moonbeam shining through the skylight – and I realise it's Jarrod. My first reflex is to go to him but when he hears me stir, his head turns slowly and a cruel smile stretches on his lips. He walks deliberately towards me and into the shadows again, shouldering his machine gun.

'Come out, Olivia.'

I squirm into the corner, in the pooling shadows. He keeps coming, his machine gun aimed right at me. He's spotted me, there's no point in hiding anymore.

'Jarrod, thank God, you've come to help me,' I say, forcing the words out.

'Afraid not, Olivia. I'm here to kill you.'

'But why?' My voice is barely audible, there's a huge lump in my throat. 'We're friends.'

He roars with laughter. 'You're a complete idiot, aren't you? We're not friends. You're a protective sleeve around a Programme asset. The Colonel's left orders. If there're any risks to the microchip, we're to extract it to facilitate transport.' He pauses. 'And as you can see, the microchip is clearly at risk. So… game over.'

His machine gun erupts in a deafening shower of bullets. I grab my head and close my eyes, waiting for the bullets to punch through my skin.

Silence falls like a mist.

I open my eyes and for a few seconds my vision swims with red and black swirls.

Jarrod is lying on his side and one of his eyes is gone, replaced by an oozing hole in his skull. There's a dark silhouette in the entrance, hidden by the thickening smoke. The man is holding a gun and prowling towards me. Crazed with fear, I make a run for it.

I'm nearly at the door when the man lunges at me, encircling my waist in his grip. I kick and yell, then bite his hand when he tries to silence me. He's too tall and strong and I can't do anything when he throws me against the wall, a hand covering my mouth, his forearm against my chest, holding me immobile.

'Olivia, it's me, calm down.'

It's Anthony.

He sees the recognition in my eyes and removes the hand that gags me. I fight all the harder, struggling with everything I've got.

'He's dead, I got him, calm down.' He steps back away from me, hands held up in front of him, trying to placate me.

'Get away from me!' I scream, panting, looking for something to defend myself with.

'What's wrong? Are you hurt?' He grabs my wrist and roughly pushes me to the window, to look at me under the moonlight. I try to shake free, but he's too strong. He inspects me and tilts my face up squishing my cheeks painfully.

'You're bleeding. Are you alright? Are you wounded? Answer me, God damned!'

As I back away from him, coughing and choking on the scorching smoke, my foot bumps into the corpse. Jarrod's gun isn't slung across his body anymore, it's just there on the floor at my feet. Perhaps I could get it. Unlikely I could use it before he fires though.

Anthony glances behind him at the door hanging off its hinges and seems to come to a decision.

This is when I die, then.

'I don't know if we'll get another opportunity to speak.'

I don't bother answering, I lunge for the weapon. But he's too strong. His fingers close around my wrist like a vice and I shriek as my bones crack. Startled, Anthony lets go and grabs me by the shoulders, shaking me roughly.

'Olivia, listen to me for fuck's sake.'

Holding my wrist against my chest, I recoil from the intensity and anger of his voice. His face changes. Softens. He reaches for my wrist but I flinch away.

'Sorry – I'm sorry. But, Olivia, you need to focus. Your life is in danger. The Board members have reached their decision.' He looks behind his shoulder towards the door.

'Well, now's your opportunity to kill me and earn their favour.' I spit.

'What? Me? No, I want to save you. Look. Look.'

He gestures to the spot where I crouched a moment ago. A spray of bullet holes has ripped the wall to shreds, just to the left of the spot where I hid. The bullets form a tidy line that veers suddenly upwards and then scatters haphazardly all over the ceiling.

Somewhere, through the fog of panic and pain, my mind grasps that Anthony has just saved my life.

'Listen, you're not safe anymore. I managed to get you assigned in Kampala, so I'd be able to protect you these past few months...'

'Why would you...' Pain burns in fiery shards all along my wrist and forearm. Anthony takes a step towards me and I stumble backward, nearly tripping over Jarrod's body.

'Come on, it's *me* for fuck's sake.' He groans with frustration. 'We don't have time for this. Now that the compound's been breached, we have to retreat to Camp Askaris. You'll be executed there and your microchip harvested.'

'Why should you care?'

He closes the distance between us, but this time, instead of restraining me, he gently lifts my chin and wipes the blood off my cheek. The salt of my dried tears stings but I stay silent, struggling to make sense of what he just said. After what seems forever, his hand slides to my shoulder and he takes a step back.

'Look, we need to move. Just stay close to me and I'll keep you safe, Olivia. You're really important... to the plan.'

Billows of grey smoke are pouring through the shattered door. Anthony grabs my hand and we plunge into the acrid fog, down the burning staircase.

24

DEANN

L ake Mburo National Park, Uganda, February 14, 2082

I WAKE up alone in our bed and stretch lasciviously.

Outside, miles of drought-stricken savannah spreads all around the lodge, dotted here and there with scraggly trees. Through the tent's flimsy canvas walls, the smell of burnt grass and baked earth waft in, as well as the day's building heat. The tent is like a gorgeous dream, the mosquito net draping whimsically around the bed's canopies, and old-fashioned maps and books are piled on the safari desk, which is made of dark leather with folding wooden legs.

Although the décor is delightful, the absence of people is what feels the most luxurious. I've become accustomed to the never ending crowds in Kampala, the jostling, the constant sense of suffocation. But here a huge weight lifts from my shoulders. I can breathe.

I walk over to the shower, naked, and take stock of the

bruises and aches all over my body. I was starting to think that Omony wasn't going to make a move at all, so I'm glad he finally did and relieved that we're compatible. Most of the men I dated couldn't handle me or couldn't be bothered to try. I can tell he won't be one of those.

More sensible, earth-toned clothing has appeared in the wardrobe overnight. I put on the safari gear, apply some extra makeup on my chin and the tip of my nose, gather my hair in a quick ponytail and go out in search of Omony. I find him in the main lodge, wearing a business suit and tie.

I'm ravenous. He watches me thoughtfully while I devour my breakfast.

'I have to work today. I've arranged for a driver to take you on a safari,' he says.

A twinge of disappointment rises before I can think. But I bat the thought away. I'll be out of Uganda in less than two months and won't ever see him again. Let's just take this for what it is: a meeting of minds and a good fuck.

'I don't know, Omony. Going on a safari is probably not a good use of my time, when the country is falling apart and I could be more helpful at the hospital. Could your driver take me back to Kampala?'

'Don't be ridiculous. It's only for a few hours and I'll be done with work this evening. I had to come check one of my business ventures here and thought we'd make a weekend out of it.'

'I don't know...'

'You can't help anyone if you're burned out. Go on. Take the time. What else are you going to do? Stay shut up in the tent until I come back?'

'Mmh. When you put it like that...'

'Perfect. In that case, the driver's waiting for you.'

I make an effort to smile and leave the table, pecking

him lightly on the lips. His hand squeezes my butt and I escape quickly before things get out of control again.

I skip down the stairs to the parking lot and find a driver there, in a bright green safari shirt and with a radiant grin. This should be nice change of pace. I smile to myself and climb in the front. Looking shocked and pleased that I'm choosing to sit next to him, the driver hands me a bottle of water. Then the van rattles to life and we set off. But after hours of driving through Lake Mburo Park, we've still not seen any wildlife.

After a pit stop and a packed lunch, we set off again. By now the novelty of the landscape has worn off. I glance at my driver, who's looking increasingly anxious and swiveling his head every time he sees a hint of anything moving in the yellowing bushes. 'So, Josious, I thought a safari would be chockfull of you know... wild animals,' I joke.

'That's what everybody thinks when they come here for the first time. They think it will be like before, when you could see hundreds of animals on a trip.'

'Isn't it the case anymore?'

He squirms in his seat. 'I'm sure we'll see one or two animals today.'

We pass a couple of villages on our way and he shakes his head as we drive by, sucking his teeth with a tsking sound. 'These villages, they're not supposed to be here. This is a National Park, a natural reserve,' he lowers his voice, 'but the government isn't strong enough to prevent the people from taking over the land. Also, I think they stopped caring about the animals when tourism dried up.'

'I suppose they've got to prioritize the citizens' survival over the animals'?'

'I don't think the politicians care about anyone except their Swiss bank accounts,' he whispers. Then, after throwing a quick backward glance in the mirror, he resumes in a normal voice, 'The poor keep invading the park and taking over the land. Last year this village here didn't exist.' He points to a cluster of a dozen huts surrounded by dead cornfields. 'They burn the savanna and replace it with crops. Then they build their huts and raise their families. Last week, the lions ate a cow. It's dangerous here, but they come for the land.'

'Will we see any lions?' I ask, perking up.

'The Big Five,' he grins. 'We will see if we win or lose today. That's why they call it a game drive – you never know if we'll find anything. But I'll do my best.'

'The Big Five?' I ask.

'Lions, leopards, very rare. There is still one lioness. After last week.'

'What happened to the rest?'

'The villagers got angry after the cow died. So they poisoned the carcass and when the lions came back, they ate it and died. But there's one left.' He rallies. 'The other drivers tell me she's been seen this morning and there might be a cub.' He continues to enumerate on his fingers. 'There are no more elephants and rhinos, they were killed for their horns and their ivory.'

'You're kidding.'

'The Chinese pay a lot.' He shrugs. 'They think it's a powerful medicine.'

Sighing, I ask, 'What's the fifth, then?'

'Buffalo. I can find, probably. But in the last year, the villagers got hungry and they killed most of them. I'll do my best. There are still birds and some monkeys.' He smiles again with tremulous desperation. His livelihood depends on my tip.

As we ride past, raising a cloud of dust in our wake, an

endless procession of dried-up cornfields blurs by the side of the road. The villagers' emaciated silhouettes, gnarled as Giacometti statues, watch us forlornly from the entrances of their mud huts. It's hard to be angry at them and yet I am, so angry. I reason with myself: they're just trying to survive and making five kids is the cultural norm here. They have no contraception, no education, and child mortality is probably so high that they're trying to hedge their bets and get one or two of their progeny to survive them.

But still, looking at them, I feel an impotent rage rising and looking for a culprit. I'm furious with their government for betraying them. How was Uganda planning to pull through this catastrophic overpopulation? They stood a much better chance of giving each person enough food and water if they had actively tried to reduce their population to a manageable number.

They could have educated these people's grandparents, empowered the women to choose how many children they wanted to bear, improved access to family planning and good clinics. They could have provided micro-credit loans to women and encouraged entrepreneurship. But instead their governments did nothing. As usual, when it comes to over-population. Doing nothing: the politically correct option. Now, as a result, they're all starving to death. The final symptom of a situation left to fester for generations.

The population grew so fast that it became like a wild careening monster that a small powerless state tried to tame and ride. But it bucked and kicked its master to death and now the overpopulation monster is running wild and free, completely unrestrained and destroying everything in its path.

'A lioness and her cub!' Josious happily points at two creatures, about fifty yards away.

A lone, scruffy-looking animal is lying despondently on the ground and a cub is panting by her side. Several hyenas surround them. Josious seems to realize belatedly what is going on and he tries to drive away, but I hold his arm.

The lioness has a gunshot wound in her thigh and the cub is patting frantically at her, but she can't move. She shakes her head in pain and snaps at the cub tiredly, then her gaze goes back to the circling scavengers.

The hyenas call to each other, their calls sounding uncannily like laughter. Then they pounce. First they snatch the cub and dance away from the mother, who desperately tries to swipe at them. But her paws are weak and they're too fast. When they realize that she can't even defend her young, they rip him to pieces, his heartbreaking screams tearing through the morning air. The mother roars and tries to get up, her useless leg dragging behind her. Then the hyena pack rounds up on her too, their muzzles bloody and I have to look away as they shred her to pieces. I slam my hands on my ears to stop hearing it, but it's seared into my brain anyway.

Josious drives us away, silently. I try to look back, but I can't see them anymore.

An hour later, we stop at a nearby village to take a break. The inhabitants are standing near the entrances of their crude huts, looking at us hesitantly. We must be the first tourists in a long time. No one can afford food anymore in this country, let alone leisure. They stare at us, their despairing eyes huge in their gaunt faces.

Josious chats quickly with the assembled group and they seem to shake their fear at last. An elder invites us to his hut and we sit on round rattan stools, our shoes coated in the red clay dust. He doesn't offer us anything to drink or eat, I suspect because there is nothing left. The old man starts to talk to Josious and then leaves for a moment. He comes back with two of his tribe members, carrying armfuls of animal skins, ivory and antlers. They spill the beautiful hides and I recognize, appalled, lion, leopard and zebras skins. This is worth a fortune. Another man spills elephant tusks and antelope antlers on the floor as the elder crouches near Josious again to beg for money and food. I look away, feeling nauseous.

Humanity is like a cancer on the world. Eating away at the planet and destroying everything on it – and for what? For our right to live? What makes these people more valuable than the beautiful animals they slaughtered? What is the point of survival if it happens on a dead planet where everything is extinct but us? And for how long before we succumb as well?

Josious tells me in a whisper that the older man is a witch doctor and that we have to honor him by buying something, but it's out of the question. I walk out and find myself surrounded by villagers. They stand silently, eerily all around us, covered in red dust, their huge eyes devouring us with longing, envy, anger. But they're bone tired so the crowd parts, making a path for us, as their fingers snatch at our clothes, feebly touch my hair, the iMode collar, Josious's hands.

We climb back in the jeep and start our journey again as somber thoughts flicker in my mind. I thought overpopulation didn't matter if it wasn't coupled with the destructive footprint of a developed, urban lifestyle. I was wrong. They treated the Natural Park like it was a fucking pantry. It's just in man's nature to destroy, regardless of development level.

Something occurs to me. 'Josious, where were all the children?'

He looks deeply uncomfortable and looks away.

'This is a region where people tend to sacrifice children when times are hard.'

'What do you mean sacrifice them? They choose not to have any?'

'No, I mean human sacrifice. They remove body parts to use in ceremonials and then kill them.'

My breakfast tries to come up but I swallow hard.

'What for?'

'Usually to obtain money or a really difficult favor from the spirits. Lately, they ask for food and water in exchange for these powerful sacrifices.'

'Looking at them, I'd say that didn't work. I guess the spirits mustn't have been listening.'

Josious looks at me, shocked and does a quick warding gesture with his hand. Perhaps he finds it unwise to mock the spirits.

25

OLIVIA

*C*amp Askaris, Uganda, *14 February 2082*

WE TRAVEL ALL NIGHT, leaving the burning headquarters behind and heading into the darkness, just a handful of us left, in two armoured cars. I sleep on the backseat, a fitful but welcome loss of consciousness.

When I wake up, I glance out of the car window and find that the countryside has completely withered. The roads are nearly impassable because of the thousands of refugees shuffling along them. People are walking everywhere, hobbling along the sides of the roads and jumping out of the way as we drive past. They all seem to be heading towards Kampala, whereas we're going in the opposite direction.

At last the milling mass of people thins out and we drive for another hour on a long, dusty road. The vegetation becomes sparse, just a few stunted trees here and there,

stuck between the red earth and the deep blue sky. Then I
see it. Camp Askaris.

Anthony said that's where I will be executed.

Eels of anxiety slither in my stomach and I try to breathe
deeply to keep the dread away, but it feels like someone is
sitting on my chest. High walls topped with barbed wire
surround the military camp and there are guards at the gate.
Our convoy drives in and about thirty barracks come into
view. We stop in front of the largest building and I get out,
gingerly cradling my wrist.

For a brief instant, I think of running but then dismiss
the thought. It's idiotic; I'm several hours' drive from
Kampala, in a military base, surrounded by hundreds of
men. I wouldn't manage to get ten metres away.

We're escorted to the main building and my heart sinks
even further. This is a huge military base. Not at all the same
type of outfit as the Kampala operation. The soldiers here
look grizzled, professional and well organised. How am I
ever going to escape?

Men in army fatigues patrol the perimeter, rifles slung
around their shoulders, looking alert. My presence draws a
few surprised glances at first, especially in my preposterous
pink pyjamas, but when they realise I'm with Anthony, all
emotion wipes from their faces. They know who I am: the
fattened calf.

A soldier shows me to a small room and closes the door
behind me with mechanical movements, avoiding my gaze. I
wait to hear if he turns the lock but no sound comes. Right,
I'm not a prisoner then. Yet.

The room's basic. A bed, a wardrobe and a sink. I
approach the basin, hoping for water but the mirror
captures my attention. There's blood splattered all over my
face and eyelids. Jarrod's gaping eye socket flashes before my

eyes and I vomit in the sink, but only yellow bile comes up. After a while, the heaves subside. I try the tap but nothing comes out. There's a bucket of water on the floor and a flannel, so I rub my face with the wet cloth again and again, until my skin is red and shiny and the tears are gone.

Skipping on one foot, I yank the filthy pink pyjamas off and inspect myself. There are burns on my arms and bruises and cuts all over me, but I'll live. Wrist throbbing and tender, I brush my hair, gagging on the reek of smoke. There is soot and ash everywhere, in the creases of my neck, under my armpits, in my belly button. I clean up as best I can, swiping gingerly around the yellowing blisters, trying not to burst them. Then I dress my burns with a first aid kit that I find in the wardrobe. Feeling restored, I put on the fatigues and combat boots that have been left out for me, slide the Swiss Army knife in my pocket and dust off the iMode bracelet. I lost the collar and ear bud but the thing still works.

Although I'm dressed, I feel naked. Everything I own is gone except these two objects. I try DeAnn a couple more times and check if I've received any messages. Just one from A., my Resistance handler: 'Evacuation Monday morning. Rendezvous point attached.'

A laughing sob blurts out. It's on the border with Kenya. I'm hours away, in the opposite direction. I'm never going to make it. And DeAnn doesn't even know that she needs to run for her life. We're both going to die. As my overflow of despair threatens to slosh out through my eyes, a knock on the door makes me jump. I'm wiping my eyes when Tom barges in without waiting for me to invite him to enter.

'Ready for some lunch?' he says, with forced joviality.

'Yes, I'm famished,' I answer in kind, wondering if there are microphones here as well. I struggle to strap my iMode onto my good wrist, get up and fall into step, as he starts to walk down the hall. I'm glad Tom survived. I know he's one of them, but I've lived with him for months and he was always nice to me. I wonder how I'll feel about him when he escorts me to my execution.

'Anything good on the sphere?'

'I was just checking the weather in London,' I lie. 'I'm longing for some grey and cold.'

He laughs.

'I can't believe we're finally going home.' I slant the words upward at the end, like a question.

'I know, right? Just a few more days. First they have to wrap up the other project.'

'What other project?'

'The one they're running here. It's a game changer.' He falters. 'Blimey, I've said too much already. Come on.' He speeds up, brow furrowed.

Oh dear Lord.

When we arrive at the cafeteria, the air is humming with conversation as a hundred men wearing beige and khaki fatigues hunch over plastic trays, shovelling in their food. They all fall silent as I go by, the easy chatter replaced by intense scrutiny and a sort of avid hunger. I wonder how long they've been stationed here and how many months it's been since they've seen a woman.

A voice calls out, 'Why don't you come and sit on my face, love?'

Loud laughter follows and more catcalls, which I do my best to ignore.

Blushing furiously, I hurry after Tom. He guides me to the officers' table at the back and then returns to the main mess hall. Colonel Groebler is deep in conversation with an older man with a buzz cut, Brigadier Ward, who turns out to be the head of the base. Anthony introduces me to the rest of the table; mostly scientists. One of them has long hair tied in a greasy ponytail and keeps biting his nails to the quick as he stares at me.

Colonel Groebler says, 'Stop looking at the poor girl like that, she's not steak.' All the men laugh.

Anthony leans in and whispers, 'Why are you eating with your left hand? Are you hurt?'

'My wrist is painful.'

A shadow of guilt wavers on Anthony's face. He was the one who hurt me in the cinema room, and he knows it. 'Doctor Maudsley, you'll have a look at Olivia, later on, won't you?'

'That, I'm sure he will. A good long... poke around.' Groebler guffaws. 'And why don't you check that everything is still in working order, Maudsley, while you're at it?' More chortling.

I crumple up and wince a smile. 'Thank you, Colonel, that's very kind. I'm sure it's nothing.'

The rest of the meal passes by uneventfully and Anthony, Groebler and Brigadier Ward go off to have a briefing. What I wouldn't give to be a fly on the wall of that room. But instead I get to go away with the creepy doctor, who's spluttering with excitement.

'I... this is so thrilling, Miss Sagewright. I've studied your father's accomplishments and your file. You knew Doctor McArthur?'

'Yes, she recruited me.'

'Oh my! This is terribly exciting.' He bares his yellow, uneven teeth. 'You know about your father, of course? The incident during his mission is the reason why Colonel Groebler asked me to—' He stops himself.

'What about my father?' I frown.

'Oh...erm. No one has told you? Well, then it's not my place to...'

'What are you talking about? What does that have to do with me?'

'I'm sorry, I'm sorry.' He licks his lips again. 'I'm confusing you. Don't you worry your pretty little head about that.' He smiles. '

Sensing I've hit a wall, I swallow down my anger and fear and titter, 'So Doctor Maudsley, maybe you could show me what you've been working on here? I'm dying to know.'

'Yes, yes, dying to know. You're not the only one.' He makes a wet snort with his nose as he laughs, it's not an altogether pleasant sound. 'First, let's check your microchip, if you'll allow me. We have a few in our archives but it's not the same to see one, actually functioning, in vivo, from such a long time ago.'

'Erm...what do you mean, check it? I'd rather not tamper with it.' I give a weak chuckle. 'You know, we wouldn't want to mess it up.'

He shakes his head and raises his hands reassuringly. 'No, no. I'd never dream of tampering with it. I'd just like to scan it and take a blood sample. Due to the fire the year you left, some of the archives have been destroyed and we can't determine whether the chip you have is DNA specific or whether it can be used by anyone.'

Oh fuckety, fuck fuck fuck. I know for a fact that my chip isn't DNA-specific, since I'm carrying the chip of one of the agents who died by the pyramid in 2016.

He walks me through grey corridors to a frosted glass door marked Lab 4. As the sharp smell of antiseptic grabs me by the throat, we step into a large room with several connecting doors and windows looking into neighbouring labs. We're the only ones here. As I take all this in, my brain scrambling to find a solution, Dr Creepy helps me up onto a steel slab.

Somebody tampered with the records so that when my chip was scanned in de Courcy's office, my name appeared on the reader and I was logged in as an agent. But any more scrutiny than that will probably reveal me as an impostor and result in my immediate execution. And they look like they have the equipment and the knowledge to find that out here.

Come on, come on, Olivia, think of something.

'Ow, ow, ow.' I pretend to bump my wrist as he helps me lie down. Panic is starting to coil itself in my gut as goose-bumps pop up all over my skin.

He looks annoyed. 'Sorry, are you alright? Did I hurt you?'

'My wrist hurts so much. Could you check it first please?'

There's a beat of hesitation then he turns away.

Shivering on the steel table, I watch him tinker with equipment on a nearby counter and he comes back holding a scanner. Oh God. If he checks the chip in my left forearm, I'm dead.

I hold my breath and then he takes my right arm. I exhale. The painful wrist side. Thank God.

The transparent tablet hovers above my right forearm for a few minutes, displaying an image of my bones that looks like a colourful X-ray image.

'Oh, yes. It's quite broken.'

The throbbing pain in my wrist flares up, now that it has a name.

Staring at Maudsley as he prints the 3D cast for my arm, I try to think of something else to keep him away from my microchip. But nothing comes. It's nearly too late.

He carefully fits the cast on my wrist and hands me a sling.

Then, his back turned, he starts tinkering with scientific tools that I've never seen before. Shit. We're moving on to the chip analysis. Will he extract it immediately, when he realises that it's safe? How do I get out of here?

He comes back with a syringe. OK, a few minutes' reprieve. I sit up, he wraps the rubber tourniquet around my arm, the needle goes in and I pump my fist as blood starts to spiral along the transparent tube and into a half a dozen vials.

'Don't go fainting on me now. I don't usually have that problem with my... patients.' He licks his lips and I look away as his tongue passes over a pimple.

If only he knew how many times I injected myself during the IVFs. Needles are the least of my worries right now.

'We wouldn't want you to lie unconscious for what's coming next, now would we?' he chuckles.

Even his double-entendres are repulsive. I open my mouth to reassure him that needles don't scare me but then have an idea.

'I think I'm going to... oh, I'm not feeling well at all...'

'Oh blimey, miss. I'll... I'll... just wait here and I'll get... Oh, bloody hell!'

Going limp, I slide off the table and sprawl on the floor. He stands there for a short while, hesitating, then he rushes out of the room in search of help.

As soon as he's gone, I yank the needle out of my arm and, pressing a cotton ball to it, I jump to my feet and have a quick look around. The large lab connects to several adjacent rooms. I open the door at the far left corner; it's just a lab with beakers, machines that look like they can process biological samples. I take as many pictures as I can, thinking I'll show them to DeAnn later. She'll know what this is for.

I hear something and freeze. My heart is beating so hard that it feels like it's going to jump out of my chest and flop on the floor like a frenetic dying fish. Wait, the sound is not coming from outside. I rush to the next door and find a small tiled room where the air is cold and still. Torn, I glance over my shoulder, but decide to risk it and dash in.

It looks like a morgue. I rush to the windows and rattle the handles but they don't budge. They're locked and there are no adjacent doors. I should really search for a way out, but curiosity wins and my feet move of their own accord towards the polished lockers. I hesitate for a second, the unfamiliar lever cold and unwieldy in my hand, and then I grip it, flinching as the loud mechanism clicks in the sterile silence.

There is a body in there. I struggle to pull the steel tray out, cringing at the touch of the corpse's hair and finally manage to pull it out enough to uncover the face: a white man with no marks on him, only the autopsy scar, roughly sewn in coarse black thread. I open another drawer with shaking hands: a black woman's body lies in the cold, autopsy stitches puckered on her torso and no marks on her either, but there's a strong smell of vomit and diarrhoea. Oh God, I hope the condition isn't catching, I've touched them. I breathe in too close to the cadaver and have to rush to a nearby sink to throw up. No water. Shit. I'm wiping with a paper towel and spitting out, when a muffled shout makes me jump. Squeaking with fear, I slam the drawer shut and hurry out.

I'm darting towards where I'm supposed to have fainted, in the middle of the room when I hear a scratching and whining coming from another door. I realise I'm pushing it now, but I have to know. I approach the room's reinforced glass window and only have time for a quick glance in that last room, but that's all I need.

Metal cages. Steel bars, chains and padlocks. Test subjects. Crouching, dejected, crying. They're not mice or chimpanzees.

They're human.

None of the prisoners see me during the few seconds I look in on them. None except one. He screams and shakes the bars of his cage, but barely a sound pierces through the glass separation.

Panicking, I rush back to the centre of the lab, lie down on the floor and close my eyes. Not a minute too soon.

Maudsley barges in and rushes to my side. The smelling salts burn a path through my nostrils.

I jump up, gasping and knock my head against his, in the process.

I apologise. He apologises. We both apologise and I try to laugh but the sound sticks in my throat and tears start to swim in my eyes. He can see them too and a look of power-less panic spreads on his face. I usually try so hard to hold back my tears. It's so inconvenient to be a crier at work, where lawyers have to take you seriously. I have techniques now. Like looking up at the ceiling so my eyes reabsorb the tears and they don't spill out. Or locking myself in the bath-room for ten minutes and just allowing myself a little cry, one that barely leaves a trace on my makeup. But this time, I completely let go. I think of how powerless I was to stop Rosebell's death, I think of not being able to connect with DeAnn. How much I wish I could help baby Jonathan and all these poor people starving to death outside these walls, and how I'm probably going to be dead and on a slab next door in the next few days and how inept I feel. Tears are positively jumping out of my eyes now and I just let it all out, ugly crying, snot and all.

Dr Creepy looks completely panicked, as I hoped he would. I don't want this guy anywhere near my chip and I have no intention of letting him rip it out of me.

He watches me sob, wringing his hands and when I get up, grab the sling and dart towards the door, he protests feebly that he still needs to scan the chip, but I make a big show of needing a tissue and ask him for one. And in the end I just leave and he walks me back to my room and promises to scan me tomorrow.

As soon as he's gone, I wedge a chair under the door handle, as the images of what I saw in the last room flood back to me. Trying to get my breathing under control, I wash my hands compulsively, using nearly all the water in the bucket. My brain is like a mouse in a maze. Frantically trying to find an exit. But there is none. Not for me. My chip is coming out tomorrow and then I'll have outlived my usefulness as a walking, talking vessel for it. Fumbling with the sling, I manage to put it on, then I sit on the bed and, smoothing my trousers down, focusing on breathing in and out. In and out, as I rake my fingers through my hair.

My singsong voice starts singing again: *Make it stop. This is too hard. I want to disappear and I want all of this to go away. I want to go home now. Please let me go home.*

I tell the snivelling voice to shut up and try to think as I glance at the sun setting the sky ablaze outside my window. Breathe in, breathe out. Dylan Thomas's lines of poetry come back to me: 'Do not go gentle into that good night.' I won't let them kill me so easily. I can't give up so easily. I'm a Programme Agent, I'm a member of the Cassandra Resistance. I am Olivia Sagewright, daughter of Alastair Sagewright. Biting my lip, I whisper, 'Rage, rage against the dying of the light,' and make my decision: I need to free the prisoners.

I bring up the photos and zoom in on the padlocks of each cell. I have no idea where the keys might be. Rooting around the first aid kit one-handed, I extract a couple of safety pins. Maybe I can pick the lock on those cages? I wasn't exactly MacGyver during training but I know how. I've got to try.

I text everything to DeAnn, Madison and A. with sweaty, shaking hands. If I die, at least someone should know what I witnessed here.

It's dusk outside by now. Right, there's no good time to do this anyway. I'm so likely to get caught I might as well do it now. I open my bedroom door carefully and sneak into the deserted corridor.

Flinching at every sound, I walk around the hallways and get slightly lost. Oh God. I'm going to get caught.

Then, as I'm starting to panic in earnest, I find the frosted-glass door of Lab 4 and try the handle. It's open. I hurry to the back and look through the separating window. They're gone! I rush into the room and look everywhere. But there's nothing left, just two empty cages, grimy marks on the floor where the other two cages were and the lingering smell of piss and fear.

Stepping back into the main lab, I try to think what to do next, when I realise that the two autopsy slabs now have bodies on them, covered in white sheets. They weren't there earlier, I'm sure of it. A shiver climbs up my spine as I approach the tables. I uncover the first body; it's one of the Ugandan men. His skin is ashen just like the woman I saw earlier in the morgue drawer. There's no wound marks anywhere on him but a trail of foamy vomit has slid down his cheek and over his shoulder.

When I replace the sheet over her face, I accidentally touch her and recoil, swallowing bile. Breathing in short, panicked breaths, I approach the other slab and lift the sheet; it's the white woman. Her blonde hair spills out over the steel table, clumped with blood, which makes her look oddly red-haired. Her throat has been slashed. Her eyes are open and seem to stare right at me like a macabre mirror image. I was lying on this table not an hour ago.

There's a sound behind me. I crouch, expecting armed men to burst in looking for me. Heart beating, I wait as the minutes slide away. What if I'm next? The woman's bloodied locks are fanning out a few centimetres from my face as I remain very still, listening intently as I grip the steel ledge. But no one comes so at length, I find my courage and get back to my feet. With shaking hands, I place the sheets back over the woman's corpse. Time to go. I can't do anything for these poor people anymore.

Wiping my good hand frantically on the beige fatigues, I close the laboratory door carefully and sneak back into the corridor. I'm a few doors down when a soldier rounds the corner and bumps into me. Startled, an involuntary yelp escapes me. When I look up, I recognise him.

'Olivia?'

Anthony stares at me, frowning.

'Dinner's ready. I was on my way to get you.' He cranes his neck, looking down the darkened corridor behind me, eyebrows furrowed. 'What are you doing here?'

'Lost, as usual,' I let a smile waver on my face.

He looks like he wants to say something. I wait but nothing comes. We start down the corridor but when we reach a set of steps, he stops abruptly and pushes me under the staircase recess, his face conflicted as he bends towards me. For a panicked moment I think he's going to kiss me, but as he leans in, pushing me against the wall, he whispers in my ear.

'Olivia, they've decided to remove your chip and execute you first thing tomorrow morning. I had a plan to keep you alive but the Board voted for Groebler's solution instead. More efficient. Cleaner. They don't understand...' He shakes his head, a bitter slant to his lips.

'What? But I—'

He overrides my protests. 'They were spooked by the near miss yesterday. You could have burned in the fire. They don't want to take any more risks that your chip will be damaged. You need to escape. Tonight.'

'What about DeAnn?'

'It's too late for her. Her chip's about to be secured. She's as good as dead.'

'But no, we have to—'

He grabs my good wrist and swipes his iMode against mine, our hands shielded from view, as he presses me against the wall.

Then he does kiss me.

It's a rough, ravenous bite rather than a kiss. His mouth hungrily tastes mine and his stubble chafes against my chin. He drops my wrist while his hand slides under my shirt and around my naked waist, bringing me close. His hips are grinding me against the wall as fear, surprise and desire swirl uneasily in me.

The sound of a dry cough makes us both jump.

Colonel Groebler is standing behind us, glaring at Anthony and me. We slink out of the shadows and as I feel my face go beetroot red, I wonder how long the officer's been standing there and how much he's heard.

Anger is radiating out of the Colonel when he says, 'Dismissed, Captain.' Anthony hesitates and then leaves, looking anxious.

'What did he want?' Groebler starts walking.

'I should have thought that was pretty obvious,' I say, caressing my burning lips.

He glares at me, eyes narrowed. I swallow and try to grin. The smile comes out lopsided but it probably does the trick because the Colonel looks away with a sneer.

We walk the rest of the way to the officers' mess in prickly silence.

DINNER IS TENSE. Doctor Maudsley looks subdued and expectant, like we have unfinished business. Which I suppose we do. Shuddering, I pretend to be absorbed by the conversation I'm having with one of the scientists about the misadventures they've had driving in the savannah. But I'm actually listening to Groebler and the base leader as they discuss the technicalities of the tests.

'Today's experiments went well. All lab tests are conclusive, in a controlled environment. We're very close, Colonel.'

They must be talking about the weapon. I didn't hear any loud explosions today, what kind of armament is it? Maybe a real Programme agent would have looked for a hangar where the weapon might have been stored instead of going on a wild goose chase and trying to save the poor souls in the cages. I'm so woefully unqualified for this mission, I'm pathetic.

As I think of my blood-haired twin who looked at me with her dead, filmy eyes and the young Ugandan man whose life was cut short, lying on slabs a few doors down from us, the food I've eaten starts to make its way back up. I force myself to smile at the two scientists. I can't lose the plot now. I need to continue looking like a perfect empty-headed Nazi-groupie.

'Everything in place for the field test?'

'Yes, we're a go Colonel.'

Dinner ends late. It must be at least midnight by the time the men decide to smoke cigars in celebration of their day of successes. I pretend to have a migraine and head back to my bedroom. I can finally look at what Anthony swiped on my iMode during our kiss.

Car keys!

The exit to the barracks is easy to find. Two guards look at me curiously and I giggle about being too hot and wanting fresh air. They let me through and I walk calmly out.

As soon as I'm around the corner, I start running towards the cars parked fifty metres away, at the back of the camp. The iMode fails to open three parked cars. Suppressing a groan, I nearly trip over my own feet as I sprint to the fourth car. The back of my neck tingling with foreboding, I press the bracelet against the door.

'God, please, please, please'

It flashes blue. With a whoop, I open the door and take stock of the jeep. Bugger. How am I going to drive with a cast?

I'm not a very good driver at the best of times. I only got my driving licence out of principle and haven't driven since. That was about ten years ago. The absurdity of stealing a car when you can barely drive and heading into the pitch-black night in the middle of Africa doesn't escape me, but there isn't any other option. So I remove the parking brake and let the car slide forward as quietly as I can, walking beside it, my good hand on the steering wheel, my cast forearm pressing on the door jamb, so I can push.

When I reach the back of the base, I open the wire-mesh gates and slip out, thanking my lucky stars that no patrols are within sight.

In front of me, the red dirt track snakes away from the camp and into the savannah. Quashing a tremor, I tell myself that I'll be safer out there than at the base and, steering as I walk, I push the vehicle down the slope, lights off, very slowly, knuckles white, looking back every few seconds, expecting to hear cries of alarm. None comes. Nobody's noticed my escape yet.

Once I'm far enough away from earshot, I jump in the car, close the door very carefully and turn the car on, wincing when the engine starts to purr. But still no one comes. Driving in the darkness, I remember a recurring nightmare I used to have. There was an emergency; my brother was dying and only I could save him, but I had to drive. And I couldn't drive. Yet in the dream I did anyway, to save him. The panic was so strong that I use to wake up drenched in sweat.

The same feeling of being in over my head grips me again. My brother is long dead but I'm really driving a car in the night and the anxiety is as strong as it was back then. The nightmare has become real.

I can't remember how long I drive. The silent electric SUV is like a huge tank, it feels like I have barely any control over it. My good hand is cramped from holding the wheel so hard and my right wrist hurts like hell. My elbows and shoulders are locked in place, feeling stiff. I stick my head out from time to time to get some air and check that the road is still there, as my headlights are turned off. The road is still passable. No rain, no crowds of refugees shuffling, no road blocks or sirens behind me. So far, so good.

I have no idea how to get back to Kampala though. I have to programme the map to take me to the French Doctors' hospital. I must save DeAnn before Groebler has her killed. I hope I'm not too late. I wonder who is supposed to execute her. Probably an assassin who will be sent from in Camp Askaris. If I'm quick, I should be able to arrive before any of them, and DeAnn and I can escape together.

I try to activate the map functionality on my iMode but I'm in the middle of nowhere and I guess internet coverage in 2082 still matters. I'm driving and fiddling with my bracelet, wincing at the pain in my wrist, when a bushbuck crosses my path and I swerve to avoid it. The last thing I see is a huge tree. Then nothing.

26

DEANN

B *windi Impenetrable Forest, Uganda, February 15, 2082*

AFTER I CAME BACK from the safari yesterday, we set off for a different region. We drove for hours and finally we reached a lodge perched on the edge of a mountain.

Today is our last day. Then back to Kampala where reality will hammer down on me and all trace of wonder will evaporate. One last day to live this strange and breathtaking adventure. A smile playing on my face, I throw on my clothes and hurry to the lodge's lobby, where I find Omony immersed in conversation with a small group of tourists to whom he's showing his charming British face.

The group of older women laughs uproariously at something he's said and he turns toward me as I arrive.

'This is DeAnn, my gorgeous other half. Not only is she a talented geneticist but she also volunteers at the French clinic in Kampala.'

He loops his arm around my shoulders and I melt into his embrace, feeling absurdly elated.

'Hi there.' I smile at the old ladies.

'Oh, you're American, dear,' one of them says. 'What an awful accent. You should try to sound more like your charming husband. Americans always do sound so stupid.'

I press my lips together and say nothing, wishing it was still possible to get coffee in this future. But it isn't.

Omony wasn't best pleased with the way my safari went yesterday. According to him, better guides could have found wild life. So today, he's coming with, to make sure everything goes smoothly. It's sweet.

We all walk down to the tourist center, where a few tourists are already waiting with intense expectation. They're all wearing semi-professional hiking gear, shin protectors, gloves, walking sticks. Either I'm under prepared or they're overdoing it; it's just a hike after all.

Omony and I seem to be the youngest ones here and the only people of color except for one elderly tourist, who is part of the group of old biddies staying at our hotel.

I walk over and sit next to her on the parapet, as the guide intones her well-rehearsed spiel about the dangers of what we're about to attempt then we all sign disclaimers saying nobody will sue if we die.

'You need a walking stick, dear.' The old Indian woman gestures to her porter and she procures a carved stick for me.

'Thank you.' I smile. 'If you don't mind me saying, you don't seem to fit in that group.'

'Who, me? Oh, I just needed company for this trip. Most of the time I tune them out. So should you, dear.'

'That strikes me as very wise.' I smile again.

'I'm Chuni, by the way.' She shakes my hand the old-fashioned way and I return the handshake warmly, liking her already.

'Do you think we're in the easy group?' she asks, looking anxiously around. 'I asked to be in the easy group.'

She enquires but no one seems to know what she's talking about. She's frail and I wonder why she'd do an activity like this. She doesn't look well.

Finally when the doom and gloom lecture's over, we pile into our respective jeeps and set off. The mountain's increasingly steep slopes unfurl like a carpet in front of us, the green patchwork of tea plantations repeating the leafy geometric pattern over and over. Tea harvesters, dwarfed by the large baskets on their backs, straighten as we pass, staring hostilely at us. Through the rolled-down window, the cool air caresses my face, as I breathe in the soil's rich scent.

The soldier who climbed aboard our jeep finishes his coke, burps and throws the plastic bottle out his window.

Hayley, one of the old ladies, blurts out, 'What do you think you're doing, young man?'

He shifts in his seat and gives her a look, as a strong smell of sweat wafts toward us. He doesn't bother answering, he just fondles his machine gun's handle. His name is etched in the wood, like a perverted carved heart. The letters are crude and the etching old. He glares at Hayley who clams up, then he looks away and the rest of the ride passes in silence.

After a while, we reach the mountaintop and get out of the jeeps, where a crowd of desperate people accosts us, pushing misshapen carved trinkets in our faces. Children flit around the group, wearing torn, filthy clothes and begging. None are wearing shoes, some don't even wear bottoms, only grimy t-shirts that are too big for them and look like dresses on their emaciated bodies. Their faces are covered in dirt and snot and they don't look healthy, so I start to kneel in front of one of them, to examine him out of habit, but Omony pulls me to my feet.

'Behave normally. Don't shame me.'

Surprised, I dismiss his comment and turn back to the child but his mother has grabbed him already. Hiding behind her, he gawks at me, eyes wide. With a sigh, I secure my grip on the tall walking stick and hurry to catch up with my group.

The rough walking stick feels dry and prickly in my palm, as we climb for half an hour, skirting tea fields, out in the pummeling sun. All around us, the red earth contrasts with the deep blue sky and the green shrubs in stark strips of color. I stop at the hilltop to drink some water and notice the guide, porters and soldiers throwing quick glances at Omony, who is standing apart from the group. One of them spits and does a small gesture with his hand behind his back and the rest chatter between themselves in hushed tones. Frowning, I think of asking the guide what this is about, but we're already moving. Maybe later.

Soon we leave the tea plantations behind and dive into the jungle; its earthy smell envelops us as the soldiers begin to swish their machetes ahead of us to clear the lianas in our path. Red mulch crumbles under my boots as we start to go down the slope toward the dense green foliage.

Our group of old ladies is silent, groaning with the hike's effort and even I'm sweating and panting. I wipe my forehead and flap the back of my shirt to let some air in and steal a glance at Chuni; she's the one who's having the most trouble; the old Indian woman is wheezing and stumbling. Her porter has spread her arm around his shoulders and he's pulling her, practically carrying her, along the narrow path.

'Break!' the guide yells and we collapse on nearby logs and tree stumps and get our plastic water bottles out.

'Are you alright, Chuni?'

She inhales deeply, looking every minute of her eighty years. She leans in and whispers, 'I have stage four cancer, dear. This is on my bucket list. I can't give up now.'

Startled, I force my eyebrows down and consider the woman with a new level of respect. I take her hand and whisper back, 'Don't worry, I'll look after you, I'm a doctor.' My fingers slide from her hand to her wrist to take her pulse discreetly; it's all over the place. So I rummage in my bag and extract a small bottle, handing it to her. 'Here, Chuni, have more water.' She looks up at me gratefully.

Just then, Omony looks over at us and I feel an odd reflex to hide what I'm doing, but I complete the gesture anyway and give her my bottle. He frowns.

We climb down the slope for another fifteen minutes or so, our porters encouraging us and supporting us every few steps. I'm drenched in sweat by now and the jungle is everywhere around us, pulsing with menace, humidity and moving shadows.

The soldiers have swung their rifles to the front and are walking cautiously, aiming with sudden gestures. Their anxiety spreads through the group like an electric current, as we stumble forward.

Our feet get tangled in roots and thorny branches grip my shirt and trousers as we pass by.

Our soldier still hasn't cracked a word, he looks intensely ahead at the moving bushes, sweat pearling on his forehead, eyes narrowed. Silence shrouds us, only broken by the rhythmic whack of machetes and occasional grunts of effort.

'Stop!' the guide says with an urgent whisper, holding her hand up.

We all freeze, eyes on her. The soldiers tighten their grips on their AK-47s, looking tense. Then the guide walks over to a tall tree covered in vines and starts chopping at the trunk. The blade's thuds against the bark resonate in the surrounding darkness. Soon, the tree is irretrievably damaged; it starts to vacillate and we all back away, looking up with apprehension.

And that's when I finally see them.

A furry shape starts to move, lumbering slowly down the trunk, then another, and another. The forest around us comes to a standstill and Chuni grabs my hand, her eyes welling up.

'Gorillas,' she whispers. 'As I live and breathe.'

I return her squeeze and stare, awestruck as well.

The band of gorillas passes by, silently, lumbering with deliberate, slow movements, eying us suspiciously. The old women in our group squeal and start taking photos of the animals, getting too close, pushing each other aside to get the best shot.

The guide, the soldiers and the porters look on, a tired, disabused look on their faces. I see my group through their eyes, ridiculous and absurd. Their country is dying, starving to death, and we come here like vultures, to snap pictures of animals, while we care nothing for their children dying just a village away. Only the promise of our money is keeping this patch of jungle safe, as the country disintegrates all around it.

They guide us on, carefully stepping through the under-growth, machetes and rifles at the ready, and we follow the animals into a clearing where tall grasses grow waist high and the sun pounds down on us. The old British women speak loudly, excitedly, trampling the roots and the plants we were explicitly told to steer clear of. This is the apes' territory, their food source. We should show more respect. More awe. Worry gnaws at the back of my mind. Pushing it away, I try to dive into the moment and try to enjoy this unique experience.

The gorillas are grunting, waving us away, hiding in the tall grass. They clearly don't want to be disturbed. The training we received at the center warned us about this: we need to stay back, give the animals space to retreat. But the guides have a desperate look on their gaunt faces. Our tips will feed their families. So they chop the patches of grass the gorillas try to hide behind, push aside the bushes to let us take the photos, call us so we can get closer. More photos, closer, more, more.

This isn't right. It feels like a voyeuristic invasion. Vaguely nauseated by the whole distasteful display, I notice that the animals are turning their backs when one of us gets too close. Some of the large apes are starting to shake their arms at us, grunting with fear. Most of the group are females and their young. This is dangerous. Why isn't the guide pulling us back?

A loud yelp startles me out of my somber thoughts.

'Oh my God, they're all deformed.'

I catch a glimpse of the female gorilla Hayley is pointing toward, as the animal limps away, carrying its baby, looking terrified. The mother's missing a limb and the young gorilla who is barely hanging on to her has discolored fur.

More cries of surprise and revulsion ring out in the clearing, Kendall runs away from one of the creatures; it has a concave face, it's as if it were bent inward. Its teeth seem to be missing and its face is sagging and covered in purulent eczema. The old woman makes disgusted sounds. The gorilla next to Chuni and me has a cleft lip, his nose is missing and his ears are pointed. Just looking at him makes me queasy.

The guide looks peeved. I guess she didn't track the right group of apes. She yells something abrupt to the soldiers and they push us further into the jungle. I catch Chuni as she struggles against the soldier's grip.

'No, no, it's fine, we don't need to see any more. It's OK,' I say.

But he's too desperate to be paid and rules seem like a flimsy barrier now, almost theoretical. Who would know, back at the tourist center, if a few rules were broken?

'Look, it's alright, let them be. Let the gorillas go,' I start to say, digging my heels in to try to stop the soldier's advance into the jungle ahead. But just as the words come out, an enormous silverback crashes through the jungle's curtain of green and careens over to our spot, grunting, his nostrils flaring. He bowls Chuni over, then stands looming over her, shoulders rolling as he roars.

The old woman has fallen on her rear and she shuffles back as quickly as she can in the bent grass. The creature screeches and paces, clearly intent on intimidating us, but making no movement to get any closer or hurt the old woman.

The gorilla's pungent smell is overpowering, as his cry of defiance resonates in the small clearing. I'm barely three feet away from Chuni; she's frozen with terror, lying on her back, staring at the huge animal as it looms over her. She's whimpering, her lips moving silently as she prays.

Crouching very slowly, I motion to Chuni to stay put. 'It's

OK, it's OK,' I whisper, inching closer to her as gradually as possible.

The enormous creature is about to turn around and leave, having made his point, when a soldier accidentally shoots. The silverback roars as the bullet punches through his shoulder. Straightening to his full height, he falls on the young man and dislocates his arm, pulling the machine gun away from his grip. Chuni's just managed to scramble back to her feet, when the other soldiers, panicked and yelling, shoot at the creature.

Chuni's eyes widen as her chest is riddled with bullets. The gorilla shrieks and falls backward and the old woman collapses in the high grass. It all happens so fast that I barely have time to drop on my stomach. I crawl over to the spot where she fell, as shots continue to burst deafeningly through the air.

Omony's voice rumbles, the ring of command clearly audible and just as I reach Chuni, he emerges, swinging his machete and bringing the blade down. I think for a second that he's come to rescue Chuni and me. But he hasn't.

The blade glints in the harsh afternoon sun and hits the gorilla's wrist with a loud thud. Blood spurts, dousing us as the majestic beast's hand is chopped off. Terrified, the other gorillas yap and flee into the forest. I stare aghast at the fallen animal and then turn back to the old woman.

'Chuni?' I take her pulse. But I already know. She moans as blood seeps into her shirt like ink on paper. She is convulsing now, as her breath rattles hoarsely. Then the breaths stop and silence descends on the clearing.

'DeAnn, get away. Let them take care of the *muzungu*.'

The guide comes over to our spot and, taking in the dead silverback and Chuni's mangled body, spits on the ground, a bitter slant to her mouth. Omony returns the machete to one of the soldiers and takes his gruesome souvenir away.

Wiping an angry tear off my face for Chuni, and for the majestic creature lying on the bloody grass, I watch my boyfriend's broad back as he walks away, his bald head shining in the sun.

'Everyone out of the clearing, now,' the guide yells.

One of the soldiers slings Chuni's corpse over his shoulder in a fireman's hold, while the rest form a protective cordon around us as we struggle back up the slope, sliding on the crumbling hilltop's mulch and tripping over the roots in our haste.

'Well, I'll definitely be asking for a refund,' Hayley mutters, as she climbs, readjusting the see-through visor of her pink cap. 'How could they let these horrible animals get so aggressive? It's really unsafe.'

'It's your fault,' I hiss.

She looks up at me, startled, as we walk up the narrow path, back toward the jeeps.

'You should all have stayed back. Now Chuni's dead, all for a stupid photo. We should never have invaded these poor animals' home.'

She scoffs, 'It's not the gorillas' home, it's ours. This is basically a zoo for rich people. We only allow the beasts to live for our entertainment.'

The other one, Kendall, snorts as she grabs a liana and pulls herself to our level. 'Oh, come off it, Hayley, I wasn't even expecting there to be any gorillas left. The locals will have probably eaten the lot of them by the time we ride away. Deformed limbs and all.'

As Hayley grumbles something about the deformities being another good reason to be reimbursed, Kendall bends over, panting, hands on her knees. 'Apparently it's because of the pesticides from the tea plantations. They contaminate the water and plants all around.'

These old women are actually younger than me, probably millennials. They grew up hearing about how the world is going to hell in a hand basket and how nothing could be done by anyone to stop it. All they've ever known is ruin and decay. I'd probably be bitter as well, if I were them. I sigh and look away, glimpsing Chuni's lifeless body, as she bounces on the soldier's back, on her way up the slope.

BY THE TIME we return to the lodge, twilight has started to dim the sky and the vast jungle seems to wait with bated breath for prey to venture into its depths, and a gray fog thickens in the gathering darkness. In the room, our things have been arranged neatly. This morning's playful mood has evaporated and I spend far longer than I should in the lion-clawed, cast iron bathtub, trying to wash away the day's horrors, in vain.

When I pad out of the bathroom, wrapped in a robe, the room is plunged in darkness except for a few candles. Omony ignores me and I can't hear any of his conversation as he's isolated himself in his iBubble. It makes him look oddly like an astronaut, his head completely enclosed in the soundproof, tinted glass sphere. The black glass reflects my distorted silhouette, which blends with the elongated image of the flame along the curved surface. It looks like I'm burning in the flames of hell. Shaking off the absurd thought, I chide myself for my overactive imagination.

Just as I'm turning away, the iBubble retracts, making me flinch. Omony removes the torque from around his neck and walks to the bathroom, still ignoring me. Startled by his coldness, I'm abruptly aware that I'm in the middle of nowhere, with a relative stranger.

I should probably at least tell Olivia where I am. Not that she could do anything to help me, the little idiot, but at least she should know, if something happens to me. We're partners after all, for better or worse. I feel, oddly, that she's the only person I can count on right now – and that's preposterous of course. Kitsa is waiting for me at the clinic, I can count on the Programme agents as well... and I still have to find Rosebell.

Rosebell's face flashes before my mind's eye. A shiver slithers down my spine and I tighten the bathrobe around me. Someone's in the room with me. But there's no one here. The curtain billows as a gust of wind pushes open the window and spills a glass, breaking it.

I'm getting off the bed to take care of the glass when Omony rushes out of the bathroom, naked, alert, looking for the source of the noise.

'No, DeAnn, you'll cut yourself.'

He's dripping with water and the drops are shimmying down his skin. His eyes change as he stares at me, bending to pick up the broken glass; and I realize belatedly that my robe is gaping open. The next moment, his hand is cupped around my breast, rubbing my nipples as he bites my neck and I moan helplessly as they harden against the terrycloth.

Plucking my breasts out, he sucks them now, circling one of my burning nipples with his tongue while he kneads the other urgently. I let myself be carried away by his voracious kisses.

He's built like a statue. All the angles on his body are hard and chiseled, but his strength feels real, not like someone who goes to the gym for aesthetics. His thighs are muscular and his neck is wide and powerful. I lick him and kiss him all over, and he allows himself to be adored and pleasured; then he takes over and ploughs through me roughly until he comes with a long, loud groan.

I fall back exhausted and wonder how it happened that I serviced him today. Normally it's men who try their damndest to make *me* come. I should feel released but instead, I lie on the bed next to him wide awake, staring at the severed gorilla hand on the night stand, as he sleeps.

Listening to the jungle's breath through the mosquito net windows, my unease grows but I can't pinpoint exactly why. I wish I were back in Kampala. I feel like a fly caught in an invisible web. And the worst part is that I don't know why I should feel this way or how to free myself.

27

OLIVIA

K*ampala, Uganda, 15 February 2082*

I COME TO WITH A START, disoriented.

The jeep crashed into the only bloody tree for miles.

For the love of God and all that is sacred, can't I catch a bloody break? Something warm trickles on my forehead. I check the mirror. Brilliant, I'm bleeding.

I clamber out of the giant SUV and stretch, massaging my painful neck and the small of my back. The car is completely totalled, the bonnet has crumpled around the tree trunk and a small trickle of smoke is billowing up.

I pee behind the tree, the sharp blades of grass tickling my bum, as my brain blinks slowly awake. It's awfully dark. Bloody hell. I'm in the middle of the savannah; there could be lions for all I know. I pull the fatigues back on as quickly as I can and dart back into the SUV, abruptly aware of how very alone and vulnerable I really am.

Back in the car, palms tingling, I try to roll up the window but the battery is dead. Shit. The iMode is the only source of light and it's displaying 5.15 a.m. I passed out for nearly five hours. This is not good. Not good at all. Am I even far enough from the base? They could be catching up with me, right this minute. I need to keep going and it looks like I'm going to have to continue on foot.

Pushing down the rising panic, I rummage through the car. OK, that's a good start: a torch, a canteen of water and a protein bar. Maybe if I wait a little longer, the sun will rise. Racking my brain to remember if lions hunt by day or night, I gobble down the chewy bar and turn on the flashlight, holding it pinned between the cast and my shoulder so I can survey the landscape and determine which direction to go.

The road is pretty clearly delineated; I decide to follow it away from Camp Askaris as it must logically lead somewhere. Otherwise it would have been erased by now. So someone must be using it regularly.

Cursing the SUV's driver for not having left anything else in the car, I check that the little Swiss Army knife is still in my pocket, drink a mouthful of water from the canteen and try to think of another excuse not to get out into the night. Finding none, I leave the SUV reluctantly, feeling like I'm abandoning a lifebuoy in an empty ocean.

Every movement in the surrounding darkness conjures up images of me being devoured by animals. Every noise is potentially a lion that might spring from the bushes, or the soldiers of Camp Askaris catching up with me. And when I'm not imaging my own death, I wonder how on earth I'm going to get back to Kampala and after that, how I'll get out of the country and back to London. My mind tries to plan but it has nothing to latch on to, so it whirrs on empty, coming up with increasingly far-fetched escape plans and daring heroics. But the reality is that I can't even drive a bloody car or programme an itinerary for that matter.

After about thirty minutes' walk, the sky starts to lighten. The sun isn't up yet but I don't need the torch anymore. Heartened, I accelerate my pace when a fighter plane comes out of nowhere, flying low. Heart pounding, I hide under a large bush and peek carefully through the canopy. The small military aircraft passes by at high speed.

They can't possibly have sent a military plane after me, can they? I mean, come on! The aircraft swerves just after passing me. Is it going back to the base, has it spotted me?

Suddenly all my thoughts are blown away by an enormous explosion. A gust of wind flattens all the vegetation around, as I'm knocked off my feet and projected on my back in the red dust. I try to get up but the wind has been knocked out of me. I struggle to breathe, but my lungs won't work.

I am going to die. I panic and hit my fist on my chest hard and finally my diaphragm moves and blissful air comes in. My heart is beating frantically as I suck in long gulps of air, grateful to be alive.

Wait, what on earth happened? The planes bombed something? But we're in the middle of nowhere, lungs burning. I run towards the small hill. The explosion came from there. I'm expecting to find a crater on the other side of it. But when I arrive at the top, there's a small village and it's intact; just a couple dozen mud huts and no crater. Could the explosion have been the planes passing the sound barrier? Nothing is destroyed, there is no damage, no destruction at all. I check the village from a safe distance behind the ridge of the hill and observe. There doesn't seem to be anyone there. Nothing moves. Where is everyone?

Finally, I can't stand it anymore and run down the hill towards it, determined to find some help.

When I reach the outer huts, there's no one there. No one inside. No one outside. Odd. I walk towards the village centre, at first looking in every shack and then going faster, as there is no one at all in the small shacks. It's eerie.

Finally, the village square comes into view; all the villagers seem to have gathered there but they must have fallen asleep. I walk towards them, as a growing sense of foreboding screams for me to run the other way. But I can't. I need to understand what's happened.

The smell of vomit and faeces hits me first. They're lying on the ground. Men, women, children. A foamy discharge on their lips. Their skin turning grey. Glassy eyes. I rush to the side of a mud hut and clutching the rough wall, empty my stomach until my throat feels raw. Then, wiping my hand compulsively against my thigh, again and again, I step among the bodies, looking for a survivor.

Time has slowed down to an eternity. Flies on their faces. Acrid smell of vomit. Open eyes, unseeing. Children's little hands grabbing their mothers. A man sheltering his wife from the blast with his own body. Red dust coats everything, like powdered blood. There are at least sixty people here. Stunned, I'm unable to take in what I see. Now I'm on my knees. Did I fall? My hands are shaking a toddler, shaking him awake, but his skin is cold under my fingers. Flashes of baby Jonathan flicker, superimposing on this dead baby's face as I shake him. Wake up. Wake up.

No, no, no. I scream and pound on the young boy's chest, the CPR compressions devolving into sobs and exhausted pushes. No one moves. The child lolls back to the ground. He's not Jonathan. My sobs are the only sound here. Everything is blurry.

'Help!' The faint voice insistently tries to pierce through my mental fog.

I wipe my eyes.

'Is anybody here?' A man's voice.

I try to snap out of my trance and shake my head slowly, dazed.

'Over here, over here! Please help me!' he shouts.

Trying my best to avoid walking on the bodies, I approach the shack, wiping tears off my cheeks, hesitating. But as I get close, I hear shouted orders and the sound of heavy boots approaching.

Squeaking with terror, I dive into the closest mud hut and hide in the shadows. My back to the dried mud wall, I cling to the uneven surface, taking in the pungent smell of straw, the overturned stool, the thatched roof. An old man's gaunt form is sprawled on the dirt floor. He stares at me, his ashen face frozen in surprise.

'Clear.' A man's low rumble makes me flinch. So close.

'Clear.'

The sound of running soldiers coordinating their approach grows in the dead's silent village. I slide along the wall and crouch, unable to see what's happening outside, as there is no window. Through the bright sun-drenched entrance, the jumble of bodies beyond looks strangely expectant. As if they were all looking at me with their glassy, empty eyes. Out of the jumble of limbs, dead fingers seem to point in my direction: *She's here, she's here, hiding in that hut.*

Shrieks tear through my thoughts. I think I hear gurgling sounds. Then silence.

Shrinking in the shadows, I grab a heap of torn fabric and crawl under the makeshift bed's wooden frame, hiding myself under the pile of coarse rags.

'Take him away, back to the lab. Take one of these as well.'

Men's black boots pass by the hut opening. I clamp my good hand over my mouth, squeezing myself tighter into the cramped space.

My breath comes in small panicked bursts. My heart frantically tries to punch a hole through my ribcage. The old man's corpse reaches towards me, his arm outstretched, his hand curled up in a claw, accusing.

I'm sorry. So, so sorry.

'Over here.'

Did I leave any trace? Did they hear me?

'The tracker says she's somewhere around here. Search these three.'

Fatigue-wearing calves appear in my field of vision, canvassing the room. The man's breath seems so loud in the small space that I hold mine and squeeze my eyes shut.

Oh my God. If they catch me, I'm dead. I'm dead. Oh God. A small whine is threatening to burst through my lips so I grab a handful of filthy rags and press them against my mouth, willing myself to remain silent.

'Clear.' The boots recede into the square.

There's a strange smell I can't identify, seeping through the blankets.

'OK, move out.'

I get a glimpse of one soldier as he lifts his tattooed arm up and makes some kind of sign. Other soldiers appear holding automatic rifles, walking in formation. In the rear, four of the soldiers carry two body bags. They're leaving!

I stay as still as I can, but it's suffocating and so hot under the jute blankets and something smells...

Fire!

My eyes widen, as I spot smoke tendrils snaking on the

floor, licking the old man's cadaver. I fight with the blankets, struggling to free my limbs and crawl out from under the rickety tinder bed just as the whoosh of flames engulfs the thatch roof.

My hair starts to curl and singe, my arms, face and neck are showered with sparks. I scream and all rational thoughts vanish as I rush through the threshold of the mud hut before the burning straw falls on me.

Shrieking and flailing, I run outside and trip on the bodies strewn there. They've been doused in gas and when the small embers fall from my clothes onto the dead, they ignite.

Backpedalling, I try to get back on my feet and fight the inert grimacing corpses, their limbs tangled with mine as the air itself catches on fire.

A hand grabs a handful of my hair and lifts me up. Something hard connects with my temple and darkness engulfs me.

28

DEANN

ampala, Uganda, February 16, 2082

THE PILE of rubble smolders in the afternoon light. It's all that's left of the Kampala Programme compound. A plume of smoke rises up toward the deep blue sky, obscuring the sun.

Through the debris, I can make out the gruesome carcasses of burnt bodies. What if Olivia is dead? What if they're all dead and I'm alone in 2082, stuck in this world of violence, fire and death?

I need to find Kitsa. Fear for her strikes me suddenly like a thunderclap in a clear blue sky. I ruffle through my purse to find the iMode. I shouldn't have removed it. I just wanted a weekend away from all the madness. What if Kitsa or Olivia tried to call? The damn thing is getting no reception. I shake it with frustration and throw it back in my bag. The driver comes back and has a few words with Omony.

'We need to go, this isn't safe.'

I didn't like Olivia but I didn't want her to die like that. I'm starting to think that maybe I should have hung around with her more often. I should have tried to hear what she was trying to say to me, instead of shutting her out.

'Look, there is nothing more we can do here this afternoon. We're both tired from the trip and we need to get to safety before night falls,' Omony says.

I climb in the armored black sedan and the driver takes us away. The silence in the car is tense. We look out of the windows, trying to spot where danger might come from. The driver is talking on an old-fashioned walkie-talkie to someone. The iModes don't seem to work anymore. How do they work anyway? Maybe the cell phone tower has been knocked out, or whatever.

Things have gone from bad to fucking worse in Kampala in the space of two days. The population was already out of control before we left, but nothing could have prepared me for the state of the city today. There are dead bodies littered through the streets; they must have dropped dead and their bodies just remained where they fell. Sometimes people have moved them into piles by the side of the roads.

Could it have gotten this bad without me noticing or did it just escalate beyond recognition over the weekend? Oh God. Please let Kitsa be alive. Please. I rack my brain to figure out whether I left her any water and come up blank. What if she's...?

The walkie-talkie crackles and a gush of words pours from it. The driver listens intently and relays it back to his master, in rapid Acoli, their eyes locked in the mirror.

Omony translates for me: 'There is no water at all anymore. The city has had no water for the entire time we were away.' He taps the driver on the shoulder and they immerse themselves in another long conversation I can't understand.

Aghast, I stare out of the window with renewed horror. The human body can only last about three days without water. And death by thirst is a nasty way to go. The symptoms make sense now. Some people are already scratching themselves frenetically; others talk to the air, agitating their hands, probably already in the hallucinatory stage. The dusty, crazed figures bat away at the air, their eyes sunken and hollow, like walking skeletons.

Most of the cadavers have a swollen, protruding tongue. I never even thought about what it might look like when I memorized the symptoms in med school. It seemed simply impossible in green, wet New England that thirst would ever touch us.

My hand has gripped Omony's and he squeezes back. He's the only thing standing between me and certain death. As my eyes remain fastened on the window, my lips start moving and after a while, I recognize what I'm whispering. It spills out of me in a loop and I can't stop myself: 'The Lord is my shepherd; I shall not want. He maketh me to lie down in green pastures: he leadeth me beside the still waters...' A strangled laugh mixed with a sob. Still waters. We drive past an old woman being clubbed to death by a teenage girl, who pries a half-empty bottle of water from her fingers.

Omony gives brisk instructions to the driver, who nods, eyes fixed on the road.

'What did you say to him?'

'To stop for nothing and no one.'

'But my friends? What about the hospital?' I need to get to Kitsa. Anxiety rumbles inside me like an approaching thunderstorm, urgent and terrifying.

'Absolutely not.'

There's a part of me that wants to agree with him. The part of me who wants to survive at all costs. Surely, as desperate as this mob gets, it will still be in their self-interest to have medical care? They wouldn't burn the hospital down, would they?

I wrench myself away from the slippery edge of cowardice and force myself to say, 'We're only a few streets away from the hospital. Please just let me get Kitsa.'

'Who?' he frowns.

'The little girl I rescued. I told you about her before.'

'What, your pet? I can get you another, cleaner one, from better stock.'

How cheap life has become in this overpopulated world. No one is special anymore. No one is irreplaceable. A person has become a low value commodity and they matter little, only to a handful of loved ones. To everyone else, they're competition or hindrance. Just an obstacle to survival. I can't become that person; I won't.

'Omony, you don't understand. If we don't go get her right now, I'll get out of this car and go fetch her myself, on foot.'

His large eyes focus properly on me then, assessing my resolve, weighing my value to him. I feel like an object whose worth is in the balance. Then he speaks brusquely to the driver and we make a sharp turn. The car climbs the steep slope and the gate appears at the top. The hospital is still standing.

I run out of the car as soon as it stops and sprint inside the building. My colleagues are all completely absorbed in what they're doing so no one notices that I'm here. I run through the packed hallways straight to my room. I slam the door open and it bounces against the wall.

'Kitsa! Kitsa!' I cry, my heart in a tight vise; she's not here.

I rush down the corridor, looking into every room, grabbing every child who looks like her, lanky arms, scraggly hair, about as tall as my elbow. Come on, come on! I need to find her before Omony leaves us both here. Where is she?

Finally, I burst into one of the operating theaters and she's there. Wearing that stupid stethoscope, floating in too-large pink scrubs, pumping an ambu bag. A strangled laugh bursts out of me, she's OK, she's OK.

I grab a nurse, place her hands over the respirator, then grab both of Kitsa's wrists. The kid fights me at first, then sees that it's me and throws herself in my arms. My heart unclenches and I remember how to breathe.

'Doctor DeAnn, you came back for me. You came back!' she half cries and half laughs, and we hug. The doctor yells at us to get the fuck out and I grab her by the hand, pulling her toward the exit.

When she understands that we're leaving, she slips out of my hand. 'Wait,' she says, patting herself and retrieving a piece of paper from her pink scrubs' pocket then she puts it back in her pocket and follows me, this time willingly.

We run hand in hand and I push her into the car and slam the door closed. Omony yells at the driver to go and we tear out of the driveway, tires screeching. On the way down, we drive so fast that a group of men has to jump out of the way to avoid us. I look back to see if any of them are hurt. They're all carrying machine guns and machetes and a few have torches. They're on their way to the hospital. They don't have any wounded among them. I reach for my iMode to warn Dr. Herault of the impending attack but, of course, it's dead. Pushing down the fear and shame, I wrench my gaze away from the hospital and hold Kitsa closer. At least I arrived in time to save her.

Half an hour later, the black sedan skids to a halt in front of Omony's house and he jumps out of the car, yelling instructions to his men then follows them without a backward glance for me.

As the afternoon sun slowly dims and the day draws to a close, I glance at the city from our view point; several columns of smoke slash through the yellow cap of smog; it looks like... I don't even want to think it... it looks like the end.

The heavy metal gates of Omony's compound close ponderously with a metallic clang, snapping me out of my gloomy thoughts. We're on top of one of Kampala's seven hills. We'll be safe here. Won't we?

As the driver ushers us inside, Kitsa looks around, swiveling her head about and taking in every detail with little birdlike motions. I keep her really close, holding her by the shoulder in front of me, as we dart through the corridors toward my room.

I should know the driver's name, but I've never bothered to learn it. I really didn't give a shit before, but maybe I should have.

'Is something happening?' I ask him.

In reply, he glares at me and holds my door open, completely silent. We go in and I half expect to hear the lock to click in place. But it doesn't.

Kitsa stands frozen in the middle of my bedroom, taking in the beautiful furnishings, the books on the dresser, the plate of sweets on the table. When she sees the carafe of water by the bed, she lunges at it and drinks the whole thing thirstily. I kiss the top of her head and empty my purse on the bed. An assortment of useless crap tumbles out: a half-empty bottle of water, my dead iMode, Rosebell's leather-bound notebook. There's the glove-full of white powder that Kitsa picked up from the water treatment plant and my white French doctor jacket, which I balled and crammed in at the end of my Friday shift. How incredibly far away Friday seems now.

There's nothing that would be much use in an emergency. I shake the jacket and drape it over a chair, leave the iMode on the charger and cram everything else back in my purse. Slinging the bag across my shoulder, I head for the door; I need to gather some water, food. A weapon, just in case.

'Oh, Doctor DeAnn, I forgot! Your friend Olivia came.'

'Where? When?'

Oh please God let her still be alive.

'At the clinic on Friday, she was looking for you. She was very upset. She left this note.'

Kitsa takes out the piece of paper I saw earlier in her pocket and hands it to me. It's an official-looking memo requesting an authorization for a multinational company to do business in Uganda.

Frowning, I skim over the text, as anxiety nibbles. This is useless. Why would Olivia give me this? I need to figure where she is. Not what some pharma company did years ago. Kitsa pulls on my sleeve and turns the sheet over; there's a note scribbled on the back.

My guts writhe as I read and the pieces fall into place. Oh fuck. Olivia says the Programme has turned against us and wants to harvest our microchips. She says to contact her as soon as I get this note and not to come back to the compound; too dangerous. How did I miss all this? Did they kill her already? Anxiety rises like a wave.

There's another page of notes. She says the Programme is building a weapon of some sort, somewhere in Bwaise. She adds that she saw blue barrels at the military compound but she doesn't know what they're for.

Blue barrels?

Oh my God. It's the white powder we saw at Mazzi. I rummage through my purse and extract the knotted glove. This has got to be it. She thinks the Programme is building a weapon but after what I've seen in Mazzi... I turn the memo around and my thoughts slide into place like Tetris blocks.

The pharma company is testing the drug and putting it in the water with the Programme soldiers' help!

Our investigations ran in parallel. I thought she was an idiot but she was my partner. And now she's probably dead. With a pang, I realize that if only we'd spoken earlier, she might have survived. We could have figured it all out together. She had one half of the puzzle pieces I needed, and I ignored her.

Olivia's earnest face flickers before my eyes, as she tried to tell me about the murder. I believe her now. The Programme soldiers executed Rosebell. After Itungo took my friend to the Mazzi water treatment plant, she must have figured out that Burke and his men were lacing the substance into the water. Poor Rosebell. She died trying to confront Burke about the experiment. I remember her telling me that the White Man will always treat us like chattel. That People of Color are just test subjects to them and that they want us to die. She was right. She was right.

Now that I think about it, this is the perfect country to test the substance in. No one would notice a missing person, a sick family, or even a localized epidemic. No one would question what was in the water because people are too desperate and need to drink it to survive. No matter what it contains. It's the one thing that people can't live without in this country. Drinkable water.

This is big. Omony will know what to do. He's the only one I can trust now. He'll be outraged when he learns what the White Man has done to his compatriots. I need to go talk to him.

'Kitsa, stay here, OK?'

'I want to go with you.'

'No, you stay here and eat and drink some more. I'll be right back. I'm going to go talk to Omony about this.' Her little face looks dubious. 'Stay here. I'll be back for you later, OK?'

I close the door behind me and head toward Omony's study like I've done fifty times before. On my way, I stop to look outside; the grounds are quiet. The soldiers patrol the perimeter, alert but silent. No immediate danger then.

My feet slow down of their own accord as I near Omony's office. Maybe he's busy. This seems so important to me, but given the situation outside, maybe he won't have time for a conspiracy theory. He'll be outraged, though, I'm sure. He suffered so much during his time in England. The racism, the ostracizing, the belittling and bullying. He'll see this for what it's: an outrageous attempt by the White Man to once again kill People of Color.

Now, I'm at the hidden door I always use. It's part of an access route that links Omony's office to an adjoining suite that he reserves for meetings with important visitors. He showed me how to get through this way a few days after I first arrived, so I could come and go when he was on calls without going through security at the front.

In the dim reception room, I make my way around the sofa and to the door that connects with his study and lift my hand to knock but I sense a movement; Kitsa has followed me. Frowning, I open my mouth to tell her to return to my room but just then, a voice drifts over from Omony's office. A really familiar voice.

Signaling to Kitsa to be quiet and to stand next to me, I

peer through the narrow gap; I can't see Omony, but I can just about make out Burke's profile.

The Captain whistles. 'That's ballsy, mate, I'll give you that. But you know and I know that my command structure won't pay.' His ankle is resting on his knee as he leans back, seemingly at ease, but his foot is jittering up and down.

Omony says nothing and narrows his eyes.

Burke laughs uneasily. 'Look, mate, you did a great job for two years. Don't get me wrong, I know you kept up your end of the bargain, but you have to unders—'

'Bollocks! I went above and beyond that, Burke. You know I did!' Omony erupts. 'Not only did I provide you with the test subjects but my men also captured them for your autopsies. Buried any leads in the press. Quashed the rumors. You'd never have succeeded here without me.'

No. No, it can't be. I feel like all the air has left the room. Not Omony.

Burke tries to temper Omony's rising anger. 'Yes. But that's all in the contract, mate. You can't just double the price on the last day.'

'Tell me, *mate*, how do you plan to get out of this country alive, if I don't allow it?'

Burke's foot freezes and his hand starts to inch toward a gun holstered to the side of his thigh.

There's a strain in his voice now, as he banters, 'Come on, man, don't do anything you might regret. You know who I work for. I only came back to Kampala to secure the remaining stock after ours burned. What do you think will happen when I don't make it back to Camp Askaris? Or worse, if the shipment never makes it to St. Louis?'

There's a pregnant silence.

Then Omony says, 'This is much bigger than you've let

on. There's something special about the two women, isn't there?'

'Omony, my friend, you really have an overactive imagination, don't you? You did a good job keeping your girlfriend distracted and out of the way. That's all we asked of you.' He adds, as if it's an afterthought, 'Oh, and while I'm here, I might as well retrieve a small piece of technology from her arm before I leave the country. To be honest, I don't give a monkey's arse what you do with the bitch after I'm gone. There's nothing special about her.'

That stings.

Burke continues, 'I thought I'd take the red-head with me, but on reflection, I'll leave her here after I'm done with her.' He pauses. 'I'd be willing to pay you extra to dispose of her body.'

Olivia is here! Kitsa tugs on my sleeve and mouths: 'Miss Olivia.' She gives me a hand gesture for searching and darts away before I can catch her. Cursing inwardly, I watch her slender little form as she slips through the back door. Frustrated, I try to focus on the conversation, as I can't stop her now.

Omony laughs and, for the first time, I think it sounds very unpleasant.

'That's nice, Captain. Leaving me the leftovers, you must think I'm an idiot. An attaboy and some fucking pussy? You think that I'm going to let you go so easily? I have a better idea. Why don't I kill you and keep everything. The chemical, the autopsy results, the technology... and the women.'

Burke sits back, one arm spread over the back of the chair, but his other hand hovers over the weapon as he lets out a tense laugh. 'Come on now, Omony, you're one of us, aren't you? Raised in my country. You understand the concept of fair play. We've been partners these past two years. Don't ruin it now.'

'This technology must be really important for you if you came back all the way from Camp Askaris to get it from DeAnn's arm. It must be really *precious* to you.'

Burke's jaw clenches. 'Listen, I'm going to get into a lot of trouble if I don't bring back my company's property. It's only a small implant, so we could track her location. It's worthless to you. It's just a trace of our presence that we'd rather not leave behind, that's all. You know how my company operates.' He laughs. 'It's all very hush hush.'

'Double the price or you can forget it. You and your implant will never leave Uganda.'

Burke takes a minute to think about it then gives a big theatrical sigh. 'OK, fine, mate, you win. I'm wiring the money now.' He taps on his wristband and there's an answering ping on Omony's iMode. Then he stands up.

'Good decision. Have a safe trip back,' Omony says, deadpan, not getting up.

The Captain's jaw clenches. 'Can you get someone to bring DeAnn to me in the cellblock? I'll be there retrieving the other... the GPS tracker.'

'Of course. Give me half an hour, I'll arrange it.'

They shake hands and Burke leaves through the main door. He's going to kill Olivia. I need to stop this. I start to retreat but someone opens the main door of Omony's office and I freeze.

The driver is holding Kitsa by the elbow, looming over her. She's fighting him but his hold on her is too strong and she looks heartbreakingly small and bony in his grip.

29

OLIVIA

ampala, Uganda, 16 February 2082

PAIN, dull and insistent, jolts me awake. I try to sit up but a shard of bright, blinding agony shreds through my broken wrist. As my lids blink slowly open, I realise that my hands are tied to my ankles behind my back, arching me painfully backward.

I'm on my side, my left cheek pressed against the raw cement floor. The right side of my face is on fire. I remember vaguely that I bumped my forehead in the car crash yesterday. Groebler's men must have knocked me out as well.

Not a good day, so far. A hysterical laughter starts to bubble up but my lip cracks and the taste of blood spreads in my mouth.

I twist and turn, ignoring my shoulder's protests and the burns on my arms. I must have gotten the blisters when the hut I was hiding in was set on fire or maybe when Anthony and I escaped the burning compound. I don't know. All I know is that everything bloody hurts.

Trying to get my mind off the pain, I survey my surroundings and come up blank. Am I still in Camp Askaris? Where am I? Through the barred window, I can see the sky. It looks like late afternoon. The grimy walls are encrusted in ominous stains; the only source of light comes through the bars of a metal sliding door. When I stretch my neck and push up with my good elbow, I can see a corridor beyond it, but nothing else. I let my head back down, gingerly pressing my cheek against the rough floor. A few inches from my face, a sinkhole marks the centre of the room. The sight of it sends a shiver up my spine.

I flex my arms, trying to fight the restraints but they don't even budge and the rope digs in and chafes against my skin. Where is Groebler? Oh God. Is this it? Am I going to die today?

I try to wriggle out of the rope but it doesn't work. I can't even sit up. Who am I kidding? I'm no James Bond. I'm a bloody lawyer who works in a bloody law firm and I'm going to die today because I'm bloody incompetent.

I flail against my bonds and scream with frustration, only succeeding in cutting open the skin of my left wrist. The 3D printed cast encasing my right wrist squashes the broken bones tight and the more I struggle, the tighter the cord seems to bite into my ankles. Salty tears sting my busted lip.

An hour passes or five minutes, when a slow clap makes me jump out of my skin. I twist, the coarse rope digging into my bleeding wrist as I crane my neck. Anthony is there, leaning sideways against the doorjamb of the cell.

'Olivia Sagewright, the English Nancy Drew. Who would

have thought?' He looks amused as he slides the bars open and steps into the cell.

'Oh thank God, it's you, Anthony. There's been a terrible misunderstanding, Colonel Groebler thought I'd...'

'I'm really impressed, you know.' His smile congeals on his face.

'What are you talking about, Anthony? Where are we?'

'In Kampala. But it really doesn't matter anymore. Does it?' He waves the information away with a dismissive gesture. 'I thought you'd fallen for me.' He walks over, an unpleasant smile on his face, and nudges my face with his boot.

Shocked, I recoil and try to crawl back. 'Anthony, I do care about you. And I know you care about me. You said we're in Kampala? If you'd wanted me dead, we'd be in Camp Askaris right now and one of Colonel Groebler's men would have slit my throat. I know there's good in you, I've seen it. You can change, you can do the right thing...'

A brutal kick in my stomach robs me of all thought. I choke, sucking in air but nothing reaches my lungs. Finally, something unlocks and a shaky breath seeps in, as tears start to roll sideways on my face.

'Please, Anthony, it's me, you know me,' I plead. 'I'm harmless.'

'Oh, don't give me the act, Olivia. It's too late to play dumb.'

He crouches next to my face, pushes a strand of my hair out of the way and observes me thoughtfully.

'The funny thing is, I did want to go ahead with the plan. Even after Groebler's men found you in that village and dropped you off like a trussed up pig with strict instructions to execute you. Even then, I was going to save you. That's why I brought you here.'

'You see? I knew you were a good pers—'

'DeAnn was going to have an unfortunate accident and during the next few months, I'd have manipulated your feelings until the idea to offer me her microchip finally occurred to you. Then we'd have lived happily ever after in 2017, where I'd have infiltrated the Programme. You were going to be smitten with me and none the wiser.' He says, caressing my face. 'I probably would have enjoyed the con too.'

I can only stare at him, aghast, as his fingers brush against the burns on my cheek. His mouth takes on a bitter slant.

'Then I saw your iMode while I was driving over.' He throws my iMode on the floor in front of me and it falls with a definitive little thunk on the cement floor. 'Fucking waste of four months' work.'

His voice changes, all trace of feeling erased. 'How long have you been corresponding with the Cassandra Resistance?'

'Who? I don't know anything, Anthony.'

He ignores my pleading and climbs on top of me. His weight crushes my bound hands painfully against my back and I start to panic, my breath coming in short pants. A tear slips out of the corner of my eye and slides into my ear.

'Whatever they've told you, it's not true...'

'STOP. PLAYING. DUMB.'

Straddling me, he grabs my head and smashes it against the ground as he bellows with incoherent rage. A flash of white light explodes; the back of my head feels like it's going to split open.

I whimper, hating the sound of my own helplessness. No one's ever hit me before, my mind can't process this new reality.

He's still holding the sides of my face, my hair pulled painfully in his grip. His face is too close.

'OK. Let's try again, you fucking cunt. Who do you work for?'

'I don't know... I don't know her name...'

He shakes his head, talking to himself more than to me. 'I never get this wrong. This is my thing. I assess people and manipulate them. You made me look like a fool.'

'Please don't hurt me, Anthony. I didn't mean to...'

'I told them you were stupid and malleable. I convinced them that I could control you. I'll probably be demoted because of you. YOU FUCKING BITCH.' His fist has already connected with my jaw before I've even seen it moving. My lip splits open completely this time, as my face smashes into the rough floor.

'We have the ID and location of your contacts. So you weren't a total loss after all. Even if you don't know their names, I'll find them and execute every last one of them, thanks to you.' He breathes hard, anger and contempt etched on his features. 'Just a small thing left to do before I slash your chip out.' He pauses. 'I think I'm going to enjoy killing you.'

My breath catches and I start to pray silently as a broad smile stretches on his lips.

Our Father, who art in heaven.

I struggle to break free, wriggling under the weight of him. He sits back and knocks my head against the floor again. Hard. Dizziness engulfs me and a wave of nausea rises, as the floor seems to tank abruptly under me.

Hallowed be thy name.

His hands slide along my neck and wrap around my throat.

Thy kingdom come.

I struggle for breath, my nostrils obstructed with snot and blood.

Thy will be done on Earth as it is in Heaven.

His fingers are pressing down on my throat as I squirm under his weight, struggling against the rope.

Give us this day our daily bread.

His stranglehold tightens around my flesh like a steel vice. Tighter. Tighter.

And forgive us our trespasses.

My broken wrist slips free of the cast.

As we forgive those who trespass against us.

He seems to enjoy the look of terror on my face. His breath warm on my face. He's holding me pinned. I frantically try to push him away with my injured hand but he doesn't even budge.

And lead us not into temptation.

My lungs feel like they're exploding. Long rasping breaths scorch their way into my lungs. But barely any air goes through.

But deliver us from evil.

There's something between me and the floor, a hard object digging into my ribs. I grope around in my pocket with my free hand and feel a small shape there, warm and smooth.

For thine is the kingdom, the power and the glory.

His face starts to blur and the cell around us dims.

For ever and ever.

30

DEANN

 ampala, Uganda, February 16, 2082

'Omonykuu, I'm so sorry, I was lost. I didn't mean...'

The driver interrupts Kitsa's pitiful excuses with a rough shake. The stupid stethoscope bounces off her little chest.

Omony's profile comes into view as he leans forward on his desk. He's reading something on his iMode and barely looks up.

'I found her in Building Four. She saw the white woman.' The driver's English is faultless. They must have been speaking Acoli in front of me, all this time, so I wouldn't understand what they were saying.

My heart skips a beat. What has Kitsa gotten herself into now? I'm going to have to intervene and avoid her getting yelled at or worse, maybe thrown out of the house.

Omony looks up from his reading and gazes at the child

with disgust. 'Ah. DeAnn's pet. Don't let her dirty the carpet. She's filthy.'

Kitsa tries to shake off the driver but his grip only tightens as he pulls her elbow higher. Her arm looks like a broken wing.

She juts her chin out in that gesture of defiance that I love so much. 'I heard what you said to the evil white man. I won't let you hurt Doctor DeAnn.'

Omony raises his eyebrows. He looks like a dog has decided to talk to him. I've never seen this side of him before and I feel betrayed, fooled. How could I not see this?

'You won't *let* me?' He barks a laugh. 'That's funny, little rat.'

'I am not a rat. I am a girl.' She looks so small, floating in the pink scrubs. She's just a child in a too-large costume.

This has gone far enough. Who does he think he is – talking to my lovely, smart girl like that?

I raise my hand to open the door just as he says: 'Kill her.'

The driver lifts Kitsa off the floor. Her little body so slender and fragile. Her legs flail as he breaks her neck with a sickening crunch and she falls like a dislocated doll to the floor.

Omony looks up, annoyed. 'I told you not to dirty the carpet.'

I can't breathe. I can't move. My eyes are wide and my mouth opens in a scream that doesn't come. I clamp my hand over my mouth and look at her little body, crumpled and lifeless on the cream carpet.

I can't think anymore. All my brain can manage is *Kitsa, Kitsa, Kitsa, Kitsa, Kitsa, Kitsa….*

I don't know how long I stay like that. Like a pillar of salt.

At length, something breaks through the fog.

A name.

What did the driver just say?

What was that name?

Olivia.

It was Olivia.

What did he say?

Omony is back to reading his iMode. He points to Kitsa's corpse with his chin. 'Dispose of that. Then find DeAnn and secure her.'

'Should I bring her to Burke?'

'No, of course not. If that technology is so important to him, I must have it, whatever it is. DeAnn probably knows what it's for. Just keep her under lock and key for now and make sure Burke doesn't get his hands on her.'

The driver starts to retreat when Omony adds, 'Oh, and go check whether Burke's done with the white one.'

The driver nods.

I tiptoe backward as quietly as possible, then rush out of the suite of rooms.

He said that Olivia is in Building Four. I've been coming here for months, I should know where that is. Panic rises as I run down the hallway toward the back, trying to remember, but nothing comes. It's like my brain has shut down. The bitter smell of smoke wafts in as I pass an open window, and I notice gray clouds rising in straight columns on the darkening horizon. Kampala is burning

At the end of the hallway, I barge into the kitchen, startling the staff who are huddled near a screen. Making placating gestures, I dart to the back door and emerge in the courtyard as one of them starts to yell, raising the alarm.

Outside, the sky has turned orange as the pungent smell of the burning city fills my nostrils. Popping bursts of machine-gun fire erupt nearby, mingling with intermittent yells that spike above the low hubbub of an approaching crowd. Mouth dry, pulse racing, I start running again, my purse flapping against my hip, as I hold the strap across my shoulder. Then, I remember. Building Four. I know where it is; at the back of the property, near the well.

As I get near Building Four, I hear a scream. It's a woman. I accelerate, feeling a stitch burn my side. Am I too late? Is Burke killing her? I pant as I push open the main door and run in.

It's dark here. I hold a hand out and wipe sweat off my forehead, willing my eyes to see. Hand extended in front of me, I stumble forward, barely able to distinguish shapes. It looks like a long corridor lined with cells. I run my fingers along the thick metal bars as I pass them, careful and silent. No one behind me. No one in any of the cells. Where is she? Oh my God. Please let her be alive.

Olivia's scream reverberates in the gloom and goosebumps erupt on my skin; she sounds like an animal. I run toward the sound. She must be in the last cell.

The sliding door is open.

There are two people lying on the floor.

And there is blood everywhere.

Olivia is screaming and kicking, as she's trying to get out from under Burke. Her screeches are getting more frantic as she fails to wriggle from under him. She's tied up and he's suffocating her.

As I rush over, the shapes coalesce into understanding; he's not attacking her. He's dead. There's a gory slash on the side of his neck and a pool of blood on the concrete floor tells the rest of the story.

I shove his body off her with difficulty and as soon as she's free of his weight, she crawls away frantically. One of her wrists is tied to her ankles but she drags herself on the floor and only stops when she's reached the corner. Looking wild and lost, she moans and shakes her head, as if to say 'no'.

There is so much blood. She's completely covered in it; on her face, her hair, her shirt, blood everywhere. Her drenched hair is plastered to her face and only her eyes are white, striking against the red, open wide and staring.

I think I hear her say 'Amen' but that can't be right.

31

DEANN

K*ampala, Uganda, February 16, 2082*

'OLIVIA? OLIVIA?'

As I move slowly closer, making gentle reassuring gestures, she wrenches her head up, trying to escape from me, whimpering, and struggles to get up, the rope bites into the deep gashes on her wrist and ankles. Her breath is coming in raspy pants so I unclog her nose with my sleeve. Then, I rummage in my purse and retrieve the crumpled plastic bottle. There's only three mouthfuls left. She gulps down the water gratefully but she doesn't seem to recognize me.

'It's OK, Olivia, it's me, DeAnn. Everything is OK, you're safe now.'

A crash in the bushes, outside the barred window, startles me. I freeze, but nothing else comes. Everything is sharpened by fright, my hearing, my alertness, my thinking. We must get a move on. Now.

One of her hands is free from the restraints and a small Swiss Army knife blade protrudes from her clenched fist, dripping with syrupy blood. Her fingers are locked tight around it. Gently, I open her fist, finger by finger, until I can pry the knife out and then use it to cut the rope.

As soon as she's free, she folds her knees under her chin and wraps her arms around her shins. As she rocks back and forth, I wipe her face, wincing when I uncover the mess below the slick red layer; one of her eyes is swelling, her lip is split and she flinches and whimpers when I touch her neck. Apart from her face, though, there's nothing life threatening that I can see. Why can't she recognize me? Has she been drugged?

'Come on, Olivia, we have to move.'

I help her up but she sways and vomits at my feet. And that's when I see it, the bloody gash on the back of her head. Shit. Concussion.

Cries ring outside and the staccato of machine guns erupts startlingly close.

'Olivia? Can you hear me?' I run my fingers along the base of her skull but she moans so I stop, startled to hear such a feral sound coming out of her. She's usually so sweet and chirpy.

OK, I can't let her pass out and we can't stay in the cell.

Shouts and gunshots ring out in the courtyard and, as if in answer, the roar of a mob reverberates a few seconds later. Fuck.

I dart to Burke's side and search him. It's slow and difficult. His body lolls and slumps and I have to tug to get his iMode and slide the gun out of the holster on his thigh. DNA locked. It's useless. Letting the gun drop to the floor, I survey the room to make sure I've grabbed everything we could use and see Olivia's bracelet; I pick it up and stuff it in my purse, just in case.

We start moving and it feels like helping a sleepwalker. I look at her sideways, hoist her arm on my shoulder and keep going, down the dark corridor toward the cellblock's exit.

The clamor gets louder and louder as we approach the door. I prop her against a guard's desk and wedge the door open to look outside.

Omony's men are running to the property walls with machine guns, yelling instructions to each other in the dark blue twilight. In front of me, there is an outside staircase climbing to the roof of the building we're in.

I close the door quietly and consider Olivia's form, slumped on the floor, back against the desk. I need to get her out of here as soon as possible. If she falls asleep she will probably never wake up.

Swinging my satchel behind me, I open the door again and this time, I slip out and climb, hunched over, as quickly as I can up the staircase. Once on the roof, I flatten myself on the floor and crawl to the edge.

The main gate is closed and beyond it, thousands of desperate, angry men are pounding on the doors of the property, squashed against the metal gate as bodies push and crush them from behind.

The huge crowd, carrying torches and weapons, is clamoring to get in. Their rage is palpable and Omony's men number only a handful. They have combat experience and guns, but what can they do against thousands? A sea of men is crashing against the doors, a roaring wave waiting to wash us all away.

I crawl on my stomach, to the other side of the roof, and

think for a minute; we're not going to make it very far on foot with Olivia in that state. Well, *I* could make it.

I push the shameful thought away. If I lock us in the cell block, we could probably hold out for a while if the mob breaks in. But then what? Biting the inside of my cheek, I look for another exit. There. The service entrance at the back. Now, where are the cars? There.

Back inside, I drape Olivia's arm around my shoulders, hoist her up and we sneak out, moving slowly and counting on the deepening darkness to hide us. I make a conscious effort not to look over my shoulder. If someone's spotted us, we'll know soon enough, when the bullets hit. The back of my neck tingles with dread.

We're in the middle of the courtyard now. Behind us, the mob's cries rise, fury and hopelessness laced together in a siren song of mayhem.

Bent in half, we hurry to the back of the compound and, as the cries of rage and gunshot bursts recede, the spot between my shoulder blades stops itching.

We reach Burke's armored SUV and I swipe his iMode against the handle. The beep of the opening doors is lost in the commotion surrounding us.

Hunched under Olivia's growing dead weight, I open the passenger door and get her in, leaving my purse in her lap. Then I pad cautiously toward Omony's black sedan and try the passenger door, praying for it to be open. Luckily, it is. In the glove box, just as I remembered, I find what I'm looking for.

Bending at the waist, I creep to the back of the sedan and check the situation. The guards are all covering the main gate. No one's looking our way and the back gate is plunged in darkness. With a little bit of luck... I straighten up and start walking quickly to Burke's Humvee, tapping on his iMode to activate the car key.

'There! She's there. Catch her!' a deep voice rumbles. I throw a glance over my shoulder; the large driver is careering toward me as he bellows for reinforcements.

Heart racing, I break into a run, sprinting as fast as I can. But something trips me and I stumble and sprawl. My chin hits the grainy asphalt, grating painfully against it, and my hands fly open to break my fall.

Thinking I tripped, I try to get up but realize that Omony's driver has tackled me to the ground. My heart beating uncontrollably, I kick him away and struggle to get up on all fours and break free but he grabs me and flips me onto my back like a doll.

Crushing me under his weight, he pulls out a huge serrated knife and holds it to my throat. I thrash against him but he's not even bothering to glance at me. He's looking to his right. To Olivia? No. Past Burke's car. A figure is approaching.

Omony is snaking slowly toward us, holding a machete, his slow measured walk exuding arrogance. His silhouette seems to soak in the night's darkness, as the torches' flames set the sky on fire behind him.

A cold sense of foreboding slithers up my spine. He's smiling but his eyes are expressionless. He looks at me, only me, as he approaches.

There is no doubt, no fear, no sense of urgency in his gait. Despite the mob outside, the city burning, the chaos, he walks as if all of it were under his control and happening by his design and watching his silhouette against the night's orange glow, I start to believe it. Maybe he *is* in control and I was always his puppet.

Shaking myself awake, I dig my nails in the driver's eye sockets as hard as I can. He howls with pain and the knife clatters to the ground, skittering away from us, as the driver's hands fly up and he tries to protect his face from my nails.

But it barely lasts a moment and then he's back in control, grabbing my wrists and holding them above my head as he hunches over me. I'm pinned again, but my muscles remember the Krav Maga moves even if my mind doesn't.

I jolt my arms straight behind my head and he loses his balance, as the hand that held my wrists suddenly lurches away from him. He pitches forward and falls on top of me. But I'm ready for it; my hips rise up to meet his fall and I push with my legs, unbalancing him. I roll out of the way then I lunge for the knife lying on the ground a few feet away.

He grabs my ankle and I drop heavily to a knee. He starts to pull me backward. As he drags me toward him, my stomach scrapes along the asphalt, chafing my skin raw; I kick back with everything I've got but he's too strong.

He flips me on my back again and just as he prepares to pin me down again, I plant the huge serrated blade in his ear.

The knife slides in.

I gag when the hilt hits bone.

He stares at me, stunned, then convulses and falls like a felled tree.

I scramble out from under him and stand up just as Omony reaches me. He stops a few feet away, a dangerous look on his face. A machete hangs in his right hand, glinting in the night as it grazes the ground like a pendulum, counting down the seconds until I die.

I would give anything for a weapon right now. The knife is planted in the driver's skull and out of my reach. My empty hands close into fists, as I lift my chin up.

'He was only trying to protect you. I ordered him to bring you back safely inside.'

I scoff, 'I know everything. Everything.'

His expression hardens as his features turn to stone.

'How could you do this to your own people, Omony? I can understand why the White Man would want to experiment on us and kill us. But you? You! With all your grandiose talk of African pride and how you suffered from their racism, how could you betray your own country to help the Programme?'

'I'm not helping them,' he says vehemently. 'I'm giving my country options. No matter how many times we try, we never get anywhere. Democracies are toppled, resources plundered and we continue to starve by the millions – and what do we do? Nothing! We keep getting to get poorer and poorer, and I've had enough of it.'

I glance around, looking for something to use as a weapon, while I try to keep him distracted and talking.

'What the fuck are you talking about, Omony? You're not going to pull your country out of misery by allowing multinationals to conduct medical experiments on your own.'

'My *own*?' He laughs bitterly. 'Listen to these idiots.' He gestures with his machete to the mob rioting behind him. I flinch as the blade cuts through the air, flashing in the night, so close to my face. 'They come here, to my city, and take our food, our water and bring only chaos and destruction in their wake.'

'You told me you were helping them! Instead you collaborated with GeneX to experiment on them like lab rats!'

'Help them?' He laughs. 'What will happen if we help them? They'll eat today. Tomorrow maybe. Then what? They'll all starve to death anyway! There's too many of them to even make a dent.' He takes another step toward me. 'They were never *all* going make it. The weakest were going to die anyway. I've tried to pull this country out of its never-ending poverty. I've tried to convince and cajole and finance. But in the end, the only thing they understand is force and compulsion. What does it matter if these parasites die? Let them. The fittest will survive and the country will rise up stronger from the ashes of this night.'

My heart pounds in my ribcage. My chances of escape are running through my fingers like red Ugandan dust. The air smells of fire, sweat and blood. The guards shoot into the crowd and cries of rage and pain erupt outside the gate.

Omony takes a deep breath and his eyes fall on his dead driver, sprawled on the ground.

'You're not like them. You're not like anyone else. You're strong for a *muzungu*.'

'Don't call me that.'

'Why, daughter of slaves? Would you rather I called you by your slave name, *DeAnn*?'

I remember the love in my father's voice when he told me that he named me and my blood boils.

'Fuck you, Omony. I'm nobody's slave and certainly not yours.'

'Fine, *DeAnn*. I'm not going to hurt you.' But he doesn't let go of the machete, it just dangles there. His eyes bore into my soul, dark and powerful, his deep voice seductive, as always.

'I've opened my home to you. You were nothing, your blood diluted with the White Man's blood. Your mind polluted by their propaganda. Yet, I let you in and I treated you as my queen. I gave you respect. I gave you status – and this is how you repay me?' He gestures to the dead driver on the ground. 'Killing my childhood friend? Escaping like a thief in the middle of the night?' He looks genuinely offended.

Then his face softens. 'Stay with me, DeAnn. I know that you're more than you pretend to be. Together we could do so much.'

In a way, I've been looking all my life for a man like him. A man who doesn't let himself be overrun by his emotions. A rational, logical person who is my intellectual equal.

I remember Trevor and his weak impersonation of a successful man. His wholesome goodness, his sickly sweetness. He was never worthy of me. A ridiculous man-child with a weak mind, naïve, shallow. I know I'm destined for more than the small, mediocre life that Trevor could have given me.

Omony sees me waver and continues with renewed passion, 'You've seen the life I can offer you. Money, respect and recognition beyond measure. You would never again have to dim your light. You wouldn't have to pretend to be less than you really are. You wouldn't have to beg or play by the White Man's rules anymore. You'd be free, DeAnn. At my side, you'd be powerful.'

My rational mind is tempted but my heart is trying to say something. What is it trying to say?

For a moment, I watch his face, mesmerizing and seductive. Behind him, the main gate shakes, backlit by the glow of torches, as the clamor swells. The guards fire again in the crowd. The rat-tat-tat of their machine guns sounds strangely like Fourth of July firecrackers, in a festive night ablaze with light.

I spot Olivia in the car. She's lost consciousness and her head lolls on the headrest. If only Kitsa had found her earlier, she might have...

And with an explosion of pain, my heart remembers what it wanted to say: *Kitsa, Kitsa, Kitsa, Kitsa...*

My eyes snap back to Omony and this time, my *heart* sees him, instead of my mind. He's a monster. A psychopath. A manipulator. He's violent. He's a murderer. His eyes, so mesmerizing a second ago, become pools of malevolence, his seductive lips were all along twisted in a bitter snarl. My heart is frantically tolling the bells of alarm and I can finally hear, I can finally see.

I put my hand in my pocket discreetly and root around, trying to find the object I retrieved from the sedan.

'Why did you have to kill Kitsa, Omony?'

'Who?' He looks blankly at me.

I take my hand out of my pocket and grip the small object in my closed fist.

'The little girl.'

'Oh, that,' he scoffs. 'Your attachment to that child was irrational. She wasn't your daughter. She was a parasite like all the others. She was not of our class, of our level. She'd always have remained a sewer rat. She didn't matter at all.'

I want to agree with him, I really do. Life would be so much simpler if we could only follow reason. She didn't really matter. He's right, in the grand scheme of things; orphans like her die every day and the world doesn't know or care. She'd have become one more mouth to feed. One more breeding woman in a world desperate for resources. She didn't matter in the grand scheme of things, no.

'But she mattered to *me*,' I whisper softly. I lift my head, look him in the eye and press the button. The mob roars with triumph and fury. Thousands of throats howl and the rattle of machine guns intensifies.

Omony turns around, as the gates of his property open, and the mob spills into the grounds. Desperate men run in, glistening with sweat, mouths open in incoherent screams. Some are killed mid-run. They twist, stopped short by bullets, a spray of blood exploding in the air and they collapse. But hundreds more rush in after them, climbing over their bodies, holding torches, machetes, guns.

Omony turns back to look at me and his gaze falls on my open hand. A remote gate opener is nestled in my palm.

Our eyes meet.

There are no words left to say.

The machete rises in the air.

But I've already started running. I sprint as fast as I can to the car as he hesitates between following me and defending his own life. I fumble with Burke's iMode, my hands slippery with sweat and blood. I can feel Omony running toward me and fear surges as I manage to open the door and climb in the car at the last moment.

Hands shaking, I lock the door just as he smashes into the car with a roar and swings the machete against my window. Thankfully the glass is bullet proof, so it holds.

Panting and panicked, I drop Burke's iMode. Screaming my frustration, I dive under the dashboard, patting the car floor blindly in the dark, to find the plastic band.

Omony is bellowing with rage and ramming the machete at the window again and again. Finally, I find the iMode and straighten up. The glass has already cracked and I flinch as Omony's machete bangs against the window, inches from my face.

Hands trembling, I swipe the bracelet and start the vehicle then I step on the gas pedal toward the gate at the back of the property, pressing the door opener frantically.

At the last moment, the back gates inch open and we burst through. The bulk of the mob being at the front gates, only a few dozen screaming men rush in through the opening. I push the pedal to the floor and the black SUV flies past as they run into the courtyard.

A last glance in the mirror reveals the buildings ablaze with fire against the night's backdrop. The courtyard is drowning under the mob's uncontrollable flood. Omony fights, enraged, his machete soaring and diving above the surging wave's crest.

And then the crowd closes in on him.

32

OLIVIA

 enya, 17 February 2082

STANDING in the doorway of the cellblock, DeAnn propping me up.

In the car, somewhere I don't recognise.

DeAnn parking and then wiping the blood from my face with a rag, whispering softly. The blood is dry and the towel feels coarse, tugging me and grating my skin.

Wincing.

Feeling my lip split open again.

Trying not to wince.

Thirsty.

DeAnn shaking me by the shoulders.

Staring at the moon by the side of the road. So bright and pure in the night sky. Wishing DeAnn would stop shaking me. She's trying to wake me up, I think.

I don't want to wake up.

On the road now. Looking at the gigantic trees. I remember Edigold telling me that baobabs scared her. Why was it again? They grew too tall and strong. And the gods grew jealous and uprooted the trees and threw them so that they fell upside down with their roots in the air. They're enormous. Their red bark glinting menacingly in the night, as the car's headlights brings them to life for a second. Then they blink out of existence and my mind can't remember anything but darkness.

Anthony is hitting my face again and again and again. My lip explodes, my eyes are shut tight. I want to open my eyes but my eyelids are sealed. I struggle to escape but I am powerless.

Waking up screaming.

DeAnn is shaking me with one hand and driving with the other. Nightmare. She doesn't look at me. Just the road. The red road. Slashing like a bleeding wound across the landscape.

Dead bodies on the sides. Shuffling dusty skeletons walking on either side of us.

My head throbs. Something is tugging on my hair at the back of my skull. Raising my hand and finding sticky blood.

The road ends.

DeAnn is discussing something with a man. He's wearing some kind of white uniform. I can't really remember what this means. I sit by the water. The smell is so strong and clean.

Salt.

Algae.

The sound of waves washes my thoughts away.

I lie down on the sand and stare at the morning sun play with the water.

Warming my face.

And surrender to sleep.

33

DEANN

Somewhere in the Atlantic Ocean, February 2082

MUFFLED CRIES and the sound of running wake me up.

Did I dream this? I hesitate, lying immobile on my cot, then decide to get up.

I grope my way forward in the dark, opening the small door to our claustrophobic staff cabin and look out. A long, narrow corridor extends as far as the eye can see, on either side of my door.

Neon lights blink slowly awake and I waver on the threshold, then glance back inside the cabin.

Olivia is on the top bunk, sleeping. I can't believe we made it out of Uganda alive. She looks so much better now. The bruises and the black eye have faded. There's still a scar where her lip split open but otherwise she's fully healed. On the outside, that is. The inside is another story.

I see a flash of her covered in blood in that cell. For all

my misgivings about Olivia as a partner, she has actually saved both our skins. I would never tell her of course, but I completely underestimated her.

When I looked through her iMode to search for a map or some sort of way out of that hellhole, it turned out she knew for months that the Programme planned to kill us and she'd been in touch with a woman who signed her messages 'A.'. The mystery woman's increasingly worried messages detailed an entire escape plan. And sure enough, when we arrived on the East Coast of Kenya, just like the Resistance promised, safe passage had been arranged on a cruise ship leaving that day.

If only Olivia and I had worked together, things could have turned out better for both of us.

So, as the ship makes its way from Africa back to the US, with the two of us camouflaged in plain view as members of the crew, time slows down to a crawl, we mend our wounds and plan our next move together.

We need to find out what the medical experiments are all about. What's the Programme plotting? We only have two leads: Carapadre & Dergrin, the law firm that filed the request to experiment in Bwaise, and GeneX, the pharmaceutical company that orchestrated it all.

Wrapping my jacket around my shoulders, I start to go back inside when I hear movement nearby. It's very faint but I can just make out the words. I walk toward the sound.

Maybe I should have woken Olivia? What if we're sinking? The last filaments of sleep ebb away when I open the door to the upper deck and emerge into the cold night. Vast nothingness meets me. Somewhere on the ship, crewmembers are issuing tense instructions. An iceberg floats by, just a few feet away from my extended fingers. Then it recedes into the void, the voices die down and soon the deck is silent again.

I breathe in the frigid night and shiver, but can't bring myself to go back to the confined cabin yet.

Maybe if we can find out what the medical experiments were for, we can go back to our own time and prevent it all from ever happening.

Go back to 2017. Right. Like that's ever going to happen. I laugh but it comes out wrong. A ball of something painful is lodged in my throat.

How will we ever go back? The Programme wants us dead and there's no way we can get access to the Cambridge pyramid now. My mouth dries up as I realize how far away from everything we are, in the middle of nowhere, just the two of us lost in this horrible future. So helpless. So hopelessly underqualified for this mission.

I wrap my arms around me and push the somber thoughts away.

There's no way I'm letting all these people die.

Kitsa's small face flickers before my eyes.

There's no way I'm letting *her* die.

And the only way to save her now is to go back to 2017.

We'll find a way.

We must.

The ocean stretches out, infinite and empty. I shiver and stare at the vast expanse as the black sky weighs down on me, crushing me with the overwhelming certainty of my own insignificance.

ALSO BY O. M. FAURE

Olivia and DeAnn's story continues in the next book of *The Beautiful Ones* Trilogy: *United.*

THE BEAUTIFUL ONES (TRILOGY):

Book 1: Chosen

Book 2: Torn

Book 3: United

If you enjoyed *Chosen*, then you will love *The Disappearance*, the action-packed prequel that explains how the Time Travel Programme got started.

Grab your FREE copy of *The Disappearance* today simply by visiting www.omfaure.com!

BIBLIOGRAPHY

This book is based on scientific studies, UN forecasts and real data. If you would like to know more, please consult the sources listed below.

A list of book club topics to discuss is also available when you join the Readers' Club at www.omfaure.com

Overpopulation Analysis:

• Cafaro, P. and Crist, E., Life on the Brink: Environmentalists Confront Overpopulation, Athens, Georgia: The University of Georgia Press, 2012.

• Ehrlich, P., The Population Bomb, New York: Ballantine Books, 1971.

• Emmott S. 'Humans: the real threat to life on earth', Guardian, 29 June 2013.

• Furness, H., 'Sir David Attenborough: If we do not control population, the natural world will', Telegraph, 18 September 2013.

• Jowit, Juliette, 'Three's a crowd', Guardian, 11 November 2007.

• Meikle, J., 'Sir David Attenborough warns about large

families and predicts things will only get worse', Guardian, 10 September 2013.

• Remarque Koutonin, M., 'Isn't it Europe that is over-populated rather than Africa?', Guardian, 11 January 2016.

• Roberts, D., 'I'm an environmental journalist, but I never write about overpopulation. Here's why.' Vox, 29 November 2018

• Bloom, D., 'Demographic Upheaval.', Finance and Development, a quarterly publication of the International Monetary Fund, March 2016.

UN Forecasts on Population:

• United Nations, Department of Economic and Social Affairs, Population Division, 'World Population Prospects: The 2015 Revision'.

Poverty in Uganda:

• Kelly, A., 'Soroti District named one of the poorest in Uganda', Guardian, 10 February 2009.

Human Child Sacrifice in Uganda:

• Akbar, J., 'Snatched on their way to school then castrated or decapitated: horrifying rise in child human sacrifice in Uganda at the hands of witch doctors', Daily Mail, 17 June 2015.

Ape Deformities:

• Krief, S. and Wasswa, J., 'Agricultural expansion as a risk to endangered wild life. Pesticide exposure in wild chimpanzees and baboons displaying facial dysplasia', Science Direct, 15 November 2017.

• Locklear, M, 'What's warping the faces of monkeys in Uganda?', The Verge, 25 August 2017.

Rebel Groups at the Ugandan-Congolese border:
- Plaut, M., 'Profile: Uganda's LRA rebels', BBC, 6 February 2004. Retrieved from: news.bbc.co.uk.

Médecins Sans Frontières:
- Documentary: Living in Emergency, produced and directed by Mark Hopkins, 2008.

Communicable Diseases and Mortality:
- Report by the World Health Organization on: 'Maternal and child health in Uganda'.
- Report by the World Health Organization on: 'Projections of global health outcomes from 2005 to 2060 using the International Futures integrated forecasting model'.
- Report by the World Health Organization on: 'Projections of mortality and causes of death, 2016 to 2060'.

Food and Water Scarcity:
- Lederer, E. M., '20 million people in four countries facing starvation, famine: UN', The Associated Press, 10 March 2017.
- Menker, S., 'A global food crisis may be less than a decade away', TED Talk, August 2017.
- Namagembe, L., 'How safe is the water we consume?', The Monitor, 20 March 2018.
- Perkins, A, 'Background: water in Uganda', Guardian, 28 March 2008.
- Wiebe1, K., Lotze-Campen, H., Sands, R., Tabeau, A., van der Mensbrugghe, D., Biewald, A., Bodirsky, B., Islam, S., Kavallari, A., Mason-D'Croz, D., 'Climate change impacts on agriculture in 2050 under a range of plausible socioeconomic and emissions scenarios', IOP Science 25 August 2015.

Religious Information:
- 'Birth Control, Catholic Answers', 19 November 2018.
- 'Christian teachings on contraception and birth control', BBC, 3 August 2009.
- 'The Guardian view on the Catholic contraceptive ban: a historic mistake', Guardian, 25 July 2018.

Medical Experiments:
- Rothman, L., 'The Disturbing History of African-Americans and Medical Research Goes Beyond Henrietta Lacks', Time, 21 April 2017.
- Shah, S., 'The Constant Gardener: what the movie missed', The Nation, 30 August 2005.
- 'The true story of how multinational drug companies took liberties with African lives', Independent, 26 September 2005.
- Washington, H., 'Why Africa Fears Western Medicine', The New York Times, 31 July 2007.

ACKNOWLEDGMENTS

A huge thank you to all the people who assisted me during my research trip to Uganda and helped to make it an unforgettable experience. The 2081 Uganda I depict in the book could not be further from the lovely country I was lucky to visit in 2018.

I chose Uganda as the backdrop for this novel because it is forecast to be one of the ten most populated countries in the world by 2100 (source: United Nations, Department of Economic and Social Affairs, Population Division, 'World Population Prospects: The 2015 Revision'). Uganda is also the smallest of those ten countries, so it is likely to be the one that will suffer the most from the added pressure.

I very much hope that Uganda will avert the terrible future I depict in the book, as the people I met there were unfailingly kind and welcoming. One way to make Uganda avoid turmoil is to visit this beautiful country. Everyone I met there was extremely keen to grow the tourism industry and you'd be helping Uganda develop that little bit faster, which, as I explain in the book, is a great way to precipitate the demographic transition. So please do visit this gorgeous corner of the world – and make sure you use eco-tourism to do it.

My own research trip would never even have happened without the diligence, attention to detail and genuine care of Edmand Twakiire from Kazinga Tours (https://www.kazingatours.com/Uganda).

I was extraordinarily fortunate to travel with one of only five female guides in Uganda: Kiberinka Safinah, who was sunshine personified.

I would also like to thank the Sanyu Babies orphanage (https://www.sanyubabies.com/) for kindly showing me around and letting me help out for one afternoon.

I owe a debt of gratitude to Kafia Omar for welcoming me in Kamapala and to Lydia Lakwonyero, who helped so much in choosing the correct names for the characters.

Finally, a big shout out as well to the Uganda Wild Life Authority (https://www.ugandawildlife.org/en/) for their very professional organization of the gorilla tours. The conservation work they do is crucial to the survival of this majestic animal.

ABOUT THE AUTHOR

 O. M. Faure studied political science at Sciences Po in Paris, before obtaining a Master's degree in International Affairs at The Fletcher School of Law and Diplomacy in Boston.

She has worked at the United Nations in Geneva and has extensive experience as a change and transformation manager in several banks over the last twenty years.

Today, she is a Principal at a Scenario Planning consulting firm, and she lectures and coaches at the Hult International Business School.

Based in London, O. M. Faure is a feminist, a Third Culture Kid, an enthusiastic singer, and a budding activist.

 facebook.com/omfaure
twitter.com/OM_Faure

Printed in Great Britain
by Amazon

15821759R00178